CHILDREN
of
THE SUN

Bridgett Jackson 4/13/07

CHILDREN
of
THE SUN

Book Two

A Novel

BRIDGETT JACKSON
Author of "Secrets of a Hidden Trail"

iUniverse, Inc.
New York Lincoln Shanghai

CHILDREN *of* THE SUN
Book Two

iUniverse books may be ordered through booksellers or by contacting:

iUniverse
2021 Pine Lake Road, Suite 100
Lincoln, NE 68512
www.iuniverse.com
1-800-Authors (1-800-288-4677)

This is a work of fiction. All of the characters, names, incidents, organizations, and dialogue in this novel are either the products of the author's imagination or are used fictitiously.

ISBN-13: 978-0-595-41336-2 (pbk)
ISBN-13: 978-0-595-85689-3 (ebk)
ISBN-10: 0-595-41336-6 (pbk)
ISBN-10: 0-595-85689-6 (ebk)

Printed in the United States of America

This book is dedicated to my two wonderful sons and my husband who encourage and support me every step of the way with my writing career and every challenge I face. Their support and constant devotion to family values and the Appalachian way of life give me the courage to continue writing about the wonderful area where we live.

ACKNOWLEDGEMENTS

Many thanks go to the Tellico Ranger District of the Cherokee National Forest for their efforts to preserve the natural beauty of the woods and streams in this area and keep the area safe for all to enjoy.

Also, I would like to acknowledge the communities of the Tellico Plains, Coker Creek and surrounding areas for their efforts to preserve the culture and heritage of the Southern Appalachian Mountains.

Many thanks to local photographer Ed Prescott for his wonderful ability to capture the beauty of the Appalachian Mountains in the cover photograph.

CHAPTER 1

The grinding sound in the engine intensified as the battered old jeep struggled to climb the last 200 yards of the rugged dirt trail to the mountaintop. Dirt flew around the jeep in a huge dense cloud and blew into the window covering everything inside with a thin layer of fine, golden brown dust.

"Come on, babe, you can do it. Just a little bit further," Maggie whispered softly as she leaned forward and urged the jeep to continue. Another cloud of dust enveloped the jeep as she swerved around the last hairpin curve and lunged over the crest of the ridge. Suddenly, a burst of steam billowed from under the hood as the distinctive odor of an overheated radiator filled the air.

"Rats!" she thumped the steering wheel with the palm of her hand and brought the jeep to a grinding halt. She shuddered when she felt a huge wet nose slide across her neck and the sticky drip of drool run down her back as Max stuck his head forward from the back seat and thrust it out her window.

"Just a minute, fella," she said as she opened the door and struggled out of the jeep before Max tried to leap over her lap and out the door.

She smiled as she watched him leap and bound around the small clearing at the top of the ridge as he checked out the trees and clumps of brush for something to chase. His glossy black coat shone as he ran from one interesting place to another. As a cross between a Great Pyrenees and a Newfoundland, Max weighed over 125 pounds. He was a welcome-home gift from an old mountain friend when Maggie returned to the mountains to live. Although she was reluctant to have him around at first, he quickly became Maggie's constant companion and loyal defender. The two were now almost inseparable.

"Well, Max, this isn't exactly the kind of adventure I had in mind for us today," she said as she reached under the hood and pulled the latch to pop it open.

A huge plume of steam billowed into her face as she lifted the hood.

"Peuuu!" she tried to wave the steam out of her face and open the radiator cap with her bandana. "Too hot to touch right now, guess we'll have to let it cool off a little bit before we fill the radiator back up with water."

Maggie bought her old jeep from a yearly forest service used equipment auction when she first moved back to the mountains several years ago. A basic, no frills vehicle, it was not much to look at, yet so powerful it could easily travel over rut filled roads, or through streams and stormy weather like a dream. It was perfect for the backwoods, rugged mountain region where she lived and often pulled her through tough driving situations where most vehicles failed. Maggie promptly determined the jeep was almost as helpful as a horse would be in most situations and named the jeep 'Charley Horse' in honor of its wonderful uses and because it could often be a pain to operate.

When she looked under the hood, Maggie brushed the hair out of her eyes and accidentally rubbed against some engine oil that left a large streak of black grime across her face. She turned around to look for Max and saw the leaves under one of the bushes shake when Max tried to squeeze through them. A small squirrel soon darted out of the brush and quickly scurried across an opening on the path with Max closing in quickly behind him.

Just as Max came within grasp of him, the squirrel quickly leaped onto the side of a hickory tree and climbed to the safety of the upper branches. He fussed and chattered angrily as he ran. He left Max to sniff around the middle of the clearing and wonder how his query disappeared so suddenly. He was used to chasing critters on the ground but never quite grasped the concept to look up in the trees to find his prey. As a result, squirrels usually escaped him.

"What's wrong buddy, did he get away?"

Maggie asked as Max looked up and wagged his huge tail. He had a quizzical look on his face as if he still wondered where the critter had gone so quickly.

"Hey, Max, I'm going to hike the rest of the way to the lookout. Digger should be there soon and we don't want to be late. Ready to go?" she called as she grabbed her water and bandana, then strapped on her backpack and headed up the dusty trail that led to the lookout on the edge of the mountain. Max quickly left the clearing and ran along the trail beside her, happy to be on the move again.

"Even at seven years old, you have enough energy for both of us, Max. I wish I had half of your energy."

As she watched him run along the trail, she wished often for some of his get-up-and-go. At forty-six, Maggie was still an avid hiker and backpacker, but learned to shorten her treks and lighten her packs through the years. She quickly tied her long, dark hair into a braid and wrapped the end with a tie. She noticed the streaks of gray in her hair sparkle in the sun as she braided it.

'Of course, my lack of energy has nothing to do with age,' she smiled smugly to herself, 'It's merely common sense, or maybe I could call it a technical obstacle. Umhmm that term would work ...' Maggie was never one to feel overly concerned about her age or the process of getting older as long as she could continue to hike and explore the woods, especially when she had the opportunity to hike with Digger.

Digger was like a father to her and helped her Grandmother raise her by teaching her how to hike in the woods, and survive in wilderness conditions. He and her grandmother taught her to respect nature and cherish the ancient heritage of each culture, especially the mountains surrounding their home. She knew that each time she hiked with Digger she would learn something new or discover some type of ancient artifact.

After her grandmother's death, Maggie graduated from a local community college and moved to a large city to work with a mental health agency. She couldn't bear the thought of living in the mountains alone without Grandmother and threw herself into her work. Life in the city was often difficult for her because she was away from her beloved mountains. She longed for the peace and harmony she felt when she lived on the mountain and knew she would someday return when the opportunity was right.

At work, she often dealt with people who were very hurtful to each other and inner city children who were in crisis because of choices their parents were making. Although Maggie loved even the most challenging cases, twenty years of practice with families in crisis left her spirit zapped. She longed to return to the mountains as soon as she was financially able and did so when she was able to purchase her grandmother's log cabin. After her move to the cabin, Maggie continued to write articles for children's magazines, parenting manuals and nature books to supplement her income.

Her favorite diversion continued to be hikes she often took with Digger. Her grandmother's friend kept in touch with her throughout her college and adult years and often hiked with her when she was home for holidays. Now that she returned to live in the mountains, they were able to hike on a regular basis.

Maggie loved the hikes because they gave her an opportunity to learn more about the mountains and gather information for her articles.

She paused by a large oak tree to cool off and take a drink from her canteen before she climbed over the stone ledge that led to the overlook. The heat from the late afternoon sun was sweltering and caused her clothes to feel damp and sticky against her skin. She wiped her face with a bandana.

'It's amazing the air could be so humid and still not rain', she thought as she used her bandana to tie up her long curly hair and get it off her shoulders.

Max suddenly appeared from under the bushes and plopped down beside her, exhausted from the heat and his investigations. Maggie scratched him behind the ears as she poured some of her water into the lid of the canteen so he could get a drink while she took off her backpack and placed it under a tree.

"Tired, Max?"

He greeted her with a sticky swipe of his tongue and thumped his tail slowly against the dusty path before he crawled into the shade to cool down away from the afternoon sun as she looked across the trail for some sign of Digger.

"You stay here and rest, Max. I'm going ahead to the lookout until Digger shows up. I'll be back in a little bit," she said as she climbed over the rocks and scrambled to the small ledge that overlooked a section of the Appalachian Mountains and valleys along the Cherahala Skyway.

A sudden wave of nausea and dizziness rushed over Maggie when she first saw the vast expanse of the valley as it gaped before her. She quickly lay on her stomach and gasped for breath just as her knees began to feel as though they would turn to rubber and buckle beneath her. As soon as she felt the security of the ground beneath her, she closed her eyes then slowly and deliberately counted backwards from ten until the feeling of panic passed.

'Ohhh, these heights still get me every time I hike in a place with a steep overlook. At least the panic attacks don't last as long as they used to when I first started hiking with Digger'. Slowly she regained her composure as she opened her eyes and began to brush the dust off her clothes. With the humidity so heavy, it was difficult to brush the dust off her clothes, it just seemed to stick and smear into everything.

"Good grief, you'd think with all the rugged mountain training I've had I wouldn't do something wimpy like this and get woozy over heights anymore. This is so silly! I'm just going to have to practice standing near high places until I get over the panic attacks!"

Determined to continue, Maggie lay on her stomach and slowly inched across the stone overlook. As the vast valley and mountain range came into view again, she broke into a cold sweat. The palms of her hands began to per-spire as she grasped the rim of rocks at the edge of the trail and pulled herself to the very edge.

"Oh, Wow! This is incredible!"

She looked out over the view. In the distance, the peaks of the Snowbird Mountains rose up so high they seemed to disappear into the hazy blue sky itself. Wispy, white clouds clung to the peaks along the ridges of the mountains and gave them the smoky appearance that the Appalachian Mountains were famous for throughout history and hence the name, 'The Great Smoky Mountains'.

From her perch on the ledge above, she allowed her eyes to follow along the folds of the mountain ridges as they deepened and darkened on their way to the valley below. The hazy blue shades of the mountain peaks turned to darker teals and greens as the base of the mountains broadened and the foothills began. The dark green of fir and pine trees and lighter greens of oak, hickory and hardwood trees filled the mountainside and foothills giving it the look of a lush, luxurious multicolored carpet.

A lone hawk soared over the valley in search of dinner. Maggie held her breath and watched it glide along effortlessly through the air. With its wings spread out and tail feathers open, it seemed to float as it zigzagged across the sky. She smiled and wondered if it was the same hawk she saw at Doc's house so often.

'Probably not, we're pretty far from his house, but it's a happy thought any-way'. She smiled at the thought of seeing him, again. They were spending a great deal of time together in the past few months. Their friendship was begin-ning to develop into something deeper and more meaningful as their lives now often intertwined in many areas. Briefly distracted with thoughts of Doc she paused, then quickly returned to her thoughts of the treacherous ledge with the enormous personal challenge before her.

"Ok, Maggie, time for the big move," she told herself as she squeezed her eyes shut tightly and pulled herself closer to the rim of the ledge until her very head hung over the abyss. She could feel the nervous tension build inside as her stomach tightened. Her mouth felt dry and her palms began to sweat as she took one big gulp of air and held her breath before she opened her eyes just a peep.

The mountainside dropped a sheer 300 feet from the shelf, to the valley below her. Huge piles of rocks and dirt had tumbled along the sides of the mountain where sometime in the ancient past; nature had tumbled the earth onto the valley floor. A jumble of bush grew at the base of the mountain then cleared to a small field that led to a hidden valley. Lush green grass grew along the sides of a small stream that sparkled in the sunlight and flowed along the base of the ridge that lay across the valley floor.

Maggie gasped when she was finally able to open her eyes completely and see the beauty below her. She was astounded when she saw the beauty of the valley filled with the dazzling array of colors. Every color, every smell, every movement seemed so alive it almost jumped right out and touched her. Her body tingled as she tried to drink in everything she could see.

Bright green fern filled the hillside and looked so soft she almost wanted to jump down on it and see if it felt like a feather bed. Small bunches of white field daisies dotted the sides of the mountain and scattered through the field. Their brilliant white petals with sunny yellow centers seemed to nod and wave a greeting with every breeze. Black Eyed Susan grew in huge masses along the base of the mountain; their dark brown centers made the rich golden petals that surrounded them seem to burst forward in a jubilant display as they reached toward the sun.

Native field flowers garnished the field and filled the scene with a dazzling array of brilliant color. Orange butterfly weed, white Queen Ann's Lace, Pink Coneflowers, deep purple Ironweed and so many more all grew with such complete, carefree abandon. The entire valley looked as though it could have been a living version of a French Impressionist's painting someone hid in this secret valley for safekeeping.

A movement in the tall grass caught her eye as a full-grown deer appeared at the edge of the clearing. The deer stood motionless for a few moments as it glanced around the field and looked for danger. She held her breath as the deer took a few tentative steps into the field. It was the soft golden color of summer and seemed to blend into the grasses and field flowers as it moved. Maggie watched the deer's tail began to twitch when two small fawns daintily stepped into the clearing beside it.

"Oh, it's a doe, and she has two little babies!" Maggie excitedly watched the mother deer and her two fawns as they grazed on the grasses and wildflowers in the field. "They're so cute!" she whispered to herself.

Suddenly, the doe's tail began to twitch and her head popped up quickly. Maggie noticed some movement in nearby brush just before the mother deer and her fawns disappeared into the woods as a loud commotion erupted on the trail behind Maggie. The deep baritone sound of Max's bark echoed through the entire valley when a loud metallic clatter filled the air followed by the distinctive sounds of a donkey bray and an old man's angry yell. The commotion disrupted the serene beauty of the valley below.

"Digger!"

Alarmed, Maggie quickly forgot about her discomfort with heights and quickly scooted backwards off the cliff. She scrambled down the rocks to the path where the commotion seemed to originate. As she rushed into the clearing, she saw Max apparently have the time of his life as he joyfully leaped and barked around Digger's old pack mule, Nugget driving the mule into a frantic bucking frenzy.

Maggie couldn't help but laugh at the sight of Max and the donkey in the mist of their disturbance. Max obviously thought the donkey was playing with him as he barked and lunged towards Nugget. No matter how much Nugget kicked and pranced around, Max was able to remain just outside reach of the donkey's powerful hoofs. Total chaos erupted as pots and pans flew through the air from the packs when the old donkey kicked his hoofs up and brayed in protest at the noisy black beast that circled him. Supplies, bedrolls and pans quickly littered the clearing as they scattered all over the ridge top when they fell from Digger's packs.

"Max, MAX! Come here, boy. Stop, now, you leave Nugget alone!" Maggie called as soon as she was able to stop laughing at the comical site.

Max briefly paused his activities long enough to look at Maggie and wag his long tail in greeting before he turned back toward his new playmate again and resumed his harassment of Nugget.

"Dag-nabbit!" Digger shouted to Max and Nugget as he picked himself up from the trail and began to dust off his worn overalls with his felt hat. "What have you been feeding that critter lately, Maggie? He's full 'o spit 'n vinegar t'day."

Digger grinned at Maggie from under the brim of his warped felt hat after he tried to knock some of the dents out and re-adjust it on his head. His bright blue eyes sparkled with amusement over the commotion with the animals.

"It's good to see you too, Digger," Maggie giggled. "It's about time you guys got here. We were about to run out of things to do while we waited for you to get here," she teased as she walked over and gave him a big hug.

Digger tried to shoot her a stern look and ended up laughing.

"Well, he shore did surprise us t'day, 'specially 'ole Nugget. Gonna take me nigh on to sunset to git him back ta normal agin, if he ever does," Digger grumbled as he rubbed the stubble of gray beard on his chin.

"You know Max. He likes to play with Nugget. You probably just surprised him, Digger. See … he's wagging his tail and trying to be friends again."

They turned to see Max wag his tail and try to get close enough to Nugget to lick the donkey's nose. His entire body trembled with the excitement of this new vigorous round of activity with his old playmate.

Nugget seemed to be less sure of the tentative truce and began to back away. As he attempted to get away from Max, he caught the remnants of his backpack on a tree and scared himself so badly he began to kick wildly and bray again. The backpack slid under Nugget's belly as he continued to thrash and kick his way through the brush. Max evidently thought Nugget was ready to have some fun again and began to bark and prance around the donkey once more.

Still laughing, Maggie quickly jumped up, ran over to Max and pulled him over to the side as Digger tried to grab Nugget's halter and calm him down before everything in the backpack was lost or completely ruined. With two final kicks in the air, a snort and a bray Nugget finally began to calm down enough to give Digger the opportunity to loosen and remove his packs.

Maggie ordered Max to stay under a shade tree several yards from Nugget. He reluctantly lay down, placed his head between his paws and looked up at her through dark soulful eyes. When both animals were finally calm, and resting under separate shade trees near the clearing, Maggie and Digger began to pick up the scattered items from his packs.

Digger and Maggie were friends for life. He took her under his wing when she was five years old and first came to the mountains to live with her grandmother after her parents died. As one of her grandmother's best friends, Digger took it upon himself to become Maggie's mentor and teach her all the things he felt she should know in order to take care of herself in the mountains. Although never formally educated, he was a brilliant teacher of the ways of nature, the mountains and often of people and their ways.

Digger taught Maggie how to hike, locate food in the woods during any season, cook, find her way out of the woods if she became lost, pan for gold and most important of all … how to love nature and appreciate the native ways of doing things. Maggie couldn't remember a time when she and Digger had not been friends. It felt like he had always been a part of her family.

Some of Maggie's favorite memories involved the times when she was young and sat around the fireplace in her Grandmother's little log cabin. There she listened to Digger and Grandmother when they told stories of long ago days when the mountain folk and the Native Americans lived in harmony with each other. In fact, their Native American friends named her Grandmother and Digger Cherokee names when they were children themselves. Their native friends named Grandmother Wani'Nahi', which was the name for a beloved woman in the Cherokee language. Digger's name, Yan-e gwa, was the name for a big bear.

'Whoever named them must have known exactly what they were doing because those two names fit them to a tee', Maggie thought to herself. 'I can't think of more appropriate names for them'. Maggie loved to call them by their Cherokee names and learn about history the way it 'really' was, instead of how history books usually portrayed American history.

Digger was now almost eighty years old and continued to stay active with his hiking and explorations of the mountains. His favorite passion was panning for gold in the streams throughout the mountains or digging through quartz in one of his gold mines. He always had some new discovery to show Maggie when she could explore the trails with him. Easy to pick out in a crowd, he always wore a pair of faded overalls and an old felt hat no matter what the season or weather might be at the time.

When they finally had all the supplies and gear picked up and repacked in the saddle bags, Digger and Maggie sat down under a tree to cool off and take a long drink from their canteens. The late afternoon heat and humidity was almost suffocating and both were drenched with sweat from their work.

"So, what else are we going to do this afternoon, Digger? You can't have anything else as exciting as this planned!"

"Anything more exciting than this, 'n ye might jest have to pack me on the back o' the mule ta get me home!" Digger laughed. "Saw yer jeep back on the ridge, Maggie. She break down on you?"

"I think it just got a little overheated. The combination of the heat and the steep trail was a little too much I think. Thought I'd wait 'till it cooled down a little and add some water to the radiator. This has got to be the hottest day of the year so far, don't you think?" she said as she wiped the perspiration from her face with a bandana.

"Yep, it shore is hot; hotter than I kin remember. These are whut they always called the 'dawg days' o' summer," Digger started.

Maggie smiled, "And the 'dawg days' are …?" she prompted him.

"Dawg days' are when it gets so hot nuthin' wants ta move a'tall. Not even the flies, 'n the only reason the flies keep a' movin' is 'cause if they was to stop somewheres they'd stick on whatever it was they landed on," he said as his eyes began to twinkle.

Maggie grinned. She could sense a tall tale develop as they talked.

One of the things she loved most about Digger was he always had a tall tale or a yarn to spin. She couldn't think of a single time she was with him that he didn't come up with some wild story about something that related to whatever they were doing.

The first time she met Digger, she was five years old and surprised him when she joined in on his tall tales without batting an eye. Digger never expected anyone to jump right in and pick up where he left off. They became side kicks ever since and often told tales when they were together. They seemed to have a knack for being able to grasp each other's ideas and expand on them at the drop of a hat. Much to the amusement of anyone who listened, it was difficult to tell the difference between facts and fiction.

"That's pretty hot, Digger," Maggie grinned and prompted him to continue. "So how hot is it?

"Yessirree, it's so hot t'day, that folks is gonna have to keep thar chickens in the shade ta keep 'em from laying hard boiled aiggs, 'n if they ain't plowed thar taters yet, they ain't gonna have ta cook em none."

"Why not?" Maggie laughed.

"It's so hot t'day, all a body's got to do is pull them taters out 'o the ground 'n slap a little salt 'n pepper on 'em cause they's gonna bake right in the ground," Digger grinned his crooked silly grin and started to fan himself with his old felt hat. "And if a body wuz to try to milk a cow … why yu'd just get pure sweet butter instead of milk."

"Enough already!" Maggie laughed as she tossed her canteen at Digger. ·

Nugget began to bray from the shade tree.

"You are so full of it today! Any more excitement and I won't be able to stand being around any of you," she said with a smile.

Max looked so sad from the place Maggie ordered him to sit under a shade tree. When he noticed her look in his direction, he sat up and moaned, then placed his head between his paws. His huge brown eyes looked pitiful in hopes that Maggie would see him and invite him to come over and join her and Digger. He took the moment she looked in his direction as an invitation to run across the clearing, leap into her lap and cover her face with wet sticky kisses.

"Max, you big baby!" Maggie fussed as she tried to move the huge bundle of fur off her lap and stand up again. "You've caused a lot of trouble today, you rascal!"

Max sat down in front of her and looked at her with huge sorrowful eyes then held up his paw in an effort to shake hands with her. She smiled at him as she shook his paw. "Thank you, Max. Now go say 'Hi' to Digger."

She ruffled his neck before he bounded across to the shade tree where Digger sat and tried to lay in his lap. Digger playfully wrestled with him for a few minutes, then gently pushed him aside and stood up.

"So, what are we going to do today, Digger, anything special? I got excited when I got your message about going hiking again. I'm glad you are feeling better and ready to hit the trails again." Maggie watched him stand as she remembered the near death experience he had in one of his gold mines after a flood last spring and the lengthy recovery that followed. As much as she loved to hike and explore with him, she wanted him to be healthy enough for the trip.

"T'day, we's jest gonna be lookin', that's all." Digger got up and repositioned the saddlebags and packs on Nuggets back as he spoke.

"Are we going to be looking at anything in particular?" Maggie strapped on her pack as they prepared to hike down the mountain.

"Well, you know how I've always told ye 'bout how the Cherokee lived in this area before the settlers ever came over the mountains," Digger began.

"Yes and how most of the pioneers wouldn't have survived without their help and friendship." Maggie commented. "The Cherokee were friendly with the settlers in general weren't they? I think they tried to adopt the settler's lifestyles and culture in many ways."

"Well, the Cherokee were friendly, but there weren't always Indians here that were friendly with the white folks. Some of them could see what was coming in the future and wanted to keep the white folks outta here, so they fought with 'em. Those are the ones all the white folks called 'savages' or 'hostile' Indians. They did everything they could to get rid o' them and as a result, the white folks considered them hostile."

When they had all of his supplies loaded on the mule again, Digger grabbed Nugget's lead rope and began to head down the switchback trail that led down the backside of the mountain. Max took off in front of the group so he could lead the way, determined to protect the crew that followed him down the path.

"Were they here at the same time the Cherokee and the white settlers were here?" Maggie asked as she followed along behind Digger and the mule.

"Nope, the Indians I'm talking about were here way 'afore the white folks settled in here. Some folks believe they wuz sum of the first travelers to ever cross through this area although they aint much of a way to prove that anymore. These wuz a group of folks that came from somewhere far, far away called the Yuchi Indians. They wuz different than any other kind o' Indian that lived in these here parts. In fact their name even meant, 'Children o' the Sun, frum Far Away'. Nobody really knows where they came from and there are very few of 'em that are still alive."

"I knew there were Indians before the Cherokee, but I didn't think the Cherokee were the ones who ran them off," Maggie commented as she grabbed a tree limb to balance herself while she maneuvered around a particularly steep section of the trail.

"This tribe no body seems to know much about anymore. They were different from all the rest 'o Indians that lived here at the time, they were Sun worshipers. They had different customs and different ways o' doing things than any other local tribe. Some of the white traders didn't like 'em too much 'cause they traveled across the Unicoi Trail 'n raided the supply wagons that came up from the settlements on the Carolina coast when pioneers were coming across the mountains."

They reached the bottom of the mountain and walked out into the little valley Maggie saw from the ledge above. As magnificent as the valley was from her ridge top view, it was even more impressive to walk through on the valley floor. The grass in the meadow grew about as high as her hips and seemed to roll and sway like ocean waves when the wind blew. She paused briefly. The beautiful flowers Maggie saw from above were even more vibrant and colorful as she passed by them. Bees and butterflies bobbed from one plant to another as they followed the sweet fragrance of the field flowers and wild herbs that filled the air.

They walked across the lush valley floor to the small stream that flowed along the edge of the field. There they allowed Nugget to get a cool drink of water from the stream. Max found the stream before the rest of the crew and was already nose deep in the water. He seemed to be having a wonderful time as he lay in the sand and allowed the cool waters to rush over him. He looked almost like an otter or a beaver as he slithered and rolled along in the current with nothing showing but the tip of his black nose. Even Digger and Maggie took off their boots and socks so they could stick their feet in the stream to cool off. When everyone had their fill of fresh cold water, they put their boots on again and continued on their journey.

"Tell me more about the Indian tribe, Digger. I haven't heard much about them. Almost everything I learned in school from the history books about this area doesn't mention many tribes except the Cherokee or the Mississippi

Mound Builders that some people believe came through here with Desoto on one of his treks. What were the people of the tribe you are talking about called?"

"This tribe wuz called the 'Yuchi' tribe. They wuz here fer a long time before the Cherokee got here. No one knows much about where they came from or anything. All's we know is that the Cherokee helped the white folks git rid of em."

Digger paused to catch his breath and wipe the sweat from his face with his bandana. The late afternoon heat was almost unbearable and the intense humidity made even breathing difficult.

"How do people know the difference in tribes who were here so long ago?" Maggie asked, curious about the history of the area. "It seems like it would be almost impossible to tell the difference between tribes that were here thousands and thousands of years after they left the area."

Digger raised his finger and pushed his rumpled hat up off his forehead just a little, his eyes sparkled. He paused just a moment before he spoke.

"No one lives in an area without leaving a trace, Maggie. They's always some sign 'o their passing. In this case, it was the way they buried their dead."

"Their graves were different?"

"Yep, there was this ole farmer up in Coker Creek, 'n he had a place where there where some unusual burial sites like no one had ever seen before," Digger talked as he continued his journey up the little valley. "So they had some 'o them people from the University come up 'n check the gravesites out."

"They looked over his place 'n lots 'o other places in this area 'n found out lots about the ancient Indian tribes", Digger continued. "Some 'of the graves they said were from a trip a guy named DeSoto made with some Indians from Mississippi and other graves were from the ones ah'm talking about, the Children of the Sun. These University people even took some of the folks that were buried and the things they had burried with 'em 'n put it in a big museum up in the capitol."

"Was it the Smithsonian?"

"I reckon so. The government has kept 'em there for all these years. They won't give 'em back to their people for a proper burial."

"Why not?"

"Well, the government doesn't recognize 'em as a real tribe, even though they were here and left evidence that they were here. If the government officially recognizes them, they gots ta have 'em returned to their people 'n burried proper, according to their customs." Digger continued solemnly. "And that would cost 'em a purty penny."

"So they keep em classified as 'Unknown Indian Tribes' and try to forget about 'em. With this group, they ain't many of 'em left Maggie, not enough to raise a ruckus about it. When they were run off by the Cherokee, the ones that survived joined up with the Creek Nation and hid out among them for protection, so no one could find 'em. They were afraid the government would send someone to kill 'em."

"Oh, Digger, that's so sad!"

"Yep, 'n they ain't much they can do about it anymore either. The ones that survived the war were moved out west with the rest 'o the Indians on the Trail of Tears in the early 1800's. They tried to keep together even though they hid in the Creek tribe, but it was hard and now the government says they just don't exist." Digger grimly wiped his forehead again. "But they do exist. These mountains are filled with not only the spirits of everybody that passed this way, but with real evidence, too. It's all there, 'n I think I know where we can look for signs o' their passing."

Maggie raised her eyebrows in curiosity but kept quiet.

As they reached the end of the valley, they came to a small clearing surrounded by a grove of birch trees near the stream. Digger paused as he rounded the bend in the trees and quickly glanced around the area.

"How's this place look to ya, Maggie? I'm about beat for today. You ready to set up camp?"

"It's beautiful, Digger, I'm a little tired, too."

Here they could look through the entire, secluded valley without detection from strangers. With the Snowbird Mountains behind them, they set up their camp facing the east far enough away from the stream to avoid disturbing wildlife as it came down from the mountains to water in the evening. As Digger unloaded the packs from Nugget and released him for the evening, Maggie gathered firewood for the campfire so they could cook dinner.

"Better make 'er a small fire tonite, girl. Them woods are just like kindling right now because it's so dry. We don't need to be the cause of any forest fires."

Maggie dug a small pit in the soil with Digger's small shovel, then took extra care to scrape away as much grass as she could from the edge of the pit to keep any sparks from catching the grass on fire. She then filled one of Digger's pails full of water from the creek and placed it by the fire in case she needed it in to put out a stray spark if by some chance the fire got out of control.

She built a small campfire and placed an old kettle full of water near the coals to heat while she walked to the creek bank to pick some fresh mint leaves to add to their tea for dinner. As she walked, she noticed a stand of Queen Ann's Lace and pulled some roots of the plants. These plants were also known as 'Squaw's Carrots'. She carried them to the stream to wash. She cut them very finely and added them to the stew she began to brew for dinner made from dried vegetables brought from home.

She also saw the bright yellow burst of color from a Jerusalem Artichoke plant growing by the stream. Maggie recognized the bright yellow flowers and pulled a few clumps up by the root to find the thick tubers that grew just beneath the soil. She selected a few and washed them thoroughly in the stream, then cut them very finely and added them to the already bubbling stew.

While supper cooked, she returned to the small stream to wash her face and hands before dinner. There she discovered a grove of wild raspberry bushes with ripe berries on them and a few bushes of wild blueberries. She filled her bandana with as many berries as she could before she returned to the campsite.

As they settled down by their campfire to enjoy the stew, the sun began to set over the far mountain ridge and the little valley finally began to cool off from the heat of the day. Digger handed Maggie a piece of cornbread from his pack and crumbled another piece in his stew. Maggie was so hungry; she ate two bowls of stew before she began to feel even remotely full.

"I didn't realize just how hungry I was, Digger," she said as she scraped the last spoonful of the stew from her cup and held it over her mouth to catch every drop from the bottom of the cup.

"Does a body good to be hongry now 'n again," Digger grinned, his eyes twinkled as he ate some of the berries Maggie picked and sipped mint tea. "Why, I've been good 'n hongry so many times, my body aught to be real good by now!"

Maggie laughed. She was too tired to carry the joke any further. The long journey and excitement of the day left them both physically exhausted. They sat in thoughtful silence as they watched the shadows deepen in the valley and the night move in to replace the day. Nugget grazed on the soft green grass near the campsite and Max curled up near Maggie. He always seemed to keep a watchful eye on her while he listened for anything that moved in the shadows of the night.

After dinner, Digger placed his bedroll near the grove of birch trees and set-tled in for the night. He liked to sleep away from the campfire when he was camping so the light from the fire would not distort his vision at night. Maggie usually did the same thing when she was camping alone, but tonight, with Digger in the shadows of the birch trees and Max nearby, she felt safe and left security of the campsite to her companions so she could sleep a little closer to the fire.

For some strange reason she felt the need to be close to the comfort of the campfire. Perhaps it was the memories of the warm fires and happy times around her grandmother's hearth that brought her such comfort and drew her there. Maybe, it was from the slight tension she felt. She could not determine what it was. Being in a new area of the mountains was exciting at times, but this particular section of the trail was taking on an ominous feel by the end of the day. Maggie felt as if she was in an area were she was intruding. She often felt a spiritual connection to the sacred areas where they hiked and explored. Now, she felt a need to be near something familiar so she crawled into her bedroll near the campfire.

'Besides, somebody has to keep an eye on the fire all night', she smiled to herself as she curled up for the night.

The conversations of the day left her mind in a whirl of thoughts and questions. As tired as she was, she didn't think she could sleep just yet. There were too many things to think and wonder about. Maggie always seemed to be able to think more clearly about things when she was away from the worries of daily activities at home.

An eerie melody filled the air as the crickets began their nighttime chirping and the frogs near the stream began to moan and groan. Maggie snuggled into her bedroll by the fire for the evening and watched the small campfire as it slowly burned from bright orange and yellow coals down to intense red embers.

She watched the deep crimson embers of the fire glow in the night. As her eyelids became heavy, she thought of the little known tribe from so long ago, the Children of the Sun, that had been such a large part of and yet rarely known part of Tennessee history. She wondered why history books left so much of American history out of the textbooks they used to teach children. It seemed like there was a large portion of history not taught in schools and parts taught that often seemed to be inaccurate. She thought about the stories Grandmother and Digger told her so many years ago of the Native Americans and their struggles to keep their own customs and traditions.

Suddenly, the fire popped and sent a burst of sparks and tiny specks of red and gold into the midnight sky. As Maggie watched the tiny specks float away, gradually, the tensions from the day began to seep out of her mind. The crackle of the fire was soon replaced with the soft beat of her heart ... shum-pa ... shum-pa ... shum-pa ... and ever so slowly, she began to fall to sleep, and to dream ...

> ... shum-pa ... pa-pa, shum-pa ... the rhythmic beat of the drums grew louder and more distinct as the gentle whisper of buckskin clad figures slipped out of the shadows into the glow around the fire. One, by one lithe figures began to move and sway to the beat of the drums. The eerie sound of a haunting chant filled the air as shadowy figures danced around the fire. Their bodies moved as gracefully as ribbons in the breeze.
>
> As the circle of dancers increased, the drums beat louder and faster. The chant intensified as more dancers joined the heartfelt wailing tones of the song. The dancers moved quickly now. The beads and shell ornaments on their clothing began to clang noisily as they pranced around the fire. They moved quickly now, their bodies jerked and swayed in erratic frenzied motions that seemed almost bizarre and out of control.
>
> The fire was alive with movement and sound. The dance continued to accelerate until it suddenly reached a crescendo and exploded into a blinding burst of golden yellow light. Then, just as suddenly, as the tiny spark in the fire, the burst of yellow separated into a million tiny glowing crimson drops that fell to the earth and formed a river of blood that surrounded and flowed around the fire ...

Maggie woke abruptly. She began to gasp for air. She looked quickly around the campsite and tried to remember where she was. She blinked her eyes to orient herself to her surroundings. The embers of the fire almost completely burned out. Only a few tiny glowing embers remained. Not a sound could be heard anywhere in the campsite.

Maggie could make out Digger's outline where he slept on the other side of the campsite and could hear a familiar snore. In the moonlight, she could even see Nugget in the field, his head hanging low as he rested during the night.

Maggie shuddered. The dream seemed so real. She could almost feel the presence of shadow dancers still around the fire and feel their frenzied movements. The eerie chant still echoed in her mind. She allowed her eyes to move from one shadow to the next until she assured herself there were no spirits in the shadows near the campsite. She lay back down again, convinced she had experienced only a dream.

Maggie's heart jumped again when a sudden motion caught her attention beside the fire. A familiar wet nose nudged her from the darkness. She sighed with relief when Max silently greeted her. Maggie, reassured to have him there beside her, wrapped her arms around his neck and hugged him tightly.

"Hey there buddy, did you hear it, too?" she asked as Max nudged her with his head and placed his paw on her knee. "Thanks for watching out for us Max," she said as she ruffled his neck one more time before she lay back down and tried to sleep once more in spite of the vivid dream she experienced.

Her thoughts wandered to her grandmother and the ceremonies she often performed in honor of special events or certain rites. Grandmother taught Maggie how to meditate and feel connected to the earth. She believed it was important for one to honor the earth, the gifts of nature and God's blessings. For each of them, being in touch with their spiritual side was a way of life and continued to be a way of life for Maggie as she grew and learned to develop intuitive an spiritual skills on her own.

CHAPTER 2

As the first rays of sun began to peak over the mountain range, the little valley where Maggie and Digger camped began to stir with activity and motion as the day began. Birds sang and swooped through the fields in search of their morning meal. In the distance, Maggie could see Nugget as he munched on the lush green grass in the field. The morning moisture lingered in a misty haze that seemed to hang over the top of the tall grass and cling to the bottom of the field giving it a mystical, surreal appearance.

Eager to get started, Maggie threw back her bedroll, shook out her boots and quickly pulled them on her feet. She learned from experience a long time ago that sometimes unwanted critters liked to crawl in nice warm boots at night and it was better to be safe and shake them out. She gathered some of the sticks and broken logs she found laying in the woods yesterday and began to stir the campfire back to life.

As soon as she had a small fire going, she placed the kettle on to boil water for tea and began to prepare fry bread as her grandmother taught her so many years ago. She waited until the skillet was hot and added just a drop of oil, then patted the smooth, elastic fry bread dough in the palms of her hands until it was just the right size. When it was just right, she placed it in the skillet to cook.

In no time, she had a stack of four pieces of fry bread drizzled with cinnamon and honey, and ready to eat. She returned the fry bread to the pan and set it on a stone near the fire pit to stay warm while she took time to extinguish the fire. With conditions as dry as they were, she didn't want to take a chance of a stray spark igniting the grass or brush in the valley. She stirred the coals with a stick, and poured a pail of water on them so they could burn down while she left the campsite to find Digger and Max.

With one quick glance around the clearing, Maggie could see a trail around the edge of the field where something recently bent over the flowers and grass. She thought it was amusing for Digger to be gone from the campsite so early. He often disappeared and hid when they were on treks together to see if she could still track him in the woods. He taught her most of her tracking skills and wanted to make sure she kept them keen, so he often devised new lessons for her when they were in the field.

'Digger must have gone through here' she mused. 'He sure left a big enough trail. This one is obvious enough for even a novice tracker to find. What was he thinking?' She almost laughed as she followed the big clumsy trail of broken grass and flowers around the field. Maggie shook her head as she remembered the many times Digger left signs for her to follow and then hid in places near their campsite and waited to see if she could find him. It was as much a game to him as it was to her. Maggie's mind began to wander as she followed the broad trail along the edge of the field.

'He's so silly; I can't believe he would think for a minute that this enormous trail would challenge me even a little bit. I could follow trails like this when I was seven years old! That old rascal, you just wait until I get my hands on him this time!'

Maggie absentmindedly began to pick up some of the wild flowers knocked over on the trail as she walked. It looked as if something recently knocked them down.

"I'll take these back to camp just to show him how clumsy he has become with this tracking game in his old age."

Her mind wandered as she walked. She thought of Digger and her Grand-mother and the special times they had when she was a child. Maggie leaned down to pick up a beautiful pink coneflower that was broken off the stem when she noticed a clump of black fur apparently pulled off by a blackberry briar.

"Umhm, I see you're with him, Max, you big traitor. It's no fair for you guys to gang up against me like this, but don't worry, I'll find you."

She smiled as she thought of Digger and Max hiding somewhere in the brush waiting for her to find them. "I should make you both wait all morning and eat all the fry bread myself, that would teach you a lesson."

Maggie picked the clump of fur from the blackberry briar and began to rub it between her fingers when a sudden chilling realization began to dawn on her.

The fur felt funny and didn't feel like Max's fur at all. It was much too short and course.

A sudden flurry of motion in the corner of her eye caused her to freeze in her tracks. A chill of fear ran up her spine. She shuddered as she saw the mother deer from yesterday bolt from the field with one of her does. Maggie didn't move a muscle. She held her breath and quickly scanned the field, her eyes darted back and forth across each clump of brush and every tree, her senses alert for danger.

Then, straight ahead, not fifty yards away, Maggie could see the second fawn as it struggled to run through the field in an effort to escape a large black bear that chased it. Confused and disoriented, the little doe ran in circles and seemed blinded by its fear. The black bear barreled down on the fawn and pounced on its back quickly bringing it down to the ground. As the fawn struggled to stand up and get away, the bear brought her down again with one forceful swipe across the neck from the sharp claws of its paw.

"Oh, No!" Maggie cried," That poor baby!"

Impulsively she started to lunge forward to do something to help the fawn as a powerful grip on her arm forced her to stay.

"Ssshhhh!"

She felt Digger's hoarse whisper in her ear.

"Don't ye move a muscle," he whispered.

"But, Digger, we've got to do something! He's going to kill it!"

"She's a' doin' what she's supposed to be doing, girl. We're in her territory right now, an' she has to eat 'n protect her young just like everybody else," Digger whispered. "Come on now, just back away as quiet as ye can; we've got ta get outta here."

Maggie wiped a tear away from her eye and quickly looked away as the large bear began to finish off her prey. Quietly, she followed Digger back to the campsite as she remembered the beauty of the scene yesterday when the mother doe watched out for her two fawns while they grazed in the field.

"It's the way of nature, Maggie," Digger explained as he ate his fry bread. "The way God meant for it to be. Everything's got to eat. There's maybe a million critters that gets eatten up by somethin' in the woods everyday. That deer was gonna be food for somebody. If it hadn't been food for the bear, it might have ended up in somebody's freezer. It's all part of what they call the food chain."

"It was so sad though." Maggie said in a weak, sad voice, the sight of the attack still vivid in her memory. "I didn't think black bears were meat eaters," she commented sadly. "I always thought they were vegetarians."

"Usually, they ain't meat eaters, Maggie. There could be something wrong with that bear, or could be the heat has her confused. What most likely happened is that little fawn must have stumbled on the bear's den 'n startled the mother. When bears fear for their young'ns they get mean tempered."

"I'm glad you were with Digger, buddy, I wouldn't have wanted it to be you." Maggie nuzzled Max sadly thinking of the fawn.

"Bears are usually skeered o' dogs, because people use 'em when they go hunting, so bears don't mess with them unless they come face to face with each other," Digger finished his breakfast and continued to talk as he started to pack up the campsite. "Yep, it is sad to see it when it happens. Life in the wild kin be mighty harsh. Ye cain't start thinking o' every deer you see as Bambi, and every bear you see as a teddy bear. It ain't that way all the time. Every one of them critters is a wild animal, 'n don't you never forget it! It may save your life sumday. You best be respecting them and their territory."

"That's why in the parks the Rangers have to warn folks all the time to stay away from the bears. Almost every year some visitor tries to feed them or get close to them, and then, the bears attack people. The sad thing is, a bear doesn't know how to act any other way than just being a bear. But, once a bear acts out against a visitor, the Rangers end up having to put 'er down just so the visitors won't be hurt and the bear won't be a danger to humans anymore," Digger said with disgust.

"You mean they kill the bear?"

"Yep, to keep people safe even though people are the ones that's visiting in the bear's territory. Usually, when a bear attacks, it's on account o' something a human has done to the bear. It just don't seem right or fair, but that's the way it is most of the time."

Maggie shook her head sadly, when suddenly, she remembered Digger and Max weren 't anywhere around when she woke up this morning and began to follow the trail of broken grass around the field.

"Hey, where were you guys anyway? I thought I was tracking you and Max this morning when I almost ran into the bear."

Digger looked at Maggie over the packs he was tying on Nugget's back as his eyes twinkled. He finished tying the rig before he continued.

"Been waiting for you to ask … we went a'lookin' for something this morning. Come on, girl, there's something I want to show you while we're in the valley before we head back up the mountain. We need to get started before it gets too hot."

"Great!" Maggie said excited to be moving out from the area where she saw the bear, "But give me a minute to double check the campfire."

Maggie took extra care to make sure there were no hot coals left in the campfire before she left the area. She again stirred the center of the ashes to make sure there were no coals left in the center that could re-ignite after she left the area. She then doused the cool ashes with water from the stream and took the small camp shovel from Digger's pack to cover the ashes with sand.

Maggie strapped on her backpack and followed Digger as he led Nugget and Max to the end of the valley. She was more than ready to leave the Spirits of the campfire and the grizzly scene with the bear and head on to new territory. The anticipation of a mystery and an adventure brightened her spirits as she walked out of the little valley.

The area they hiked seemed overgrown with fairly, young hardwood trees and lots of underbrush. They trudged through the dense underbrush for most of the morning taking only short breaks to drink water or rest. Finally, Digger made his way through the maze of trees and foliage to an area that faced what seemed to be a low hill or rise in the ground that was perfectly round and could have been at least a hundred yards or so in diameter. The place was in an area that appeared to be undisturbed by humans for many, many years. In an area as remote as this one was, it was impossible to tell.

Finally, Digger came to stop. Obviously pleased with himself, he then turned and smiled at Maggie as he pushed his felt hat to the back of his head.

"Well, what do you think?" He said and grinned as he took off his hat a wiped his brow with the old felt hat.

"About what?" Maggie asked a little distracted as she pulled a couple of briars out of her hair and stood beside Digger facing the small rise in the terrain.

"It's 'bout what yer lookin' at rite now!" Digger beamed. "I'm pretty sure this is one 'o them ancient Indian burial grounds I was telling you about. It's just like the one I was tellin' you about that's up in Coker Creek. See how the ground is mounded up in a perfect circle. It's so big! There's trees growing on it right now, but they weren't there years ago when it was first built."

Maggie stopped what she was doing and looked in the direction Digger was pointing more seriously. Her eyes traveled around the edge of the woods to the large mound and surveyed the clumps of trees on the mound.

"Has anyone ever dug around in them to prove these were the same type burial grounds? They may be empty by now if anyone has looted it, or maybe it's just a hill."

"As far as I know, nobody's ever messed with this place. I seen this place once years ago when I was a little boy 'n thought it looked mighty strange then, almost out 'o place. I didn't know what might have caused it to look this way until I heard the University man who is here for the summer speak in town. He got permission from the forest service to document a lot of the ancient burial sites and started to talk about the ancient mounds he's heard folks talk about. He wanted more information."

Maggie's whole body tingled with the possibility of being near enough to see an ancient sacred site. Just the very thought that ancient peoples passed through this way was intriguing, but to actually see something that might be a part of their history was absolutely, sensational. This site was so unusual, yet so well hidden she might have passed by it a hundred times and never recognized it for what it was. To the untrained eye, it looked simply like a hill.

"Wow!" she sank to her knees in awe. "This is incredible! I think I would pass a place like this many times and not realize it was anything other than a small hill until you brought it to my attention. Now, it really stands out, it's very distinctive."

"It's somthin' ain't it!" Digger beamed.

"It sure is, Digger. It's amazing. I can't believe you remembered it from so long ago. How many years has it been since you saw it?"

"It's been nigh on to seventy years or more since I seen it for the first time. I've been over these here mountains all my life, but I can't say I've been in this exact spot but once. When I heard the University fellas at the BP the other day talk about the mounds and heard them talk about how they wanted to find Indian things, it got me to remembering this place. So, that's when I called you, I wanted ta check it out."

The BP was a small gas station with a country diner inside where all the locals liked to hang out and drink coffee. One could catch up on almost anything in the morning before getting the day started or at the end of the day before going home. Digger and several of his buddies migrated there from the town square after city officials removed the park benches in town where they used to spend their time. When they sat in town, they often whittled, chewed tobacco, and told tall tales. Now, they met at the BP.

"Oh, yeah, you mentioned a stranger in town? Was he trying to buy artifacts from Indian burial sites?" Maggie asked.

She was alarmed that this student's bold talk might bring out the looter in some people who needed money, or those who didn't respect the sanctity of sacred places. Although she saw many artifacts on her journeys with Digger and her grandmother, she never removed any of them. They taught her to learn from the places, respect them and leave things as they were.

"All he said was that he wanted to see some of the ancient places and was willing to pay for genuine Indian items, no questions asked." Digger stood and stretched his legs as he prepared to leave. "He made it clear he wasn't concerned about how he got them."

"But, that's illegal! That doesn't sound like something the University would have him do, he must be doing it on his own. He can't do that! There won't be a place in the whole area that's safe from grave robbers."

Angrily, Maggie stood up and began pacing back and forth in front of the mound as she talked. She quickly tried to think of things she and Digger could do to protect this area and keep it hidden from looters. The mountains and its treasures were almost sacred to her and Digger as well.

"What are we going to do, Digger? We can't let anyone find out about this. If this place is still in its original condition and never excavated, people will rip to shreds and take all the treasures away. You know very few people will respect it as a sacred place and all of its treasures will all be lost forever."

"They ain't much we can do, Maggie, except keep our eyes 'n ears open for trouble. For right now, this place is safe. Nobody knows about it. Just make sure that the next time you see your friends at the ranger station you tell 'em about the college boy 'n what he was sayin' at the BP. Tell 'em to watch out for looters."

"Have you ever found any artifacts here, Digger?"

"When I came here the first time, I found a couple of arrowheads 'n a piece of what looked like it could o' been a stone bowl of sorts, but I didn't do any digging. At the time, I didn't think about it too much so I just left things as they was."

"You said this place was similar to other places where the Mississippi Mound Builders passed through. How are they alike?"

"Back in the 1800's, 'n then again around the 1970's they had some University folks that came down here 'n ta Loudon County to investigate signs of Indians passing. They looked at old burial grounds, 'n mounds so they could study 'em and see how the folks lived back then."

"What did they find?"

"They uncovered some 'o the old graves 'n things like that. Then, they discovered there were more than one kind 'o Indians that passed thru the area. That was something they already knew they just wanted proof. What they found was that in the burial sites, there were different kinds of Indians buried. They could tell they were from different tribes because they were placed in the ground in different ways."

"How were these burial grounds different from the Cherokee or Yuchi burial grounds?"

"Some of the graves they found had folks buried together on sort of a limestone slab. There were other folks burried in a different way right on top of them. Those university folks study the way a body is laid in the ground, the direction they got the body faced and what kind of things are in the grave with the body to decide what tribe they came from when they died."

"Has anyone ever found proof of a Yuchi grave in this area?"

"Not yet, it's just a matter of time though. They did a lot of investigating down around the river bottom when the folks were buildin' the TVA Tellico Lake. Evidently, there was a huge Indian village sumone discovered at the forks of the river. Them University folks were trying to study the village and save ancient things from it before the lake waters flooded it and took away all the information".

"This is all so amazing, Digger. My head is spinning."

"Yep, in one way, you want to leave the dead alone 'n let em be. In another way, you don't want to let the lake waters flood interesting pieces of history, either," he said with a grimace, "but that's progress," he said as he wearily rubbed his back.

"I'm about beat fer t'day, Maggie. Why don't we head back to our last campsite 'n stay there before we head back up the mountain."

Maggie looked at Digger closely. Sometimes, she forgot his age when they were hiking or camping and didn't pay attention to signs he needed to rest. He usually told her when he was ready to rest, but she always felt badly when she didn't notice the signs he was tiring and brought up taking a break before he had to mention it.

She nodded her head in agreement and took one last look at the ancient mound before she turned to follow Digger and Nugget out of the valley and back to their first campsite. It felt like the trek back took longer to hike than when they started the day.

Dusk had settled by time the weary travelers arrived at their campsite. After a quick dinner, they all lay down to rest without building a campfire. It was difficult for Maggie to get a restful sleep. Her mind whirled with the new things she learned about the ancient Indian tribe that lived in the area before the Cherokee. She could not pull her thoughts from and the precious, ancient burial sacred site she and Digger saw this afternoon. She felt a sense of anxiety grow in the pit of her stomach when her thoughts returned to how they could keep the site safe.

'I once heard someone say, 'knowledge is power, but in this case, I feel as though knowledge must also be a huge responsibility. It feels like a burden. I can't take what I've seen and learned today about the ancient burial site and just store it away. I want to know more about the people who came from far away, how they disappeared and how to protect these ancient places as best I can.'

CHAPTER 3

They started their trek home just as soon as the sun was up and it was light enough to see the trail. It took most of the day for Maggie and Digger to make it to the top of the ridge where their journey began. The combination of the heat, suffocating humidity and lack of any breeze slowed them down as they trudged up the mountain.

Maggie's legs felt as heavy as lead with every step she took. By the time they reached the top of the ridge, they had to stop and catch their breath at almost every turn of the switchback trail. They both needed to rest as much as they needed to stop for drinks of water. The intense heat sapped their energy as well as their fluids.

Maggie felt like a fish out of water unable to breathe properly. With every breath she took, she felt as though she was trying to suck oxygen trough gills that weren't operating properly. She looked at Digger in amazement. He was having a rough time, too, but he was doing better than she was.

'And to think he's almost EIGHTY YEARS OLD!!! I hope that I'm able to get around half as good as he does when I'm his age', she thought then, giggled. 'Heck, Maggie, you're ALREADY getting around half as well as he is, and you're almost half his age! Get over it!'

Max heard some unusual movements down the trail and disappeared over the ridge as she and Digger arrived at the top of the trail. She didn't try to keep up with the dog because he was too fast. She was too tired to tell him to slow down, and knew she couldn't keep in step with him.

"That dog has more energy than a barrel of monkeys. You'd be rich if we could find a way to bottle it up and sell it," Digger commented with admiration. "Whatever he discovered will just have to wait until we can get enough oomph to get there, and I'm in no big hurry. It's way too hot for that."

Maggie nodded as she and Digger leaned against a huge stone and drank some of the water from their canteens. Digger took off his hat and filled it with water for Nugget to drink while they cooled off. Maggie leaned back to place the weight of her backpack on the rock while she rested, although she didn't take it off. She knew once she took it off, she would be too tired to try to pick it up again.

"You just about 'bested' me this time, Digger. I'm just about whooped," she looked up at him and grinnned.

"You ain't getting soft on me are you? What do you say we get up 'n go right back down there again," Digger teased. "We didn't take the time to pan fer gold while we where there, 'n I've been hankering to pan for a while."

Maggie rolled her eyes at him.

"Sure, Digger, I'll go whenever you're ready," she replied hoping he didn't mean today. "It's not like I have anything else to do but hike," she said jokingly.

They looked up as Max trotted back over the top of the ridge with a large man who wore the familiar khaki uniform of the park Rangers close behind him. Ranger Stratton's large frame and easy stride always made hiking seem easy. His cheerful smile and friendly face was always a welcome site when they were on the trail. He always looked like a large, friendly country boy in a Ranger's uniform. He smiled and nodded as he topped the ridge.

"Hello, Maggie, Digger. Boy, am I glad to see you two. I was beginning to wonder if I was going to have to put out a search team for you two before I went home tonight," he said as he stopped by the rock where Digger and Maggie were resting and took out his canteen for a drink of water.

"Hey, Stratton. What's up?" Maggie smiled, "I thought on a hot day like this you'd rather be stuck behind the desk than out hiking on one of these trails."

"Yeah, right, I'd rather be cool, but I'd rather be hiking than anything. This time, I didn't have much choice. They've got us checking out all of the trails this week and I drew this one to hike." Stratton adjusted his pack and leaned on the rock across from them. "Thought you might be having some trouble with your jeep, I saw it back there on the trail. It looked like it was broken down."

"Nah, it just overheated a little on my way up here yesterday. I'll fill the water tank up before I try to drive back down the mountain."

"Anything special goin' on to get all you fellas out on the trails t'day?" Digger asked, curiously. "It's been a while since they put every Ranger on the trails."

"Well, we've got two things going on really. We haven't had any rain in the area for several weeks. With the extreme temperatures we have right now, there's a high risk of forest fires so we have a ban on campfires on the trails until it rains a little. Don't want any hikers to get careless and leave a campfire unattended. It would be easy to get trapped in one of these little valleys if a fire gets started."

"You're right about that!" Digger nodded. "I've seen whole mountains go up in flames before when one o' them big fires jumps from ridge to ridge. It's easy to get trapped if you're in a valley below them."

"What's the other thing?" Maggie asked.

"Well, we've been getting reports of illegal hunting and trapping in some of the remote areas and we've been on the look out for poachers. Did you see any signs of traps or animal kills on your hike?"

Maggie looked at Digger. The sight of the bear and deer yesterday morning still vivid in her memory. She shook her head in sadness.

"The only animal kill we saw was a black bear when it killed a fawn," Maggie said sadly. "We're not sure what provoked the attack."

Digger nodded his head in agreement, as he looked in Maggie's direction.

"She was purty tore up about it, 'n had a hankering to save the deer. But, she knew to let nature take its course."

"Yep, that's always a tough sight to see when it happens." Stratton agreed. "I know you wanted to help the deer Maggie, but I'm glad you didn't interfere. It really messes up the course of nature when folks try to stop something like that from happening. Sometimes, when people with good intentions try to intervene, they get hurt or killed. They had a case like that over in the Gatlinburg area not too long ago where a visitor tried to stop a black bear from killing a fawn and the rangers arrested the visitor!"

"Really! What did they charge him with?" Maggie asked.

"They charged him with 'disrupting the course of nature' and 'endangering wildlife', I believe. The Rangers started conducting schools over there to teach the visitors how to watch the wildlife without interfering."

"That's amazing! Will he have to spend time in jail?" Maggie asked.

"He may, and he'll probably get a pretty hefty fine, too. Lots of the campers saw him throwing rocks and kicking towards the bear to try to get it off the deer," Stratton continued, "It's a good thing it was a small bear. A larger bear might have attacked and killed the man. That would have been an even bigger tragedy than it already was. The bear would also be destroyed for attacking a human."

Maggie and Digger nodded in agreement.

"Well, as long as you two are ok and off the trails, I'm going to head on out. I have quite a few miles to go before I get back home tonight. If you see any other campers on your way home, let them know about the hazardous fire conditions. Be sure you tell them that the trails are going to be closed for a while till we get some good rains if you don't mind."

"Sure will," Maggie said and waved as Stratton headed down the switchback trail. "Be careful!"

"You've got it," Stratton smiled and nodded. "Oh, by the way, there's a special program at Indian Boundary Campground tonight you two may be interested in hearing."

"Really?" Maggie paused curious about the program. "What is it about this time?" She loved the special programs designed by the Rangers for visitors and often participated herself in programs to educate children about wildlife and nature.

"Well, we have a couple of fellas from one of the universities that are spending the summer here helping us work on some of the remote trails. Their specialty in school is studying ancient Native American tribes. They're going to speak about some tribes that were in this area a long time ago.

Maggie and Digger glanced at each other.

"What time does it start?" Maggie asked as she tried to squelch the alarm that rose inside her. "That might be something I'd like to hear about."

"Should get started around 8pm when the sun goes down. We have to wait until it's a little cooler to meet with the campers; otherwise it's hard to keep their attention."

"Sounds like fun!" Maggie said excitedly, "Hope to see you there".

"Sounds like we need to show up at the campground to check out these two University men and see what they're up to," Maggie commented to Digger.

"I think you're right."

"Well, Digger, I'm beat. I think I'm ready to go home and rest, how about you? Are you heading back to your cabin?"

"I'm headed back to my cabin to get cleaned up and then I'm gonna head to the campground. If we can get an idea of what these fellers are talkin about, we'll know more how to handle them." Digger's eyes began to sparkle as he grabbed Nugget's lead rope and started to walk briskly again.

"There must be somebody special who might be at the campground for you to get cleaned up before Sunday," Maggie teased when she saw the sparkle in his eyes.

Digger grinned and tipped his hat as he grabbed Nugget's lead and headed down the mountain. His jaunty step was a little lighter and quicker now he headed downhill and the intense sun was gone.

"There may even be somebody there you might be interested in yerself!" he teased as he kicked up his heels and tipped his hat.

Maggie laughed as she headed to the jeep. She knew he was teasing her about her relationship with the retired doctor who lived near her on the same remote mountain. Their friendship was growing stronger every day and her friends kept a watchful eye.

'It will be good to see Doc again. There are so many things we both have in common, and he loves to hear about the hikes Digger and I take when he can't join us. I always feel so comfortable and peaceful when I'm with him. It feels like we were made for each other.'

Maggie and Doc already had quite a history together of danger and adventure. While living on the mountain, they worked together to help a woman who lived near them deliver her baby in the middle of a blinding snowstorm. Last spring, they also helped Rangers solve an illegal drug lab in the area and saved Digger when he almost lost his life in a terrible mining accident. It began to seem as though whatever they were involved in together ended up being adventurous and exciting at the very least.

After Maggie refilled the water tank in the jeep and closed the hood, she motioned for Max to climb into the back. She loaded her backpack in the passenger seat before she headed on the rugged service trail down the mountain. She quickly glanced in the rear view mirror, brushed one of the curls out of her face and smiled as her thoughts returned to Doc. Her heart skipped a beat and began to beat stronger.

'I wonder what time it is. It really would be fun to clean up and go to the campground for an evening. After a good hot shower, a meal and some good mountain music, I'd feel like a million dollars. Plus, if I happened to run into Doc. Well, that wouldn't be half-bad either, in fact, that would be very, very nice'.

CHAPTER 4

It took Maggie the rest of the afternoon to return to her remote log cabin in the mountains near the Cherahala Skyway. To get home, she drove almost seven miles on a rugged unpaved forest service road through an area inhabited with only two families in other cabins. Travel on the rough road was a challenge on good days; during inclement weather, it was nearly impossible. Today, the road was especially difficult because the dry weather conditions created enormous amounts of dust as she drove.

Maggie pulled into her yard late in the afternoon and parked the jeep under a huge oak tree near her cabin. Before she could get out of her seat, Max leaped across her lap and out of the door as soon as she opened it.

"Good grief, Max!"

Maggie fussed as she followed him out of the jeep and tried to brush the paw prints off her clothes. "You could at least TRY to give me time to get out before you go barreling out the door!"

Max was thrilled to be home. He leaped and jumped around in a circle then, quickly made a mad dash around the yard. He checked the edge of the woods, sniffed rocks, trees and holes in the ground for anything he could chase. From the moment Digger brought him to live with her seven years ago, Max took it upon himself to become chief of security around her and personal body guard wherever they were. His loyalty and selflessness had saved her life more than once. She knew he would risk his life to save her if need be.

It didn't take long for Max to make his way to the ground hog den where Basil, Maggie's resident groundhog, set up housekeeping. Max and the ground hog made a game of constantly harassing and pestering each other in every way possible. Basil loved to sneak up on the porch and eat food from Max's dish, and Max loved to chase him around the field and dig out Basil's den. They seemed to get into some wild battles at times, but enjoyed the challenge of the game and didn't act as if either of them wanted to stop their game.

Max stuck his huge nose and head down into the groundhog den then barked several times. His tail wagged and swayed in the air as he waited for a response from inside. Hearing nothing, he pulled his head out of the hole and sniffed the air for some scent that might tell him where Basil might be hiding. When he could find no trace of the groundhog, he remembered the stream that flowed through the woods on their property and trotted off to the creek to play in the water.

Maggie shook her head as she carried her backpack up the stone walk to the cabin. She leaned her backpack against the wall of the cabin and took her boots off before she headed inside the cabin.

"Max, I'm going inside to clean up, you behave yourself!" she called over her shoulder as she walked up to the porch. "I'm definitely going to hang this pair of shoes outside for a while. Don't want the cabin to smell like dirty socks. There's enough foul odors with you always giving me the smelly things you finds in the woods."

Maggie breathed a huge sigh of relief as the cool, clean air from within the cabin greeted her when she walked in the door. Although her cabin was over 100 years old, it didn't have air conditioning. The ancient oak timbers were so thick; they were able to keep the cabin a comfortable temperature even in the extreme heat of summer or cold of winter. The natural slate floor that covered the main level of the cabin helped keep the cabin cool in the summer. In winter, she placed woven area rugs in places that were too far away from the fireplace to stay warm. The rugs gave the room a cozy, natural feel, and also kept the cabin nice and warm. She glanced around the room overcome with a feeling of contentment.

'Umm, it feels good to be home again', she thought as she walked to the front window and propped it open. She always felt centered and connected here to the things she loved the most. There wasn't a single day since she moved back home from the city that she regretted her move. In her heart, she knew this was where she belonged.

Maggie spent over twenty years working with families in crisis in a large city until she was finally able to save enough money to return home and live in her Grandmother's old log cabin. To come back to this place was a goal of hers for many years, even though it always seemed to be impossible. She finally came to a place in her life where she decided she had enough ... enough of the sadness, enough of the hurtful things people do to each other, enough climbing the corporate ladder at work and enough of relationships.

When she discovered she could make ends meet by supplementing her income with articles she wrote for magazines, she decided to move back home again. She bought this place and walked away from everything she had in the city.

Although, she initially came to the mountain to escape from city life in general, as with everyone else, life often has other things in store for us that can't be foreseen. It was the same for Maggie. Since moving back, she found it was almost impossible to live in an area and not become involved in the community or the people who lived there. There was no escape from life and being a part of life meant one had to get involved.

She quickly discovered being reclusive was not always the best choice for anyone because people needed each other in many ways. And as much as she hated to admit it at first, she knew she needed people. She also knew she enjoyed spending time talking to people and getting to know them. She found she could learn something from everyone she met and that she really enjoyed it, too.

The construction of Maggie's cabin was similar to many of the old cabin designs. Many years ago, cabins were built as one simple large room with a large front porch. To the left, an enormous stone fireplace covered the entire end of the room. It had a massive old oak mantle built into the stones. Maggie kept an old oil lamp on the mantle to use in case of emergencies, and a variety of hand carved bears and animals that people made for her and given her through the years.

On the fireplace hearth, she kept some old, well-used iron kettles, a handmade pottery butter churn that once belonged to her grandmother and a section of a huge copper still from an old broken down moonshine still she found on her property when she first moved there. The copper still was a wonderful conversation piece because it was an actual remnant of east Tennessee history.

Although illegal, making moonshine was very often a source of income for many people in the poverty-stricken Appalachian area. In the local area, there were many folk tales told of those who tried to make moonshine and those who tried to banish it. The amazing thing about Maggie's pot was that anyone could survive drinking anything from a copper still with a two-inch seam of soldered lead.

Along the wall, a large, comfortable sofa that sat on a braided rag rug. A rough oak coffee table her grandfather made to celebrate her birthday when she was very young sat in front of the sofa. A bookshelf nearby was filled with things she had collected through the years. There was a small hummingbird nest, an old pottery vase, and a few baskets filled with feathers and rocks she found while hiking.

On the other side of the cabin a small kitchen complete with a stove, refrigerator and an old butcher block filled the end of the room. Open shelves displayed a collection of pottery dishes and food supplies. She positioned a small round oak table in front of the other window, facing the field and mountain. Maggie could sit here and watch the sunrise as she ate breakfast or the moonrise in the evening before going to sleep.

A loft above the main room contained most of Maggie's reading and study materials, her paints and most of her craft projects. It had a small desk and a day bed for guests when overnight company came for a visit. The loft was a wonderful place to read in the winter, as it was the warmest area of the cabin. Here, she looked out the window from the loft, she could see across the field to the mountains beyond.

Maggie walked into the kitchen to pour a glass of lemonade and grabbed an apple before she headed into the bedroom to clean up. Her bedroom was one large room that was built as a lean to on the original cabin when, as a young child, she first came to live with her grandmother. Her grandmother lived all of her life in the cabin as a one-room home, but felt Maggie needed more space. She enlisted the help of Digger and some other friends to build the bedroom, bathroom and add electricity to the cabin for Maggie.

'As much as I love nature and the natural life, there are some things I will always be grateful for,' Maggie thought to herself as she began to take her dirty hiking clothes off and prepared to take a shower. 'Electricity and hot water are two items that are pretty high on my list.'

The hot steamy water from the shower soothed her aching muscles and slowly began to wash the dirt and grime of the trail away. Maggie stayed in the shower until she finally felt squeaky clean again.

She sipped on the lemonade as she dried her hair with a towel and began to prepare to go to the campground program. She chose a pair of khaki shorts and white tee shirt with a daisy on the collar. Her dark hair fell in damp curls around her shoulders. Quickly she looked in the mirror. Serious soft gray eyes returned her gaze. She looked at the image and shook her head.

'Forty-six and counting, humm, not bad I guess. I suppose it could be worse, I could still be working in the city and have stress lines, or EVERY hair on my head could be gray instead of half of them!'

She laughed as she smoothed the skin on her face with a small amount of cream. She then fluffed up her hair a little with her fingertips, knowing it would dry on its own before she got to the campground.

'Wouldn't do much good to dry it or roll it anyway. As hot as it is outside, it would be all frizz and curls in an hour. At least I'm clean.'

She grabbed the remainder of her apple and headed out of the door. She glanced around the yard for Max and didn't see him until she reached the jeep. He raced up the path to greet her from the stream. Covered with mud and soaking wet from the cool water, he couldn't wait to share the cool water with Maggie. She saw him head toward her and immediately held up her hand.

"Max, NO!" She said sternly.

He screeched to a halt in front of her, sat down and wiggled while he waited for her to pet him. She taught him to halt mostly to prevent him from accidentally knocking her down when he ran to her. At 125 pounds, he was a very strong dog and could easily overpower her. He just didn't realize that he was seven years old, not a puppy anymore and too big to crawl in her lap or jump on her.

"Max, STAY!" She looked at him and pointed her finger at the ground. He knew she was serious when she held her hand up to him. "I have to go for a while, you stay here, STAY!"

He looked at her with huge brown eyes, his tongue hung out of his mouth and tail wagged as Maggie opened the door and started to climb in the jeep. Just before she closed the door, Max jumped up, shook and sprayed her with water before he trotted over to the shade tree and lay down.

"MAX!" Maggie tried to brush off the water quickly before it had time to seep into her clothes. "Great, now I smell like wet dog fur, that's going to be a real turn on for everybody near me," she said as she turned to look at Max who wagged his tail and barked. "At least YOU seem pleased you shared with me."

Maggie drove slowly and carefully on the dirt road to keep the dust level to a minimum. In spite of the heat, she kept the windows up on the jeep and ran only the fan to keep the dust inside the jeep to a minimum. She laughed when she thought how funny she would look if she arrived at the evening program at the campground drenched with perspiration and covered with dust.

'I can see the headlines of the local newspaper now, "Former crisis counselor crashes campfire program covered in mud. Everyone dashes to safety as the odor of wet animal fur permeates the air," she laughed and shook her head, "It would be just my luck to finally get up the nerve to go to a Saturday night program and have everyone run away in fear or disgust. It's the stuff nightmares are made of for reclusive people."

Maggie glanced toward the McCutchen's cabin as she drove down the mountain. No one appeared to be home, the lights were off and the boys were nowhere in sight. 'They must have gone to the campfire program. Someone must have come by to take them, or maybe Ranger Stratton came back from checking the trails in time to take them. He's really going out of his way to help Rena with the children since her husband died,' she smiled at the thought of Stratton becoming a part of the children's lives.

The McCutchens lived in one of the two other cabins on the same mountain where Maggie lived. Rena's family ancestors lived in the same place for many generations. She was raising her two young sons, Zack and Jonah and their little sister Abigail, who was less than a year old, by herself since her husband died. His death in a tragic mining accident happened shortly after Rena became pregnant with Abigail.

Maggie smiled as she thought of Rena's little family. They are so tough and resourceful, the perfect example of the typical Appalachian mountain family. In the face of hardships, they make do with what they have without trying to impose on others. They are hard working, loyal and honest in everything they do. If I ever had children of my own, I would hope they would be like Zack and Jonah, they are such great kids.

She often asked Zack and Jonah to help her pick strawberries or work in her garden and gave them vegetables or other items she knew they needed in exchange. She knew Rena would refuse to take a handout or a gift without being able to give something in return, so Maggie worked out special deals with the boys that helped both her and Rena's family, also.

If she let too many days go by without stopping to see the boys, she knew they would pull some prank or stunt to find a way to get her to stop when she drove past their house on her way up the mountain. At four and six years old, they loved to pretend they captured her and often took her in to their mother as hostage. Maggie usually allowed herself to become a captive with little resistance. She loved her visits with Rena and the children and tried to stop as often as possible. She looked forward to the possibility of seeing them at the campfire program tonight.

Maggie's thoughts turned to Doc, or Chris, as he wanted her to call him. It was so hard to change now and call him Chris since she called him Doc for so long. First names made their relationship seem much more real. She arrived at the campground around dusk and parked her jeep in one of the parking lots near the swimming area. She then began to walk the short distance to the community campfire and stage area where many of the current campers gathered for the evening program.

CHAPTER 5

Located just a few miles from her cabin, Maggie could visit Indian Boundary Lake as often as possible. A beautiful, pristine 96-acre lake at the North East section of Tennessee in the Cherokee National Forest, the campground borders the Tennessee and North Carolina state line. The state park is complete with numerous campsites for campers, a beautiful sandy beach for swimming, shower houses and a three and a half mile hiking trail that surrounds the lake along the edge of the woods.

As Maggie walked along the path that circled the lake toward the group campfire area, she felt someone come up close behind her. She turned to see Doc smile down at her. He quickly picked up his step and walked along beside her.

"Good evening, Maggie," he said. His eyes twinkled when he spoke. "I thought you might be here tonight."

Maggie felt a rush of excitement when she saw him. Her face felt warm and filled with a rosy color. She paused in the path to allow him to catch up with her.

"Hey Doc," she grinned.

"You must have heard about the special program tonight."

"Yes, Digger and I were on one of the trails when we ran into Stratton. He told us all about it. We thought it might be something we needed to check into."

"So, do you have anyone to sit with yet?' he asked with a smile.

"Well, I was kind of hoping you would be here," she said quietly as he reached for her hand and they continued to walk down the path to the camp-fire.

Maggie and Doc quietly slipped in behind the last row of campers on the log benches. The small rustic arena around the campfire and stage area was almost filled with people. A small wooden stage in front of the benches rose behind the campfire where speakers could stand slightly above the crowd. Although there were twenty-four benches, there were few places left to sit, as adults and children who camped in the National campground over the weekend filled every seat. It was good to see so many people out for the evening program.

One of the Forest service Rangers usually conducted the small presentations. Tonight, Ranger Stratton presented a program on local herbs and wildflowers native to the area that were currently in season. On the stage beside him, two small boys who wore matching outfits in colors similar to the Ranger's official attire assisted him with the program. A scruffy little mixed breed dog sat obediently between the boys on the stage.

Zack was slightly taller and obviously the oldest of the two boys. His jet-black hair fell in a straight line across dark eye brows giving his steel blue eyes a calm, sincere look. He took his job seriously, as he walked among the benches filled with campers and passed around samples of flowers he carried to campers in the audience.

The smaller and younger of the two boys was Jonah, who looked as if he had filled out some since Maggie last saw him, but still seemed small for his age. His bright red hair was ruffled and just as tussled and unruly as it was each time Maggie saw Jonah. Several dozen new freckles had developed his face and arms with the summer sun. He broadly grinned and waved from across the crowd when he saw Maggie and Doc in the back of the arena.

Jonah returned from the crowd and stood staunchly on the stage beside Ranger Stratton as he spoke. Behind them, the boy's small scruffy dog sat and watched their every move. The dog looked so odd it was difficult to tell what genetic pool he came from, although, he looked as if he could have some collie and terrier heritage. The most endearing quality about the dog was that he looked so peculiar he became instantly charming. One ear on the dog stood straight up while the other ear flopped over an eye. The fur on his face stood out in all directions as if he had static electricity in his fur. He seemed to have an uncanny ability to express emotions and frequently stole the show from his human counterparts.

Ranger Stratton discussed each plant as the boys slowly walked among the benches and allowed the campers an opportunity to see samples of native plants for themselves so they would know how to recognize them in the wild.

A soft chuckle rippled through the crowd when a little girl squealed with delight as the older of the two boys passed near her. Zack grinned and blushed slightly as he looked her way and waved. She squealed louder and stretched her arms toward him, wiggled and then flapped her arms wildly.

"Zaa, Zaa, Zaa" she called to him, "uhh, uhh, uhh!" she called as she struggled to get out of her mother's arms.

Zack lay the bundle of Jerusalem Artichokes down on the stage, walked toward his mother and took his baby sister from her arms. She immediately wrapped her arms tightly around his neck and squealed with delight again.

"Bob-oo, Bob-oo, Bob-oo," she cried as she covered his face with kisses.

A warm feeling flowed through the small crowd in the arena as everyone smiled at the tender scene. She was certainly stealing the show from the Ranger. Her love and adoration for her brother was obvious.

"Come on, Abby, you can help me," Zack told her.

He handed her part of his bundle of flowers to hold and hoisted her up on his hip then continued to walk among the campers again. No one seemed to notice the flowers she held as the pair walked in and out among the benches because all eyes seemed to be on the special bond between the two children.

After the touching scene, Ranger Stratton knew he obviously lost the group's attention as all eyes trained on his three young helpers and their dog. Stratton smiled with pride and continued his discussion on native herbs as best he could.

"In addition to its beauty as a flower, the Jerusalem Artichoke's root can be used for anything you use a potato for in cooking. Simply dig up the root, wash it and prepare it in the same way as vegetables. They can be boiled, fried or baked. Other edible root plants include a plant most of you know as Queen Ann's Lace. The beautiful delicate flower that tops the plant can be fried and eaten, but the tastiest part of the plant lives just under the soil. Just beneath ground, you will find a long slender root known as 'squaw's carrot'. It is packed with vitamins and nutrients, tastes similar to a home grown carrot and will help you survive in the wilderness if you have no food."

"There are, also, many types of wild mint growing along the trails of the National Forest. You can find these plants in abundance along stream banks and trails in the woods. For a breath freshener, simply pull a few of the tender new leaves from the top of the plant, wash them and chew on them. To flavor your drink, crush a few leaves and toss them into your tea as it brews. In addition, these plants can be used to settle an upset stomach."

folks who were unscrupulous in their searches or insensitive in their pursuits of ancient treasures would damage or destroy the sacred burial sites. She always felt some things were better off when left undiscovered and these men seemed to inspire the lust for treasure hunts in everyone.

She eyed the crowd anxiously. Several of the campers talked eagerly to each other. Many of the campers seemed to be excited about the professor's speech. The buzz among the campers intensified as the professor began to describe artifacts and explain exactly what he was looking for when he researched a site.

Maggie leaned over to Doc and whispered in his ear.

"We will have no stone left unturned on the mountain if he continues to talk like that. Every treasure hound on the mountain will think they have made a discovery with each stone they see."

Doc nodded in agreement.

Ranger Stratton closed the campfire program with a dry alert warning and reminded everyone to be safe with campsites. He also reported that until the area had some significant rain, there would be a 'no campfire' warning on all of the trails outside the official campground. As the crowd dispersed, Maggie's eyes wandered among the crowd. Everyone was discussing the professor's lecture and the possibility of unearthing some type of treasure in this remote region or maybe even in their own back yard.

Maggie's eyes fell on a pair of men who stood at the edge of the clearing. Although, she did not know them personally, she occasionally saw them in town when they came down from the mountain for supplies. The two men were dressed in their usual attire of faded overalls and soiled tee shirts. Both had shoulder length scraggly hair and long beards. They stood near each other by the campfire and eagerly whispered to each other. They seemed suspicious as they looked out over the crowd and stared at campers.

In light of the professor's lecture, Maggie was curious about what the two men discussed so fervently. She often wondered what they did for a living in the mountains, and what their current source of income was. Both men always seemed to have cash available for their purchases in town, but neither had an apparent job. Maggie often heard rumors around town, which indicated locals thought the two were involved in making and selling moonshine, but no one who would talk about it had proof of the rumor, so the stories remained simply rumors.

Maggie's concentration was broken when she felt Doc's hand slip under her elbow and guide her down the path to the front of the arena where Stratton and Rena stood with her children. The lectures were over and they were ready to leave.

"You seem to be in deep concentration tonight," Doc commented with a smile as they walked down the path.

"Oh, well, the professor's speech left me with a bad feeling that he may have inspired some people to start on treasure hunts in the forest and loot the sacred sites. As I listened to him, I watched those two characters over there. They seem to be fascinated about something. I've never seen them talk so much."

Doc laughed, "Oh, no, Maggie! Here we go again!"

"What?" Maggie asked with a bewildered look on her face.

"I can see that curious, determined look on your face already. You don't have to seek out trouble, it just seems to arrive at your doorstep when you least expect it."

"But …," Maggie started to respond when she saw an old mountain man signal her at the edge of the clearing. "Excuse me, Doc. I see Digger and need to talk to him for just a minute. It won't take long."

She quickly walked over to meet Digger, relieved to be away from Doc's observations. She was glad to talk with someone sensible and practical like Digger who didn't make her heart race or her stomach knot up like it did when she was with Doc.

Maggie grinned as she walked to the edge of the woods where Digger anxiously waited for her to arrive. He paced back and forth on a small trail that led away from the campfire area as she walked toward him. He obviously was anxious to talk to her.

"Maggie, we gots to get on the back trails as soon as we can," he began eagerly.

"Hey, Digger, it's good to see you again, too," she grinned and gave him a warm embrace. "If I'm not mistaken, didn't we just come off one of the trails earlier today?"

"I'm serious, Maggie, we gots to go. There's something we gots to check out! I heard a rumor."

"Anything you want to tell me about before we go?"

"I can't tell you nothing with all them folks around here, you know that," he said seriously. "I'll tell you when we're on the trail, 'n not a minute before that."

Maggie smiled and laughed.

"Ok, I understand. So, are you talking about a camping trip or a backpacking trip? Do you realize how hot it is this week! It's been in the upper 90's all week long and there's no rain in the forecast for at least another week.

"I ain't talking about no camping trip. I'm talking about us takin' a pack trip to the backwoods, one where we load up 'ole Nugget 'n take him, too. We'll need him to carry things with us because we're gonna be gone for several days."

"You're serious!" she exclaimed, surprised he was ready to get on the trail again so soon after their last adventure, "I thought you were teasing."

"It's important, Maggie," Digger's face clouded with a dark, serious look. "That there University feller's got me worried about something and we need to check it out."

Maggie noticed Digger's sense of alarm and fear. His expression seemed to intensify and confirm her own anxiety about the professor.

"Ok, Digger. If it means that much to you, we'll go."

"It's important, Maggie. It's dang important!" His eyes glowered and a deadly serious look crossed his face. "Bring the Doc with you, too. We may need him."

"Ok, when do you want to go?"

"First, I need to check something out 'n meet somebody in town tomorree. So, we can go the day after tomorree. That'll give you a day to get ready. I'll meet you on the trail," he said as he pulled the front of his old brown felt hat down over his eyes and disappeared into the shadows around the clearing.

Maggie watched him disappear into the darkness of the trees. She was always amazed at his ability to come and go so quickly and without notice. She felt Doc move beside her. He looked toward the woods where Digger disappeared.

"What's Digger up to today? Is he planning on getting you off on another one of his crazy adventures again?"

"He's got something up his sleeve; says he wants to go on a trek to the back country. I think something the professor said has him worried. He wanted me to see if you might be interested in going this time, too."

"I think a trek to the back country is just what I need right now," he said with a smile as they turned and walked toward Rena and her family. Abby was sound asleep on Rena's shoulder, exhausted from her evening with the boys on stage. Stratton coached the boys as they put the campfire out. Maggie smiled as she watched Jonah stir the coals and Zack pour a bucket of water on them.

"The kids were adorable tonight, Rena," Maggie commented as she gave Rena and Abby a big hug. "They had the whole audience captivated."

Rena smiled. She blushed with pride as they watched Stratton work with the boys and instruct them in fire safety. Anyone could see she felt the same way.

"He's really good for them, Rena."

"They're beginning to care for him a lot," Rena bit her lower lip and quickly looked down at the ground.

"You know, it's ok for you to care for him a lot, too," Maggie said quietly as she wrapped her arm around Rena. "Sometimes, the right person comes into our lives at just the right time."

Rena smiled and wiped a tear from her eye.

Just as the boys finished their work with the campfire, they noticed Maggie talking with their mother. They immediately ran to her side with Bandit barking and jumping along beside them.

"Maggie, Maggie, did you see us help Ranger Stratton?" Zack exclaimed as he sat down beside her. "He let us teach everyone about the herbs Mommy picks."

"Of course I did! You were wonderful and I wouldn't have missed it for a thing!"

"Did ya see me git stwangled?" Jonah asked as he crawled into her lap. "I 'bout cwoaked!" he exclaimed in his funny little drawl.

Maggie laughed, "Yes, you surely did! It's a good thing you had a Ranger there to save you!" She brushed a few strands of hair out of his face.

"He said we could help him with another program sometime, Maggie," Zack told her with such excitement Maggie marveled at the change in the usually somber child since Stratton came into the lives of his family.

"Zack, I think that is wonderful! He is doing so many great things with you and your family," Maggie said as she watched Zack's eyes sparkle as she talked about Ranger Stratton.

He nodded then jumped up to grab Stratton's hand as he walked toward the little group. Jonah and Bandit followed close behind him. Stratton paused to allow the boys to catch up with him.

"Hey, everybody! Did you enjoy the program tonight?"

"Yes, we did, but you are going to have to be careful or you are going to loose your job to your helpers. They almost stole the show tonight," Doc said as he shook Stratton's hand.

"They're something aren't they?" he said as he ruffled the boy's heads. Stratton beamed with pride. Anyone could tell he was as attached to the boys as they were to him. He reached across and lifted Abby from Rena's arms as they prepared to leave.

"We'll be seeing you around, Stratton. Digger and I are going to take a back-pack trip in a few days. Let us know if you need us to do anything on the trail while we are gone. We're going to be going to the back country this time."

Stratton paused and turned toward them.

"I'll be on the trails myself again tomorrow. I don't need to remind you, but be careful Maggie. Don't forget about the fire ban, it has been so hot and dry the underbrush is just like kindling right now."

"I'll be careful, and I'll be with Doc and Digger so you don't need to worry about me. Just take care of your family. They look like they are really close to you, now."

He smiled and tenderly looked at Rena, then nodded and turned toward the trail.

Maggie and Doc held hands as they walked silently to the parking lot. They didn't speak much on the walk because both remained lost in their own thoughts. Maggie paused before she got into the jeep.

"You know I'd like to see more of you Maggie," Doc said as he tenderly brushed a curl away from her forehead.

"That would be nice," Maggie smiled.

"So, when do you think you could get together?"

"Digger and I are planning on the pack trip the day after tomorrow, so I will probably need to come into town tomorrow to get some supplies. Would you like to meet for dinner tomorrow evening?"

"Sounds great, I'll look forward to it," he smiled and gently kissed her before he closed the door to her jeep.

Maggie said goodbye, started the engine and headed toward home. As she thought about tomorrow and dinner with Doc, her worries and concerns from the visitors at the campfire program disappeared into the background of her mind.

CHAPTER 6

Maggie woke up early, quickly dressed and went to the garden to weed and pick vegetables before the sun was high in the sky and it was too hot to work outside in the garden. There were relatively few weeds to pull because she tried to get them out before they took control of the garden. She worked in the garden for about an hour and was able to pick a basket of vegetables for herself and another basket for Ms. Cates, an elderly lady she planned to see later in the day.

Maggie then walked over to the old apple tree and picked about half a bushel of apples from the gnarled old tree. The tree was ancient and must have been in the yard long before even her grandmother lived there years ago. She took the apples and vegetables to the porch and quickly sliced the apples into thin slices, which she placed on a sheet in the sun as her grandmother did so often in the past to dry apples for later use.

Maggie then went inside, showered quickly, and sat down at her computer to work on an article she was writing for a parenting magazine. Although, her property was debt free, there was always a need for extra money and she wanted to keep from dipping into her savings when she could. Maggie often wrote for parent's magazines, children's magazines and even for the National Forest Service at times. The sale of these articles helped her with occasional need for money. She finished the chapter, and slipped it into an envelope to take to the post office when she went into town.

She then quickly checked her backpack for things she might need on her hike with Digger. Clean socks, dry shoes, a change of clothes and extra food supplies. She checked the cabinets for supplies on hand and realized she was short on some of the things she needed, so she made a brief list and stuck it into her purse. She continued to pack dried vegetables and her water bottle. Maggie decided to stick her water purifier pump in her bag, also. She didn't always carry it with her, but for some reason, thought it might be good to have on hand on this trip. With the temperatures so hot and the weather so dry she knew she might need more water than she could carry.

When she finished, she sat her camping bag behind the front door where it was always ready for a hike with Digger or Doc and then glanced around the cabin before she left. Everything seemed to be in order, so she closed the door and headed to the jeep. Max slowly walked over to greet her before she left. He still looked exhausted from the last trip they took down the trail.

"Hey, Max, I'm going to leave for a little while. You need to stay here this time and take care of things, ok?"

Max thumped his tail in response and crawled under the porch.

Maggie jumped in her jeep and headed to the bottom of the mountain. She turned right on River Road to go into the small town of Tellico Plains. The road was narrow and curvy as it wound around the base of the mountain and followed the course of the Tellico River. Originally, loggers constructed the road only as a means to bring out timber when settlers first came to the area.

The area was a Mecca for outdoor enthusiasts and the road was quickly becoming too small to carry the daily load. The National Forest surrounded the road and did not want to change the wilderness setting, therefore little work to expand or develop it and it was often filled with ruts and holes. Trails for backpackers, overnight parking slips for campers, kayak events on the river and plenty of trout fishing in the cold rushing waters kept the road busy during spring and summer seasons.

Maggie passed the area where an old mansion once stood. A man who operated an ironworks company in town before the civil war originally owned the property. The Union Army demolished the iron works company during the civil war, but the home remained undisturbed until a few years ago when fire destroyed it. There were many local folk tales of the mansion's history as a part of the Underground Railroad during the civil war and persistent tales of numerous hideouts and secret tunnels throughout and around the property. Although, no one could ever seem to prove the tales true or false, the rumors persisted through the years.

The area around the old mansion property contained camping sites, rental cabins and restaurants that operated their businesses mostly in an effort to cater to tourist crowds who vacationed in the area. Once relatively unnoticed by vacation crowds, the local area was beginning to receive much more attention as overpopulation numerous tourists affected other places in the Smokey Mountains. The result was a boom in the local population during summer months.

The air was much cooler here along the river. Maggie rolled her window down so she could smell the rich moist fragrance from the river as she drove by. The moss and damp leaves along the riverbank mingled with the delightful smell of fresh mint and jewelweed that grew wild along its banks.

Just as Maggie entered the shadows of the deeper forest and rounded the last serious curve, the figure of a man ran in front of her on the narrow road. She immediately swerved the jeep to the left to avoid hitting him, then, jerked the jeep back to the right again to prevent the front wheels of the jeep from going into a ditch. The wheels began to slide back and forth on the hot pavement and Maggie was unable to keep it from slipping off the road and into a ditch on the right side as a cloud of dust and smoke surrounded her. Her hands trembled and heart pounded as she opened the door to get out. She quickly looked up to make sure the jogger was unhurt.

As Maggie watched him continue to jog down the lane of the narrow road, completely oblivious to the problem he caused by not paying attention she knew he must be ok and unhurt by the accident.

"Jerk! He didn't even slow down to see if I was ok."

She walked around the jeep to see how serious the damage to the vehicle was and determine what she needed to do to get out of the ditch. The tires all seemed ok although two of them were in a deep rut, no dents were apparent and nothing seemed to be leaking fluids. Maggie crawled back into the jeep, put it into four-wheel drive and slowly tried to work her way out. Even in low gear, the wheels began to spin and dig deeper into the soft dirt in the ditch. She tried to put it into reverse and slowly back out of the ditch but had no luck when the wheels continued to spin.

"Well, babe, looks like we've done it this time. You're stuck pretty good and I'm not sure if we can get out by ourselves."

Frustrated, she lay her head down on the steering wheel and contemplated what she should do next. She often wished she knew more about car repairs.

'Town isn't too far from here. I guess I could walk over there and find someone to help me get out. Digger would help, or one of the Rangers.'

Maggie looked up when she heard a movement beside the jeep to see Chris lean his head inside, his bright blue eyes sparkling and full of merriment.

"Hey, Maggie, blazing a new trail today?" He said, obviously having fun with her predicament. "I heard there's a need for trail blazers with the Forest Service lately."

"Not intentionally, I was trying to avoid some guy that jogged right in front of me in the road. I guess I overcorrected when the wheels swerved and sort of took a dive into the ditch. Now, I'm stuck and can't seem to back out."

"I can see that," he grinned. "Need any help getting out? Or are you planning on hanging out here for a while this afternoon?"

"Thanks, Doc, I'd appreciate it. Looks like I need the help. At any rate, I'm not going to be able to get out on my own."

Chris backed his truck in front of the jeep, lay on the ground and hooked a chain to the main frame of the jeep before he got up and returned to his truck.

"Maggie, you just put the jeep in neutral and steer a little to help us get out then I'll do the rest." He slowly began to pull forward. In just a few moments, the jeep was out of the ditch and the two vehicles were safely sitting on level ground.

"How's that, Maggie?" Chris smiled as he unhooked the jeep from the chain and began to roll it up. "Going to be blazing any more trails today?"

"I hope not," Maggie grinned, "I was planning on going into town to get some supplies and then eat dinner with you until this happened. Now, I look like I've been out working in the fields."

"Wonderful! That's just the way I like to see you," Chris beamed at her, his blue eyes sparkled, "Mind if I join you?"

"But ..." she began to protest, "I'm really dirty now."

"And, by the way, you look beautiful when your face is flushed," he grinned.

Tall and lean, Chris had the firm, trim physique of someone who spent many years in exercise and physical labor. Although, his profession as a doctor kept him inside much of the time, now retired, he was able to spend his free time with work in his vegetable, herb and flower gardens.

Maggie blushed as her heart began to beat faster.

"Umm, yes ... that would be great! I'd like that."

She became flustered and felt as though the temperature rose in the jeep several degrees. She picked up an old envelope from the seat of the jeep and began to fan herself quickly as perspiration broke out on her face.

"I'll just follow you there," she smiled, hoping he would leave her window soon.

'Gosh, I hope he goes before I start sweating', she thought, wishing he would get back in his truck quickly. 'There's nothing more glamorous than breaking into a sweat when a man tells you how beautiful you are and asks you to join him for dinner,' she thought as she squirmed in her seat and tried to think of a way to get moving gracefully.

Amused with her obvious discomfort, Chris continued to grin at her and hang his head inside the open window of the jeep.

"Oh, I almost forgot!" Maggie blurted out when she suddenly remembered she had not uttered a word of gratitude for all his efforts to get her jeep out of the ditch. "I don't know how I can ever thank you for your help. You are very kind to help a damsel in distress on such a hot day."

"Pleased to be of service ma'am," Chris smiled, took off his cap and bowed slightly. "If you would do me the honor of keeping our date and joining me for dinner and music this evening, I would be most grateful in return."

Maggie grinned, and laughed as she started the motor on the jeep. "I'm right behind you, kind sir. Just lead the way," she sighed, relieved to have a few moments alone to get herself together again.

She followed Chris as he drove through town square to the other end of town and pulled into the parking lot of the Telehala Diner, named after the Cherohala Skyway and the town of Tellico Plains. This was one of Maggie's favorite places to eat. A small diner in the middle of a mountainous region famous for country cooking, this place specialized in gourmet food, and often had many specialties.

After becoming a vegetarian over ten years ago, Maggie found the biggest challenge to being a vegetarian was eating out. She often ended up eating only a salad or baked potato when she went out to eat in local areas because most cooks in the area seasoned everything in the traditional country way with meat drippings or some other type of grease. Here, Maggie knew the chefs and was able to order many dishes without meat or any type of fat.

Chris held the door open for her as they entered the small diner and waited for one of the waiters to seat them. All of the servers were dressed in black pants with crisp white shirts and black bow ties, fresh flowers and candles sat on each table and a piano player played soft bluegrass music in the corner of the room. Delicious aromas filled the room and made Maggie's stomach growl in protest from neglect.

Maggie excused herself to wash her hands and quickly try to wipe some of the dust from her face before returning to the table to order dinner. Chris waited at the table for her when she returned.

'He must not mind the 'natural' me, he's still here,' she thought with a smile.

"Whew, I feel a little bit better now, didn't know a person could get so dusty just driving into town on Saturday night. This place smells wonderful!" Maggie smiled, "I'm starved!" Her mouth began to water as one of the waiters brought a large basket of hot homemade rolls and two glasses of black currant tea to the table.

Chris laughed, "It's not everyday that people go to such trouble to drive beside the road on their way into town, either, Maggie!"

Maggie smiled, "I don't usually drive in the ditches, either, but that fella was right in the middle of the road and didn't show any signs of moving out of the way either."

"Was it anyone you knew?"

Maggie thought for a moment, "Come to think about it, he looked an awful lot like the man who spoke at the campfire last night."

"Do you mean the college professor?"

"Yes, I think it was the same man," she said thoughtfully, "Anyway, no one was hurt and I'm out of the ditch now."

"You must have been determined to get here," Doc said hopefully.

"In a way I was," she said as she started munching on one of the homemade rolls. "Digger and I were out on one of the wilderness trails eating camp food for a few days earlier in the week and I made the mistake of thinking about real food on my way back to the cabin. When you asked me to dinner yesterday, I started to think about the wonderful food they have here. By the time I took a shower today and got ready to come to town, all I could think about was eating," she grinned.

"Well, I'm glad we planned to come to dinner and I ran into you on the way here then," Chris smiled as he buttered a roll. "I was on my way to eat and listen to the music this weekend anyway in hopes of seeing you. Until last night, I haven't seen you around for a few days. How was your trip with Digger?"

"It was great! It is so good for me to hike with Digger. As tiresome and exhausting as these hikes are, they keep me in shape, and I always learn something when I'm out with him. He always teaches me something I don't know, too."

Their waiter arrived at the table with dinner. He placed a steaming plate of eggplant parmesan with pasta and a salad on the side for Maggie and a catfish dinner with hushpuppies and homegrown vegetables for Chris. As they ate their dinner they discussed the past week and events that happened to each of them.

Maggie took extra time to describe most of her hiking trip with Digger. Chris often traveled with them and was always interested in the conditions of the trails and any information about new rock formations they had found. He was an avid rock hound and loved to search in mines and rock quarries for gemstones. She carefully omitted the parts related to Digger's discovery of the mysterious ancient burial mounds.

'It's really Digger's to tell, when he wants Chris to know about it, he will tell him' she thought to herself.

They ate every bite of their meal, neither leaving a scrap. The music and candlelight seemed to lull them into a mood to talk. Chris told her of a new vein of gemstones he came across while in the mine he had on his property. He had a large collection of gemstone he discovered through the years that were such high quality stones he was able to facet and cut them into jewels.

Maggie glanced outside at the darkening sky.

"Oops! I didn't realize it was so late. It must be time for the music to start downtown. Still want to go?" Maggie smiled at Chris happy to be with him.

"I wouldn't miss it!" He smiled.

They paid the bill and headed outside to drive to the town square. On the way out the door, Maggie remembered she was running low on gasoline and wanted to make sure she filled up before the store closed at midnight.

"Chris I need to stop at the BP and fill up before I go back into town, would it be ok if we meet downtown a little later? I don't like to head home with a partial tank of gasoline you never know when you might need to have a full tank."

"Of course it's ok. I'll go ahead and set us up some lawn chairs near the bandstand. I want to make sure we are near enough to the dance floor so I can lure you out for a dance or two," he teased, knowing Maggie was reluctant to dance when there was a crowd around.

"Ok," she said hesitantly. "I'll see you in a few minutes," as her stomach began to ache. After living alone for so long, she often felt tense in new situations.

'Oh great, I didn't think about dancing! I was just going to listen to the music and see if Digger or the McCutchens were around! I'm way too clumsy to dance when other people are around. He may regret asking me, it's hard enough for me to just walk somewhere and not run into something or fall down. I can't imagine trying to dance!'

Maggie's self-doubt began to fill her mind as she drove to the BP station and filled the jeep up with gasoline. When the tank was full, she checked the water and oil before going inside to pay her bill. She walked around a group of local residents who were inside discussing the weather conditions and several tourists who were stocking up on cold drinks and snacks. Maggie could sense a feeling of unrest and maybe irritation among some members of the group as they talked. Heat and extremely dry weather conditions always seemed to raise tempers and lower tolerance in everyone.

The area where they lived was remote and surrounded by miles and miles of National Forest where firefighting equipment was limited in most areas or even non-existent in some places. Dry, hot weather conditions could easily turn everything in a forest from a lush, green wonderland into a dry, crisp tender-box.

She grabbed a newspaper, picked up a loaf of bread, some granola bars, a jar of peanut butter and a few other groceries before going to the counter to pay her bill. Sharon, the clerk greeted her with a broad smile and a big wave.

"Hey, Maggie, how are you? Haven't seen you around here for a couple of weeks. You been doing ok?" Sharon was a large woman in her late fifties with bright red hair and heavy makeup who greeted everyone who entered the store with a smile and a warm welcome. She knew no strangers and talked with everyone who entered the store, which probably accounted for why she knew almost everything that went on in town.

"Have you heard the latest, Maggie?" she continued without giving Maggie time to answer her first question. "I have all the latest information from the grapevine."

Maggie shook her head as she placed her things on the counter for Sharon to ring up. She didn't like to gossip herself and usually felt uncomfortable hearing gossip but it was often difficult to avoid hearing the latest without offending Sharon.

"Well, the big thing is the Rangers have closed down all the trails until it rains. They've put this area at one of the highest levels of emergency in years. All the Ranger fire stations are manned and they banned any kind of outdoor burning at all." Sharon rang up Maggie's purchases as she talked, happy to pass on some bit of information to everyone she knew.

"That's really scary. Do they have any idea when it might rain?"

"Not a drop in sight. They don't expect it to rain at all this week," she began placing Maggie's purchases in a brown paper bag as she talked. "They aren't sure when it's going to rain; it may even be another week."

"Wow," Maggie said, concerned, "I hope it comes soon, we really need it now more than ever. I know my garden is starting to suffer from the drought."

"The other thing is … how long has it been since you've seen Ms. Cates?" Sharon asked, her voice becoming serious as she looked intently at Maggie.

"It's been a few weeks I guess, is she ok?"

Over the past year, Maggie developed a friendship with an older, eccentric woman in town who often suffered from bouts of delusional behavior and periods of time when she was extremely forgetful, possibly associated with Alzheimer's disease.

"Old Ms. Cates has been asking for you. She said it was something important, really, really important!" Sharon raised her eyebrows and nodded her head, then continued, "We had to run her off from here two or three times this week because she was acting so crazy. It was something, I'm telling you."

"What do you mean crazy? What kind of things was she doing?"

"Well, you know how she dresses all the time with all those old clothes and scarves and things like that. This time her hair was down and sticking out all over the place, it looked wild. She had on some kind of knapsack and it looked like she was wearing an old pair of army boots."

"She was outside scaring off the customers one day, telling them some kind of crazy stories. People that didn't know her got upset. Sometimes she comes here so confused and disoriented she can't find her way back home. All I know is, every time she comes here, she talks about you and something important she has to tell you."

"Well, I guess I'd better run by and see her soon then," Maggie said as she smiled and paid her bill. "Thanks for telling me Sharon, I didn't know she was asking for me. When you see her again, if you don't mind, tell her I'll come by and see her."

"You're welcome," Sharon beamed; pleased to be able to pass on information that Maggie hadn't heard from anyone else. "I'll sure tell her that you're coming when I see her, maybe it will settle her down some. I'll keep an eye on her for you and let you know if anything else happens."

"Thanks, Sharon," Maggie said as she smiled and went out the door to the jeep. "I'll try to run by and see her in the next few days."

CHAPTER 7

Maggie parked on one of the side streets in Tellico Plains. The streets in the main downtown area held yellow caution tape to prevent anyone from driving through town during the Saturday night block party and harming dancers or pedestrians. She walked to the main area as it filled up with people and looked for Chris and his lawn chairs.

Many local residents who only came into town on Saturday to purchase supplies, visit with friends or listen to good mountain music filled the downtown area. A few tourists and visitors meandered in and out among the crowd as they waited for the music to start. Small groups of performers warmed up while they waited their turn on the central bandstand.

Along the sidewalks, various church and civic groups set up booths to sell food and cold drinks. A number of people brought fold-up lawn chairs or quilts and set them in an area around the bandstand so they could get a good view of the performers as they sang. Town officials designated one area for anyone who wanted to dance. It soon filled with couples who seemed anxious for the music to begin. Often, teams of square dancers performed and groups of young people performed line dances, while others who chose to dance with just one person danced the two-step along the side.

Sometimes one or two of the old timers clogged. Maggie loved to see them sway and turn as they danced. For a few moments in time they were agile again and filled with energy. The young people who learned to clog had excellent dancing skills and did a very good job when they clogged, but there was something unique and very heartfelt about the way the old timers moved when they danced. It was almost as though they were able to transport themselves back to another time and another place.

Maggie meandered through the crowd and spoke to people she knew as she continued to look for Chris. When she neared the bandstand, she noticed two empty lawn chairs that looked like the ones he owned placed near the edge of the crowd. Maggie stood beside them and looked the crowd over again.

The sky began to darken as Ranger Stratton neared the crest of the wilderness mountain trail where he hiked. He paused and leaned against an outcrop of rocks to take a drink of water from his canteen and wipe the sweat from his head. Even this late in the evening, it was still very hot.

After an early start, he completed the section of wilderness trail assigned for him to cover and switched to one of the side trails that ran along the Cherohala Skyway. Just as he was about to head back to his truck, he saw movement on that trail ahead of him. He didn't think anyone else was on the trail, but he wanted to be sure that he reached as many hikers as possible to let each one know the forest service was going to close the wilderness trails. The fire hazard was too great right now to let anyone stay on the trail and he needed to warn everyone to leave the trails for their own safety.

"Might be an animal, but I'd better keep on looking, just in case it isn't," he said to himself. Just as Ranger Stratton came to the crest of the ridge, he ran into a group of young people who were setting up camp for the night. Stratton didn't want to alarm the couples or surprise them so he called to them from the edge of the trees.

"Halloooo, the camp!" He then stepped out from the trees so they could see he was a Forest Ranger. "Halloo!"

"Hey, Ranger Stratton, come on and join us," Amy smiled brightly and invited him into their camp. "We're just getting ready to make dinner."

"Well, look what I found!" Stratton beamed. "Well, if it isn't the happy hikers! How have you guys been?" He walked over and shook hands with Josh and Justin then tipped his hat to Amy and Colleen. "I haven't seen you all since last Spring."

"We're just weekend warriors, Stratton," Justin smiled and nudged Stratton on the shoulder. "We have to go home and work now and then so we can come back and play. Not everyone has the opportunity to be in the mountains everyday like you do."

"Yes, but work is still work no matter where you are," Stratton teased. Everyone knew he loved his job and would have forfeited his paycheck to be a Ranger. "Have you been on the trail long this time? Last Spring you were hiking for several weeks."

"Nah, we just started today," Josh answered. "We were hoping to hike over to the Joyce Kilmer Forest and camp there but kind of got a late start, so we thought we would set up here tonight and take off again in the morning."

"Have you seen any other hikers on the trail today?"

"There were a couple of men who passed us about an hour ago headed northeast on the trail. They weren't too friendly, so we just let them go on by," Josh answered. "We didn't want to have to worry about them being near us when we set up camp."

"I don't blame you. If you don't know someone, it's better to put a little distance between you when you're setting up camp," Stratton replied. "I really hate to disappoint you kids because I know how much you love the mountains, but I'm going to have interrupt your trip and ask you to leave tonight," Stratton told the group.

"Oh, no! Is anything wrong?" Amy asked as she moved over to stand beside Justin. He instinctively put his arm around her.

"Well, yes and no," Stratton answered. "Yes, there is an emergency, and no, nothing wrong has happened, yet. We just want to make sure nothing wrong does happen and no one gets hurt on the trail. It would take a lot of time to conduct a rescue."

"What's going on?" Justin asked as he held Amy a little closer.

"First of all, it's very dry. We haven't had rain for over six weeks and none expected for the next week as far as we can tell. The entire area is like a box of kindling, it's very hazardous," Stratton tried to state the facts without overly alarming the two couples. "So, the forest service decided to place a ban on any outdoor fires and to close the backcountry and wilderness trails until we get a little rain."

"Oh, no! That sounds serious!" CC sat beside Josh on a rock. "What are we going to do? We left our jeep down at the bottom of the mountain and it's starting to get late."

They all silently stared at each other for a few moments.

"Well, one thing I know we can do is walk back down the ridge on the road instead of the trail and hope someone drives by and gives us a lift," Amy said. "The only problem is there aren't many people driving on the road this time of night, but we'd have more luck on the road than anywhere else."

"Or,.... if we knew where Maggie's cabin is, we could go there," Josh reminded them. "She told us to come by and camp out at her place next time we came. She really seemed like she wanted us to come there."

"I can tell you how to get there if you want to go over to Maggie's place. It's not far from here and you can probably get there before it gets completely dark," Stratton tried to help. "She may not be there until later though, I saw her at the campfire program at Indian Boundary last night and she said she might go into town for a while this evening. She'll be back sometime tonight though and knowing her, I'm sure she'd want you to set up camp at her place."

"That would be great, Stratton," Justin said. "Guess we'd better get our things together again before it gets any later. It's harder to hike at night."

The two couples repacked their gear and strapped on their backpacks as Ranger Stratton gave them directions to Maggie's cabin.

"Are you going to come with us?" Josh asked.

"Not yet, if there was someone an hour ahead of you, I can probably catch up to them and be back to my truck before midnight. I have a duty to warn them and get them off the trail if at all possible."

"Do you want any help?" Josh asked before they left.

"No. Thanks for the offer, but it's my job and if I can head you four out of here and to safety, then that's four less folks I have to worry about while I'm out here hiking," Stratton grinned and nodded to them as they headed down the trail towards Maggie's cabin. "After all, somebody's got to work."

He stood up, tightened the straps on his knapsack and cautiously headed northeast on the trail in the direction the young couples said they had seen the two men go. Although tired, he hiked quickly, eager to be off the mountain and headed to town square for the evening. As much as he enjoyed his job, Rena and her little family were quickly becoming an important part of his life and he didn't want to miss a chance to see them.

Chris reached for Maggie's hand and pulled her out of her chair as the mellow notes of a soft, country slow dance began. Couples hurried from their seats to the dance floor area for a chance to hold each other tightly and move around in the moonlight as one of the local bands played softly. A woman with a cowboy hat, dressed in a long skirt with fringe on the sides began to sing the soft notes of a heart wrenching Patsy Cline song. Everyone seemed to dance to the music or at least tap their feet in time.

"I'm not very good at the two-step, yet," Maggie protested as Chris led her to the center of the dance floor, and began to dance around her.

"Doesn't matter," Chris gazed down at her, his eyes twinkling. "You don't need to know how to two-step because this isn't a two-step song."

He wrapped his arms around her as he pulled her in close and began swaying to the music. His enthusiasm was infectious and caused her to laugh.

"Oh, really," Maggie laughed, "So, what kind of song is it then?"

"This is a 'hold on to your babe' song, designed specifically for dancing with someone you want to hold on to while the world whirls on by," he said as he smiled and squeezed her tightly.

"Sounds like my kind of song," she smiled.

'The world already feels as though it's going to whirl on by because my head is fuzzy, I have goose bumps all over my body, the lights are spinning, and my stomach is doing flip flops! If everyone feels like this while they're dancing, it's no wonder they have to hang on to each other.'

As they danced, the whole world seemed to slip away and nothing else existed except for the warm tingly feeling she had whenever Chris was near her. Maggie sighed deeply and lay her head on Chris' shoulder.

'I never thought I could feel like this about anyone, especially at this time if my life, yet this feels so right, so real. It's a wonderful feeling.' She closed her eyes, lost in thought as they swayed around the dance floor.

Suddenly, a commotion erupted along the sidewalk beside some of the vender's booths when a man in runner's clothing ran in front of the booths heedless of anyone in his way. As he ran past an older woman, he brushed against her shoulder and caused her to fall and spill her drink, then kept right on running. He startled a toddler who strayed away from her mother's hand when he leaped over her head, then ran on through the end of the square and out of town. Several people began to shout at him as they gathered around the older woman and the toddler to help them.

"We'd better go see if we can help, Maggie," Chris said as he started in the direction of the fallen woman. "She may be hurt and she was a patient of mine."

They could hear people ask for a doctor as they neared. When someone recognized Chris, the crowd parted to allow him to come closer to the woman so he could examine her. The woman lay on her back and seemed to be dazed or semi-conscious. Chris first checked to make sure she was able to breathe, then took her pulse.

"Is there anything I can do, Chris?" Maggie kneeled beside him and noticed the woman's drink spilled on her dress and face.

One of the vendors handed Maggie some napkins so she could gently wipe the spilled drink from the woman's face and dab the spill from her dress.

Slowly, she began to appear more alert. Chris continued to monitor her recovery.

In the background, Maggie could hear angry shouts from some of the men in crowd as anger and tension built over the incident. Several of the men wanted to chase the runner down and bring him back to the town square to account for his behavior. Tempers flared as they continued to argue until it sounded like a lynch mob was brewing as several of the men began to work up a fight.

Over the din and confusion of the crowd, Maggie could hear the sheriff's voice as he tried to calm the crowd down. "Come on now folks, let's settle down. We don't need to get riled up about an accident. Everybody's gonna be ok."

"What do you mean, Sheriff?" An angry man in blue jeans and cowboy boots shouted. "I seen the whole thing! It weren't no accident. I say we go take care of him right now!" He yelled as he rolled up his sleeves.

"Now, Colby, we don't need to make things worse. Let's not let this ruin our evening," the sheriff said as he placed his arm around Colby's shoulder and walked toward the bandstand with him. "Hey, Sweeny, how about starting us up with a song so these fine folks can get started dancing again," he called to the guitar player.

The band gathered quickly and began to play a familiar bluegrass song as the sheriff walked to the edge of the square to talk with Colby and calm him down.

Several of the men with Colby continued to grumble in the background but returned to their seats when the music started. The toddler continued to cry in her mother's arms when Maggie realized the woman who held the toddler was Rena.

"Oh, Doc, the baby he frightened was Abigail. If you don't need me here, I'm going to check on her, Rena looks pretty upset."

"We're fine," Doc said in a soft, comforting voice as he helped the older woman sit up. "We're just going to sit here for a few minutes and rest," he said as he patted the woman on the hand.

He looked up at Maggie and smiled, "You go ahead, Rena needs you right now."

'Gosh, he's good,' Maggie thought. 'No wonder he became a doctor, he's a natural healer. He seems to have a special touch with everyone he meets.'

Maggie watched as the woman relaxed and smiled adoringly at Chris.

'It's a good thing he was here to help out, although she looks like she might swoon from all the attention!' Maggie grinned at Chris and waved as she left to check on Rena and the baby.

Rena sat on the edge of the sidewalk while she rocked and held Abigail in her arms. She looked almost as frightened as the baby did. Rena rarely came into town when there were crowds. She spent most of her time at home, or roaming through the mountains near her house where she looked for native herbs or willow branches to make baskets for a local craft shop. Between the vegetables she grew in her garden and the extra money she made from the sale of herbs and baskets, she was able to provide for her little family. Although, very independent and resourceful, she was extremely shy.

Rena preferred to stay home in the safety of the mountains, live off the land and take care of her children without help from anyone. She still lived her life in very much the same manner as her parents and grandparents lived.

Life became a little more difficult for her after her husband died in a mining accident shortly before Abigail's birth. She became the only living adult left in her family. As difficult as it was for Rena to make ends meet, she never complained and always seemed to find a way to feed her family.

"Rena, are you ok?" Maggie asked as she sat beside Rena on the sidewalk. "How's Abby, doing?"

"Oh, Maggie, I'm so glad you're here," Rena looked at Maggie with huge round eyes that looked like a frightened deer caught in the headlights of a car. "We told Stratton we would meet him here, but he never came."

"I know he's on one of the trails, Rena," Maggie could feel Rena's whole body shake as she put her arm around her. "He was trying to get word out to all the hikers that the trails were going to close because of the fire danger. I'm sure he would be here if he could, that's just a long trail and it may take more time than we realize."

"Would it be ok if I held Abby for a few minutes and give you a break?" Rena nodded, still shaking. Maggie reached for the sobbing little girl.

"Hey, there Sweetpea, how's my little Abigail doing today?" She cooed to the baby. "Did you get a bump on your head?"

Abby gulped down a sob as she reached for Maggie, then snuggled against her neck and began to suck her thumb as Maggie held her close.

"There, there, everything's going to be just fine," Maggie whispered softly as she rocked Abby back and forth.

"I just didn't see him coming, Maggie," Rena looked as though she was going to cry. "I was holding Abby's hand when I turned around to see what the boys were doing and she slipped away. It all happened so fast."

"It wasn't your fault, Rena," Maggie said as she placed her hand on Rena's arm. "She's just frightened, she'll be ok. That man wasn't looking where he was going anyway. He must run with his head in the clouds. If I'm not mistaken, I think he's the same man who ran in front of me and caused the jeep to run off the road earlier today."

All of the sudden, Maggie felt someone brush up against her back as two warm and very sticky little hands covered her eyes. A tiny little voice whispered in her ear, "Guess who!" followed by a chorus of giggles.

"Ohhh Nooo! I can't see!" Maggie exclaimed as she squeezed Abigail in mock fear. "Somebody's got me Abby! Help me; help me! Who could it be?"

Abby began to giggle as Maggie reached around behind her back, grabbed Jonah and pulled him into her lap with Abby.

"It must be … the JONAH monster!"

She began to tickle and squeeze Jonah and Abby together until both were giggling so hard they couldn't stop.

"My goodness, Jonah, you sure did surprise me. I thought the boogie monster had me for sure!" Maggie smiled as she teased Jonah. "I'm so glad it WAS you! It isn't every day I have a handsome young man try to grab me."

"Awww, Maggie," Jonah grinned a bashful grin and stuck his thumbs under the straps of his faded overalls as he looked at the ground, "You knew it wuz me th' whole time, didn't ya?" His beautiful soft brown eyes filled with delight.

"You'll never know will you?" she teased as she ruffled his bright red hair and attempted to smooth down a stray piece that seemed to want to stand up on top. "Where's that big brother of yours? I haven't seen him tonight either."

"I'm right here, Maggie." Zack was standing with his arm around his mother. "I had to go get Mamma some water."

Zack's steel blue eyes filled with concern for his mother. Since his father died, Zack felt like he needed to take over the role of head of the household even at the tender age of six. His jet-black hair and thick black lashes made the blue in his eyes seem intense and piercing.

"I'm glad you did, Zack. A drink of water always seems to help when something scary happens." Maggie said as she watched him carefully, concerned that he often seemed so solemn and serious at such a young age.

"You're a great helper for your Mamma, Zack. I know she appreciates it. Think you could help me with something for a minute?"

Although, Zack nodded his head solemnly, his eyes began to glow with the anticipation of being able to help with something new and challenging. Maggie always gave him important things to do which made him feel more grown-up.

"What would you like for me to do, Maggie?"

"Well … I'd really like an ice cream cone, but I can't buy just one. I told myself on the way over here today that I wouldn't buy any ice cream at all unless all my friends let me buy one for them, too."

She watched each of the boys seriously.

"A person should only eat ice cream with friends, so I need one for each of us. That makes … how many ice cream cones?" She asked as she looked at Jonah.

"One, two, free, four, five … FIVE; Maggie … we need FIVE ice cweam cones!" Jonah excitedly grabbed her face and turned it toward him so he could look directly in her eyes. His sticky little fingers were warm on her face.

"That's right, Jonah. We need five ice cream cones so we can all eat together. There's only one problem, though," Maggie said as she raised her eyebrows and looked from one little boy to the other.

"What, Maggie?" Zack asked, interested in helping her solve the problem.

"Well … Mrs. Smith is standing beside the ice cream booth. She looks like an ice cream monitor. If she sees me coming to buy five ice cream cones, she's going to wonder why I'm buying so many. She may think I'm going to get fat!"

Jonah started to giggle, "Maggie's twying to git fat," he teased.

"What do you need me to do, Maggie?" Zack asked her seriously.

"Well, I was hoping you might know someone who could go buy the ice cream cones for me if I pay for them," she said as she looked at Zack.

"I will, Maggie," he said eagerly, "I'll go get the ice cream for you!"

"Whew, somehow I knew you would help me, Zack. Do you think you could find anyone else to help, too? Five ice cream cones are a lot for one person to carry."

"Me, me, me … whet me help, Maggie. I want to help, too," Jonah cried.

"Wonderful! It's such a relief to know you two are such good helpers."

Maggie reached in her pocket to get them the money for the ice cream and helped Zack figure out how much he would need to pay for five ice cream cones.

"Now, the ice cream monitor will never know just how fat I'm going to get!" she said as she tickled Jonah when he ran past her to catch up with Zack on their way to the booth. "Ask for a holder so you won't drop the cones, please."

Maggie laughed as she watched them run and bounce across the street to the ice cream booth. Both seemed happy and content with their world as it is.

"You have such great kids, Rena. You've done a wonderful job with them. I know things are sometimes tough for you, especially since your husband died."

Rena nodded her head.

"Being lonely is the hardest part but now that Stratton has taken up a friendship with the boys, it's been a little easier. I think he really likes them a lot," she said softly.

Maggie smiled, "I think Stratton took up an interest in more than the boys. It seems to me there are a couple of special ladies who live in the same house, too."

Rena smiled shyly as her face turned a deep shade of red.

"I do like his company, Maggie. He's been so good to the boys. He takes them fishin' and has started teachin' them how to track small game. Those are all the same kind of things their daddy would do if he was still alive. He treats them real special," Rena twisted the end of her dress as she talked. "I just don't want to put him out, or have him do things because he feels sorry for the boys or anything like that. The kids are takin' a real shinnin' to him."

"Rena, I know enough about Stratton to know he spends time with the boys because he really likes them and because he enjoys spending time with you, too," Maggie said as she put her arm around Rena. "He doesn't do things out of pity."

Rena smiled and wiped away a tear.

"I hope he's ok if he's still out on the trail tonight. I'm a little worried about him. He has always done the things he said he would do, and tonight he said he'd be here."

"I'm sure he's fine, Rena. Very few people know the remote trails as well as Stratton. He'll be ok," Maggie said confidently. "Why don't you let me give you and the kids a ride back up the mountain tonight? He may have to camp on one of the trails, or he may be so far out he has to wait until daylight to come back."

Rena nodded as the boys returned quickly with the ice cream cones, giggling as they ran. Rena and Maggie looked at each other and wondered what was so funny. The boys usually didn't get so tickled unless they were in to some kind of mischief.

"Did anything happen, Zack?" Rena asked suspiciously.

"When we gave the woman the money, Mrs. Smith asked us what we were doing with so many ice cream cones," Zack laughed.

"Mzz. Smiff's a ice cweam monstur," Jonah giggled.

"Monitor, Jonah. She's a monitor," Zack corrected, "and Jonah told her …" he started to giggle, "… Jonah told her …," he laughed too hard to talk.

"What did you say, Jonah?" Maggie asked a little alarmed.

Jonah grinned and tucked his bottom lip inside his mouth before he looked up at her sweetly and then giggled harder.

"Zack …?" Maggie looked to Zack for an answer as her concern grew to alarm.

"He said, 'Maggie said don't tell the ice cream monster she might get fat,'" Zack said through broken laughter, "And Mrs. Smith said …," he laughed harder, "she said, 'WHO'S A MONSTER?'"

"Mzz Smiff's an ice cweam monstur," Jonah chimed in and began to giggle; then Zack and Jonah both burst into uncontrollable laughter.

"Great," Maggie said as she and Rena looked at each other with their mouths hung open in shock, before they began to laugh, too. "Kids!" Maggie said as she laughed and ruffled Jonah's hair. "What am I going to do with you two?"

The boys continued to laugh as they sat on the curb and tried to eat their ice cream before it melted. When they finished eating their ice cream, Maggie and Rena stood up and began to gather up Rena's things.

"Boys, how would you like to ride back up the mountain with me in the jeep tonight?" They both nodded their heads in unison. "I know you were going to meet Ranger Stratton while you were here, but it's getting late and I think he may still be working on one of the trails."

"Can we ride up front, Maggie?" Jonah asked.

"Not tonight, Jonah. We need to let your Mom ride up there tonight, ok?" Maggie held Jonah's hand as they started to walk toward the jeep. "I'll take you boys somewhere another time and you can take turns riding up front. How does that sound?"

"That sounds good, Maggie," Zack nodded.

Just before they got to the end of the roped off area, Maggie remembered she left Chris to tend to the woman who had fallen on the ground.

"Oh, wait just a minute; I need to run tell Doc where I'm going so he won't worry about me. I'll be right back."

She hurried to the area by the booths where the injured woman sat earlier in the evening with Doc, and saw Chris in a chair by the injured woman. She looked much better than she looked earlier in the evening when the accident first happened. The color was back in her cheeks and her breathing and speech were normal. She was now able to even sit up and sip on some lemonade.

"Hi," Maggie smiled as she approached them. "How are you feeling?" she asked the woman.

"I'm feeling much better. Thank you for asking, Sweetie," the woman said with a smile. "The doctor was kind enough to wait for someone to call one of my family members to come pick me up," she looked at Chris and smiled.

"She's going to be just fine," Chris smiled. "She's a strong lady."

"Chris, I just stopped by to tell you that I'm going to take Rena and the kids home. They were supposed to meet Stratton here tonight and he hasn't come yet. I think he may still be on one of the trails."

"Oh, that's too bad," Chris looked genuinely disappointed. He turned to the woman, smiled and said, "Could you excuse me for a moment?"

"Of course, honey, go ahead. I'll be fine," she said as she held her head with one hand and began to fan herself with the other.

Chris held Maggie's elbow and walked a few steps away with her before he stopped and gazed into her eyes.

"Looks like we aren't going to get any more dances with each other tonight," he smiled and reached for her hand.

"And I saved the last dance for you, babe," she grinned. "Oops, let me correct that. I DID dance the last dance with you, the last dance I danced anyway."

"Guess we'll have to take this up another time then," he smiled and leaned over and kissed her gently on the lips.

Maggie felt her knees turn to melted butter and her heart begin to pound as she wrapped her arms around his neck. Whew, he's going to have to be careful or I'm going to swoon, too.

"Yes, we definitely are going to have to take this up some other time, and maybe another place, too," she grinned as the woman who was injured cleared her throat and tried to see what they were doing.

"Maybe later in the week we could get together?"

"I'd like that," Maggie smiled and quickly kissed him on the cheek. "Oh, and don't forget about the hike with Digger if you want to go. We'd both love for you to go with us."

Chris nodded and touched her cheek gently, before he rejoined the woman who sat in the chair by the vendor's booth anxiously waiting for him to return. He really is such a good, caring person Maggie thought as she left to join Rena and her children and take them to their home on the mountain before heading back to her own little cabin.

Ranger Stratton paused at the top of the mountain trail to catch his breath and rest for a moment. He began his trek early in the morning and was still on the trail after twelve hours of hiking over rugged wilderness terrain. Night had fallen and the air was beginning to cool down quite a bit. With an elevation of nearly 5,000 feet, the temperature on the top of the mountain was substantially cooler than in the valleys below.

While he rested, his senses suddenly came to full alert as fear struck him when the wind shifted and he could detect the faint odor of a fire. He stood again and sniffed the air before he strapped on his knapsack once more hoping beyond all hope that the odor he detected was from an unknowing camper's campfire and not from a forest fire.

Wearily, he shook the remaining contents of his canteen and took another drink before he continued on the little known side trail to what he hoped was a campsite with a campfire in the clearing ahead instead of the beginnings of a forest fire which would be something much worse.

As he neared the clearing, much to his relief, he saw a very small campfire with two men nearby. He stood in the trees at the edge of the woods before he hailed the campsite as he had earlier with the two young couples. Just as he started to step out and open his mouth to let them know he was there, some natural instinct deep within him told him to stop. Cautiously, he moved deeper into the forest to avoid detection while he studied the campsite a little more carefully.

From deep in the darkness of the forest, he watched the two men as they moved around the campfire. One large, muscular man with gray hair and a wiry, gray beard sat on a rock near the campfire. He had a large mallet in one hand and a metal spike or some similar type of instrument in the other hand, as he chipped away at a large stone slab.

The second man was tall, much taller than Stratton was and very thin. Stratton estimated the man to be at least six feet six inches tall. He was only slightly younger than the heavyset man and had long dark hair that hung around his shoulders. He also, was working on some slabs of stone. It looked like he applied something to them and then rubbed them down with a cloth.

Stratton hesitated, unsure of what he should do. He felt a duty to tell them of the hazardous conditions in the woods right now, yet something held him back. Something kept him from going forward to the campfire. He waited and watched the two men as they worked silently around the campfire. Then, just as he was about to put away his uneasy feelings and step forward, both men suddenly stopped what they were doing, stood up and backed into the shadows.

As the heavyset man moved, he reached beside a rock and pulled out a large handgun while the taller man quickly gathered the stones they worked on by the campfire and slid them under a bush. They both then carefully slipped silently back into the shadows and waited.

"You hear somethin', Darryl?" The heavyset man hoarsely whispered to his partner. "I thought I heard somethin' in the woods."

"Shhh, Ray!" Darryl growled. "Jest shut yer mouth so I kin hear."

Stratton froze, afraid that any movement he made might give away his location in the woods. Something was wrong, very, very wrong. He wasn't sure what it was, but he knew one thing for sure, his life was in danger.

Slowly, the campfire began to burn down to embers. After what seemed like an eternity, Stratton heard Raymond and Darryl step out of the woods and return to their campfire. Neither of the men returned to their seats when they came back to the campsite. Keeping their backs to the fire, they seemed to be moving around the entire area as they talked quietly to each other. They moved slowly, as they picked up sticks, or rearranged stones. They did anything they could to have an opportunity to glance through the forest from every angle.

Suddenly, it dawned on Stratton that the two men knew he was there and were searching for him. He knew he was in trouble once they were able to pinpoint his location. He waited for the moment when both men were on the far side of the campfire before he made his move. Cautiously, he held his breath and backed deeper into the forest away from the campsite.

Then, silently he quickly made his way through the woods to a rarely used trail that led back to the better-known trail where he encountered the two couples earlier in the evening. Although, he didn't know for sure what was going on in the campsite, he knew he needed backup in order to check it out thoroughly.

Quickly, he walked back up the steep grade of the remote trail to the crest of the mountain before he paused to rest for a moment. He glanced over his shoulder and shuddered. His internal alarm signals were still going off as he rounded the boulders in the area where the path narrowed on the top of the ridge.

The hair raised on the back of his neck as a rush of movement came from behind him out of the darkness. Suddenly, two assailants surrounded and overpowered him. He put his arm up defensively as he felt a crashing blow against his head and suddenly felt himself tumble and fall down ... down ... down ... to somewhere far below. Rocks, trees and dirt surrounded him as he slid and tumbled deeper and deeper into darkness.

CHAPTER 8

Maggie pulled into Rena's driveway a little after ten o'clock and decided to stay and help her get the children ready for bed, as they were all exhausted from their evening in town. Abigail was fast asleep in her baby seat tucked between both of the boys who slept slumped over in the back seat of Maggie's jeep.

"You go ahead and take Abby, Rena. I'll bring the boys inside," she urged.

Rena nodded, then gathered her things and slowly walked up the little dirt path that led to her cabin and turned on the porch light so Maggie could see her way. Bandit waited on the porch to greet them. He wagged his tail and barked at Gertrude the cat when she sauntered out onto the porch.

Maggie leaned into the back seat and gently shook Zack and Jonah.

"Hey, boys ... we're home. It's time to go inside."

Zack opened his eyes enough to see his way down the path to the house. Jonah lay down in the seat and curled up. Maggie smiled, then reached inside the jeep and pulled Jonah into her arms and carried him into the house.

While Rena was changing the baby's clothes and getting her snuggled in bed, Maggie took a warm, soapy washcloth and cleaned a little of the sticky goo from Zack and Jonah's hands and face.

"I'm not sure if that's from the ice cream, the watermelon or the cotton candy," she smiled, "at least some of the sticky stuff is gone."

As soon as she had them as clean as possible without a full bath, she covered them up with their sheets. Both boy were sound asleep almost instantly with Bandit quietly curled up on the floor beneath their beds.

As she waved goodbye to Rena and walked out the front door, Gertrude McFuzz, jumped off the rail in front of Maggie's feet, arched her back and began to rub against her legs. Gertrude was one of the largest housecats on the mountain.

"Hey, girl," Maggie reached down and picked up the large calico cat. "Have you been lonesome this evening with no one here to play with you?"

The cat rubbed Maggie with a cold wet nose and began to purr. Maggie pet her for a minute when Rena came to the front door.

"Maggie, if you hear anything about Stratton, would you let me know? I hope he's ok," Rena asked softly. Care and concern filled her voice.

"Of course I will Rena. I'm sure he's fine. He's one of the best men they have on the trails. When I go into town tomorrow I'll stop by the Ranger Station and see what I can find out ok?" Maggie tried to smile a reassuring smile.

It was unusual for one of the Rangers to take so long to get back to the station, but there was a lot of territory to cover. Most of the Rangers were very thorough when they hiked the trails and wanted to make sure everyone was safe.

"Besides, it was only this morning Stratton started at the beginning of the trail Digger and I hiked earlier in the week. He may have not had enough time to be finished with that trail, yet."

She waved goodbye and headed up the mountain to her cabin. As she drove on the dusty unpaved road, her eyes became heavy and driving seemed to take longer than usual. Each curve seemed longer than the last.

'Guess I'm just not used to staying out so late,' Maggie thought to herself. As the need for sleep grew, she tried to keep her mind busy to keep herself stay awake.

'Next time,' her mind rambled as she drove, 'Maybe I'll just go for dinner and skip the town square party. Anyway, I like to be home on my own front porch when the sun goes down, although it was nice to see Rena and the kids. Plus, there was the wonderful dinner with Doc …, or, Chris. It still feels a little funny to call him Chris.'

Maggie finally arrived home and pulled the jeep under the oak tree in her yard. She rolled the window up to keep the inside from getting wet on the slight chance there might be rain during the night. She also wanted to keep any critters from climbing in the jeep overnight. Wearily, she started toward the cabin when she heard Max rush through the field to get to her. He was so excited to see her he ran full speed toward the jeep.

"Whoa, there buddy," she called as he neared. "Slow down there some."

Max immediately began to leap and bark when he saw Maggie. He dashed towards her and darted back out into the field several times as if he wanted her to follow him. When she continued to walk toward the cabin, Max barked louder and ran around her until she finally stopped walking.

"Oh, Max," Maggie sighed, "Whatever it is, surely it can wait till morning. I am too tired to go traipsing off through the field with you tonight."

Maggie tried to get Max to sit down so she could pet him for a minute and calm him down, but he wasn't interested. He wanted her total attention.

Max continued to bark louder and face the field. Exasperated, Maggie decided to see what was in the field that was so exciting. She stopped by the jeep to reach inside and get her flashlight from the glove box before she followed. Maggie knew to listen to Max when there was something he wanted her to do. He saved her life several times when he insisted she follow him. Instinctively, she knew she had to follow him. So tired, she could hardly walk another foot, she followed.

"Ok, boy, what is it this time. What did you find in the field you want me to see?"

Maggie thought she heard voices when she followed Max across the field.

"I must be crazy. I'm too tired to follow this crazy dog across the field just so he can show me something he's caught. It's probably a squirrel, an opossum or some critter he's never seen before. I am so tired; I'm beginning to hear things. It's a good thing one of my friends from the mental health agency isn't' here right now, they would most likely try to commit me to a psych ward somewhere."

She shook her head and laughed at the idea when she heard one of the voices again! She immediately stopped, every sense alert, and listened more carefully. She felt like kicking herself. Every time she ignored Max when he tried to tell her things she regretted it. She knew it was important for her to listen to him when he was so persistent.

She carefully looked around the edge of the field. In the soft moonlight, it was difficult to see much, but she thought she could see the outline of some tents along the far side of the field. Max ran ahead. He leaped and bounded across the field as if he was excited to have her finally follow him.

'He doesn't seem to sense any danger or any reason to be alarmed. In fact, he seems happy to see whoever is there. I wonder who it could be? Digger usually waits on the porch until I get home if he shows up here.'

Maggie could feel no sense any danger. She knew Max would alert her if there were any sings of danger In fact, she thought she could hear someone laugh when Max neared the area. She walked a little closer before she decided to call out.

"Hallooo, the camp …"

A chorus of laughter and giggles erupted from the tents followed by the sound of a girl's voice as she tried to talk through the laughter.

"No, Max! Noooo! Stop licking me … gross!"

'I know that voice—where have I heard it before?' Maggie tried to place the young woman's voice when a man's voice called out form the tent, also.

"Hey, Maggie! It's us …" Josh called as he climbed out of one of the tents and began to walk toward her with one of his hiking partners, Justin.

"It's Josh and Justin, too! Oh, wow … my hiking friends. What a wonderful surprise! How have you been?" She greeted them with a big hug each.

Before either could answer, another commotion began with Max. Maggie could barely make out Max with his tail and rear end sticking out of the end of the tent. His huge tail swung from side to side in excitement as he crawled deeper into one of the tents. More squeals and laughter burst from the tent when suddenly, it collapsed with the campers and Max inside. The tent then looked as if it had a life of its own as it rolled and writhed on the ground with the girls squealing and Max playfully barking inside.

Maggie and Josh got so tickled, they couldn't help but laugh as they watched the hilarious scene. They had so much fun watching the calamity; they didn't try to help the girls out of the tent.

Justin then jumped in the tent and tried to pull Max out so the girls could have a chance to get untangled. When he finally pulled Max out of the tent, he wrapped his arms around him and tried to calm Max down. He then tried to keep him from licking the girls long enough for them to get out of the tent.

It took a few minutes for the girls to get untangled from their sleeping bags and out of the collapsed tent. Both girls giggled as they emerged from the tent with their hair tangled and clothes in disarray from their struggles. Max sat by Justin, his whole body wiggled in anticipation.

"Max!" Maggie called out sternly to the dog. "Come here!" Max looked at her and wagged his tail, yet did not move. He wanted to stay exactly where he was.

"Max! Now!"

He knew she meant business now and reluctantly walked across the camp-site to sit beside her and lay down. He looked up at her through huge sad brown eyes.

"I'm sorry girls, I hope you're ok. I think he was just excited to see you. Max loves visitors," Maggie greeted the girls.

"We're fine, he just caught us by surprise," Amy laughed as she brushed off her clothes. "We didn't have much room to move around to begin with and then when he crawled inside, there was no way we could get out."

"I don't think I've ever had so many doggie kisses before," CC giggled. "Does he ever get tired of licking people?"

"If he does, I haven't seen it. That's the only way he can show people how much he likes them and evidently he really likes you girls," Maggie smiled.

She looked sternly at Max.

"Are you going to behave yourself? You've caused quite a commotion here tonight." Max looked up at her and wagged his tail. "If you can behave yourself you can get up now."

As soon as she motioned for him to get up, Max jumped and ran to the girls again. He began to wiggle and wag his tail in an effort to get their attention.

"It may take him a few minutes to calm down," Maggie said. "Has he acted this way the whole time you've been here?"

"He was excited to see us, but stayed pretty calm until he knew that you were home," Josh laughed as he started to pick up the tent. "I think he just wanted to wait until you got home to play with us. Maybe he wanted you to be a part of the celebration, too. He knew we'd all have fun together."

"This makes the second time today we've had to regroup our campsite." Justin commented as he helped Josh put the tent back in place and reposition the stakes and supports. "We are getting used to it now."

"Were you camped on one of the forest service trails?" Maggie asked as she sat down by the girls in order to keep Max calm.

"We just set up camp on one of the trails this evening when one of the Rangers came by and told us about the fire hazard. He said we needed to be off the trail as soon as possible," Josh commented.

"We weren't sure what to do because it was about dark and too far to walk back down the mountain to our jeep. We hope you don't mind us stopping by here," Amy explained hopeful that Maggie would not object to their campsite in her yard.

"Of course not, I'm thrilled you did stop by. Please know that you can always stay here whenever you want. I think I offered last time I saw you didn't I?" Maggie tried to remember their last conversation, but exhaustion from the day's activities was taking a toll on her.

"We remembered you offered the last time we were in the area," Josh said, "And we were going to stop by after our hike this time but with the trails closing, we just came by a little earlier."

"You said one of the Rangers stopped by your campsite? Do you remember which one it was?" Maggie asked.

"It was Ranger Stratton," CC said. "He remembered us from the last time we were here. He knew you told us it was ok for us to come by, so he gave us directions to your place. He said you might not be in until late."

"He was right! Which reminds me, I'm about to turn into a pumpkin," Maggie smiled as she stood up. "If you kids don't mind, I think I'll turn in for the night, I'm really tired. It's been a very long day."

"We don't mind, you go ahead," Justin said, "We can catch up tomorrow."

"Thanks guys, I hope you can get some rest tonight. I'll take Max back to the cabin with me, but I won't guarantee he will stay there. Since he knows you all are here and knows how good the girls taste, he may come back," she grinned as she started toward the cabin. "G'nite."

"Night, Maggie," they all called.

Then, Maggie remembered Stratton.

"Did you say which Ranger stopped by your campsite? Was it Stratton?"

"It was Ranger Stratton," Justin commented.

"Oh, good, we were looking for him earlier. Did he happen to say where he was headed after he left your campsite? We kind of thought he would be back in town for the music tonight, but he didn't show up."

"There were a couple of men on the trail about an hour ahead of us and he said he was going to go let them know about the trail closing," Josh said. "I think he expected to be off the mountain and back in his truck by ten o'clock or so. He said he wasn't planning on camping on the trail tonight."

"Ok, thanks, I'm glad he was ok. I'll see you guys in the morning."

Maggie thought about Stratton on her walk back to the cabin. She knew he was careful when he was on the trails and extremely conscientious about safety of each hiker in the mountains. Of all the Rangers, she could think of, Stratton was the one person she knew would stay on the trails until he made sure everyone was safe if there was a danger somewhere. His dedication to his job was only part of it; he was just a really, nice person.

CHAPTER 9

After a long, hot shower, Maggie snuggled into her bed, closed her eyes and almost immediately fell into a deep sleep. So tired, she felt as though every muscle ached. Yet, in spite of the physical exhaustion, sleep proved to be elusive for her. The events of the past few days began to replay in her mind over, and over through her dreams:

She walked though a mountain meadow filled with beautiful, fragrant summer flowers. She wore a long, gauzy dress the color of the golden sun that flowed in the breeze as she walked. Summer daisies and sunflowers filled her arms. She watched as in the distance, the fields of hay swayed like the roll of an ocean wave when the wind blew. Blue birds swooped back and forth over the field in play while a family of deer nibbled on fresh green grass. Not a single cloud appeared in the crystal blue sky allowing the sun to shine down on everything she could see. The whole world seemed to sparkle and come to life.

She smiled as she turned around in the meadow, filled with a feeling of peace and contentment with everything as far as she could see. Suddenly, the ferocious roar of a beast interrupted the beauty and serenity of the scene. She looked across the field to see an enormous hairy beast devour one of the deer. The sky darkened, and heavy gray clouds covered the sun as bright red blood began to cover everything in the field.

Maggie gasped for air, unable to breathe as she woke from her dream. She felt as if the dark clouds covered her and suffocated her. A cold sweat broke out over her body as she sat in bed, tried to get her bearings straight and remember where she was.

'Gosh, that was so real,' she thought as she got out of bed and headed to the kitchen. 'I haven't had a dream that vivid for a long time.'

She put the teapot on the stove to heat and reached in the cupboard for some herbal tea. When the water was hot, she steeped some chamomile tea with lemon while she went to the bathroom to wash her face.

"I'm too tired and too old to be awake this time of the night, it must be 3am or more. This seems to happen when I'm extremely tired."

She shook her head at the face in the mirror then returned to the kitchen to get her tea. Quietly, she slipped out on the porch and sat on the swing to drink her tea. When her eyes adjusted to the night, she was able to see the stars from where she sat. The moon already passed over the cabin on its journey through the sky. Peace finally began to return to her as she listened to the sound of the crickets as they chirped and the creek as it flowed over the rocks.

Maggie watched the stars as they twinkled and sparkled in the sky. It looked like a million stars were in the sky. The stars seemed so much brighter on the mountain, clearer and purer. Suddenly she saw the fleeting tail of a shooting star burned out and faded almost directly over her head.

"How beautiful!" She whispered to herself.

She watched intently for another shooting star while she finished her tea. Here on the mountain, far from city lights and haze, shooting stars were easy to see. When none appeared and finally, relaxed once more, she returned to her bed and lay down to get some sleep. Although, she tried to get the frightening dream out of her mind as she closed her eyes, she knew the dream was somehow related to the bear she saw with Digger. She knew that scene was so frightening and gruesome it was bound to trigger some dreams. Yet, even as she closed her eyes, she knew the dream had some deeper meaning than the incident on the trail.

'I'm too tired now to try to figure it out. I'm going to do the Scarlet thing and think about it another time.'

She finally drifted off into a light, restless sleep where some vague thought continued to nag at her inner consciousness.

Maggie woke to the loud sound of Max as he barked and ran after something in the field by the cabin. The sound of the chase became louder and closer until she heard a loud thump land on the porch and scamper across the front followed by a crash as Max followed closely behind it. Maggie quickly got out of bed and ran to the door to see Basil dive over the woodpile and crawl under the tool shed in the yard. Max frantically began to dig under the shed where he saw the groundhog disappear.

"Max! Stop it!" Maggie called as she ran down the steps to the tool shed. "You are going to HAVE to leave that poor critter alone!" She grabbed Max by the collar and pulled him away from the shed.

"I don't need any new holes dug under the shed today. Now, come over here and behave yourself!" She fussed as she walked with Max back to the porch as she glanced across the field to see if the two young couples were stirring from their tent yet. Seeing no movement, she looked down at Max.

"Have you been to the creek today, Max?"

He wagged his tail and looked at her expectantly.

"Ok, come on then, let's go see if the water's deep enough for a swim," she said as she walked toward the creek, knowing with so little rain; it was most likely too low to swim. "If it isn't deep enough, we'll just wade for a while."

Max leaped up and raced ahead of her. He loved to swim in the creek, especially when Maggie was with him. He didn't hesitate for a moment when he reached the edge of the creek; he just plowed right through the middle of the creek and splashed everything in sight. He then climbed over the rocks to the large boulder that sat in the middle of the stream and waited for Maggie to catch up.

Maggie waded through the cool stream in her bare feet. She gingerly stepped over the slippery rocks until she was able to make her way to the large boulder where Max stood and wagged his tail as he waited for her.

"You certainly were ready to go swimming weren't you buddy?" She laughed at him when she reached the boulder.

"You go first!"

She pointed to the deeper waters behind the boulder where a natural swimming hole formed through the years when stones around the boulder built up after floods and formed a natural dam.

Max immediately jumped off the boulder into the stream and covered Maggie with cold water. She shivered as the cold water drenched her hair and nightshirt causing it to stick to her skin. She started to pull her nightshirt off, but remembered she had visitors camping in the field and decided to leave it as it was.

"No skinny dipping for me today!" She laughed. "Ok, boy, here I come," Maggie called as she jumped off the boulder into the stream with Max.

The cool water felt wonderful against her skin as it rushed over her. Max was ready to play when she emerged from under the water. She splashed him and tossed a stick for him to chase until he finally tired of play and lay down on the boulder again. Then, she finally had some time alone.

She reached down to the bottom of the creek bed for a handful of the fine sand that lay underneath the rocks and began to rub the sand against her skin. Every pore tingled with the cleansing. When she finished, she climbed back on the boulder in the creek and twisted her hair to wring the water out of it when she heard the sound of voices behind her. She turned to see Amy and Colleen standing by the creek bank.

"Hey, girls, the water's great! Come on in," she called to the girls.

"Would it be ok if we swam?" CC asked, with anticipation.

"Sure! Morning is a wonderful time to take a dip. I'm sure the guys would like it, too. In fact, while you all swim, I'll go get us some breakfast together."

"We don't want to put you out," Amy said earnestly.

"You aren't at all. I'm thrilled to have you here. You all enjoy the water while I go change. I've been in here long enough for my fingers to pucker," she said as she looked around for Max, to take him with her, but he was upstream looking for something to chase.

Maggie went back inside the cabin and quickly changed clothes. She towel dried her hair and slipped on socks and tennis shoes before she headed to the kitchen. She quickly put some blueberry muffins in the oven made with wild blueberries she picked earlier in the week. She then poured orange juice while she waited for the coffee to brew and the water to warm for the teapot. She carried everything out to the wooden table on the porch so they could eat outside in the fresh air.

From the sounds of the squeals and giggles, she heard come from the creek, it sounded like a large water battle was going on between the guys and gals. Somehow, she knew Max was most likely also involved. Maggie smiled as the deep baritone bark from Max rang out as he joined them, followed by a chorus of yells. She couldn't tell if he joined the guys or the gals team but, it was beginning to sound like a free-for-all..

"It sure sounds like they're having fun."

She sat on the swing and drank some wild raspberry tea while she waited for them to finish their morning swim. Finally, one by one they began to emerge laughing and giggling from the creek. Maggie smiled.

"Good morning!"

"Hey, Maggie!" Justin called. "That was a great way to wake up this morning."

"I'm glad you enjoyed it. I made some breakfast for you whenever you're ready. The coffee's on, too," she smiled.

"Thanks, Maggie," Josh smiled. "We'll dry off and change clothes, then be right back." He and the others ran across the field with Max right behind them.

Soon, they all came back across the field fresh and clean from their morning swim and joined Maggie on the porch. Max ran along beside them to make sure they found their way without getting lost.

"Looks like you've made permanent friends with Max," Maggie smiled.

"He's a great dog," Josh said. "He really likes the girls. He especially liked to play with, Amy. He wouldn't let her get out of the water."

"Yeah, every time I tried to go to one of the banks, he ran over and jumped in front of me. He loves to splash," Amy smiled.

"He's used to playing in the water with me and the McCutchen boys when they come up to the cabin. He really gets into it with them and they love it," Maggie laughed. "Help yourself to the food. There's plenty to eat here, and more if you eat all this."

"Wow, we didn't expect all this!" Justin immediately sat down and began to fill a plate. "We sure lucked up when Ranger Stratton told us we had to leave the trail. I can't remember when the last time was that I had homemade blueberry muffins." The rest of the group joined him at the table and began to fill their plates.

"Well, now that you know where the cabin is, please feel free to come by here anytime you're in the mountains. I'm usually here unless I'm out on the trail with Digger or Doc." Maggie handed them the dish of butter and a jar of homemade jam for their muffins. "So, what are you guys up to today, anything special?"

"There's not a whole lot we can do with all of the trails closed," Josh said. "CC and I brought our kayaks with us, so we may try to make a run down Baby Falls if the water is deep enough."

"Just be careful if you try it. The water is so low right now that some dangerous rocks are exposed you usually don't have to worry about. You're all welcome to stay here tonight if you're still in the area. I have to make a short run to town, but I'll be back this evening."

"Thanks, Maggie. That would be nice," Amy said. "We're not sure if we'll be here but if we are, we'll come back."

"Could we catch a ride with you down the mountain when you go into town?" Justin asked, "We left our jeep in front of the Ranger's station."

"Sure, just let me get these things put away and I'll be ready to go."

"Ok, thanks Maggie," Justin stood up. "Come on you guys, let's go pack up camp in case we don't get a chance to come back."

They all thanked Maggie for the breakfast and headed to the tents to gather up all of their camping equipment. Maggie quickly put away all the food, scraped the dishes and stacked them in the sink.

"These can wait until I don't have anything better to do," she grinned, "and I can always think of at least a dozen better things to do than wash dishes and clean house."

She quickly brushed her hair and put on some lipstick, then changed her shirt into something a little nicer. 'Nicer, because it doesn't have any stains on it,'she grinned, 'I doubt I'd ever wear anything truly fancy, this will do just fine.'

By the time, she returned to the porch the two couples headed across the field with their gear. They all crammed into the jeep as Maggie started it up. Max barked in protest because so many fun people were going somewhere without him, especially because three of them were sitting in his seat!

"Max, you stay here! I'll be back later, STAY!" Maggie looked sternly at Max, who finally sat down in the shade and wagged his tail as they drove away.

"He sure minds well," CC commented.

Maggie laughed.

"Not always, if there is something he really wants to do or if he knows I'm going hiking, there is practically nothing in the world I could do to keep him home. He knows I'll be home this evening because I don't have my backpack with me."

They drove with the windows up on the jeep to keep the dust out as much as possible. The mountain was already beginning to warm up even though it was only mid-morning. Maggie slowed down to a crawl when they were about half way down the mountain and close to the place where the McCutchens live.

"Is anything wrong?" Josh asked.

"No," Maggie laughed, "We just have to be careful of the McCutchen Gang around here. They're notorious for finding ways to get me to stop the jeep. I just want to make sure they aren't in the way when I drive by their house. Keep your eyes and ears peeled. You never know what's going to happen around here. Sometimes they are in the road and sometimes they are in the trees, you just never know."

Maggie began to peer through the trees. Curious about what she meant the four young people looked at each other and then shrugged their shoulders while they watched the road and forest banks. As they neared the McCutchen house and tried to understand what Maggie meant they looked for obvious clues..

"What are we looking for?" Amy whispered to Justin.

Justin shrugged his shoulders and then looked intently out the window for some sign of danger.

"Ahh, there it is," Maggie whispered as she rolled the jeep forward.

Ahead of them were four small tree branches arranged into a square in the middle of the road. She pointed to the branches and began to laugh.

"What is it?" CC asked.

"It's a pretend trap," Maggie whispered.

She searched in the small bush beside their driveway until she could see both of the boys hiding in the bush.

"See, we have a couple of bandits in the bushes over there."

They all giggled when they looked into the bush and saw two little boys as they hid there and waited for them. Maggie slowly rolled over the leaf and branch square that lay in the middle of the road.

"It's ok, just follow my lead," she whispered as she stopped the jeep and turned the engine off, then rolled down her window.

"Oh, NO! What are we going to do?" She exclaimed in exaggerated alarm. "We're caught in an enormous trap! How will we ever get out so we can get go toward town again? Who will save us now?" She motioned her hand for the two couples in the jeep to join her. They all began to pretend to fret and worry at the same time.

"Louder," Maggie whispered.

They all continued to fret and moan a little louder about being caught in a trap until they were loud enough for the boys to hear.

Suddenly, with a loud yell, the two little McCutchen boys jumped out into the unpaved road, their faded overalls dusty from hiding in the bushes. Both wore old cowboy hats that were several sizes too large, bandanas around their necks and carried large sticks in their hands. They began to yell as they ran in a circle around the jeep.

"Oh, no! We're caught!" Maggie exclaimed. Then, she looked sternly at the boys and demanded, "Take me to your leader!"

As she began to get out of the jeep, she quickly turned to the two couples whispered, "Sorry guys, this will only take a few minutes and then we'll leave."

They all laughed when the two boys pointed their sticks at them. They didn't budge from their positions until not just Maggie, but all five passengers climbed out of the jeep and followed the boys to the house.

"Put your hands behind your head," Zack ordered as he tried to see from under the rim of his hat. "You're all our prisoners, now."

Everyone did as told and tried not to laugh. Zack was very solemn as he marched down the path with his captives in front of him. He carried his stick high on his shoulder and never cracked a smile as he quickly walked.

Jonah was so excited about capturing not one person but five that he ran ahead of the group as fast as he could to get to the house first and inform his mother of his feat.

"Mamma! Mamma!" He shouted, "Hurrwee up, we gots us a bunch of 'em! Mamma!"

When Rena came to the front door and saw Zack and Jonah with their captives, her face turned a deep shade of red.

"OH, I am so sorry, Maggie," she was so embarrassed and painfully bashful that she was afraid to look at any of the captives in the eye. "I hope everybody's ok and the boys didn't do anything to hurt you. I'm so sorry if they did," she looked sternly at the boys as she wiped her hands on her apron.

The girls couldn't stop giggling.

"No, we're fine. They are so cute!" Amy said as she and CC sat down on the porch steps where Zack ordered them to sit, as good captives should.

When Josh and Justin reached the house, they suddenly began to break out of rank and chased the boys around the yard until they captured them. They then tickled them until the boys couldn't stop laughing. They hoisted them on their shoulders and then toted them back to the porch as they kicked and squealed. The boys giggled and laughed with the rough and tumble play with the older playmates until they were exhausted. Finally, after they rested and caught their breath again, the boys took the two couples over to show them their new tree house built by Stratton in a tree near the stream. It felt wonderful for Maggie and Rena to see the boys have so much fun. They sat on the porch and watched the boys show off their new playhouse.

"We're headed into town, Rena," Maggie said as she picked up the baby. "Is there anything you need for me to pick up for you while I'm there?" She held the baby's hands while she stood up and bounced her in place. "She looks like she's about ready to walk, Rena. Look how strong her legs are!"

The baby cooed and smiled at Maggie while she bounced.

"Yes, she's getting stronger everyday. She's about nine months old now, so she could start to walk early." Rena hung her head down and was very quiet for a moment. She twisted the towel in her hand and smoothed it out again.

"Could you do one thing for me Maggie?" Rena asked hesitantly, "Could you stop by the Ranger Station and make sure Stratton is ok? I still haven't heard anything from him and I've been getting kind of worried."

Maggie looked up. She could see the stress and worry lines on Rena's face.

"Of course I will, Rena. I meant to tell you, the two couples with me were setting up a camp on one of the trails yesterday when Stratton found them and told them the trails were going to close until the fire hazard was over. So, I know he was ok as of ten or eleven o'clock last night. He probably ran into some other hikers he had to warn and then ended up having to stay on the trail."

Rena sighed, "That's such a relief. I didn't want to be a bother."

"You're never a bother, Rena. Is there anything else I can do for you while I'm there? I have three errands I need to run. First, I'm going to the Ranger's Station to see if Sam has any news about Stratton. Second, Sharon told me Ms. Cates has been asking for me, so I need to stop by there for a few minutes and then last, I'm going to stop by the grocery store. I should be back before dark. I could bring something by from the grocery if you need it."

"No, I'm fine, Maggie. Thank you anyway."

"Ok, then, if you don't need us, we're going to go on. These kids have some things they want to do today."

She looked across the yard for the boys. Jonah was all smiles as he pushed CC in the tire swing. Zack was busy giving Josh a lesson in how to find salamanders in the stream.

'I hate to bother them; the boys look like they are having so much fun. They seem like they're starved for attention. Maybe some other time we can stay longer but for now, I know these young people have other plans, and I'm beginning to worry about Stratton, too. It isn't like him to stay out so long.'

"Are you guys ready to head out?" She called to them.

They all stopped what they were doing and started to walk to the house. They looked like they made some long lasting friendships with each other in the short amount of time they were together. Jonah was holding CC's hand as they walked and Zack made sure he was exactly between Justin and Amy. He blushed slightly every time Amy looked at him.

Maggie looked at Zack and Jonah very seriously when they finally reached the house. She stood in mock attention and saluted the boys.

"Officers, do I have your permission to take the hostages into town now? Its time for their next assignment and I don't want them to be late. I promise I'll make them behave exactly as they should."

They both nodded in agreement.

"When ya gonna brang 'em back ta play sum more, Maggie?" Jonah drawled out as he started to swing CC's hand.

"Well, I don't know, Jonah. That's up to them. It's hard to tell when they'll be back, but for now, you'll have to let them go and tell them 'see ya later', because they have some things they need to do."

The boys nodded in agreement and watched as Maggie and the two couples got ready to leave. Both boys seemed pleased when Josh and Justin walked over and shook their hand. They then turned a crimson red and blushed from ear to ear when the girls gave them a hug before they left. Jonah smiled and tucked his lower lip inside his mouth as he looked down at the ground. Everyone said goodbye and the five former hostages headed to the jeep. The boys picked up their wooden sticks and oversized cowboy hats again, and followed every step Josh and Justin took to the jeep. The boys tried to imitate every step and every gesture they took.

Maggie got tickled and finally had to ask.

"Are you boys pretending to be Josh and Justin? You're walking just like them."

"No! It's not that," Zack exclaimed, "We're following your trail! See?" Zack demonstrated how he could look at the ground to see Josh and Justin's footprints and follow them right up to the person.

"Oh, I see," Maggie said, "That's a good skill to learn."

"We gonna twak us sum wild aminals like Wainjur Stwatton. Him taught us how!" Jonah said his eyes large with excitement.

He looked at the ground bashfully as he walked up and stood beside the girls, then grinned. Everyone laughed.

"Well, keep up the good work. It looks like you're on the right track, just keep practicing," Maggie smiled as they all bundled back in the jeep and headed down the mountain again.

"That was so much fun, Maggie," Amy said, "Thank you for stopping."

"I appreciate the amount of time you all spent with the boys. They love and need all the attention they can get. Sometimes life is hard on them but they love their life exactly as it is and don't want to change it."

"What's the story behind them?" Josh asked.

"Well, their father died in a mining accident when Rena was pregnant with Abby," Maggie began as she drove down the mountain. "Rena's ancestors lived in this same place for so many generations no one can remember how long it has been since the first pioneer got here. So, leaving the mountain isn't really an option for her. She owns the land and makes financial ends meet by gathering herbs in the mountains or making baskets and pottery to sell in one of the gift shops in town. She's a very honest, hardworking person. I admire her a lot."

"Is there anything we can do to help them out?" Justin asked.

"She won't take handouts, she's too proud to do that and it sort of goes against her culture. She doesn't want to feel like she owes anybody anything but I know she has things she needs. What you may want to do is make a trade with her or barter for services, something like that."

"What kind of trade?" Josh asked.

"Well, like in the fall, she will need wood for the winter. So, you may want to tell her that you've seen some of her baskets in town and like them quite a bit. Then ask her if she would be willing to trade a load of wood for one of her baskets, or something like that. Or, you could ask her if she would dry some fruit for your backpack trips. She preserves all her food already. I'm sure you can think of other things."

"That sounds like fun! I'd like to see the boys again," Amy said. "Plus, I didn't even get a chance to see the baby. Maybe she would let us spend some time with the kids and give her a break."

"Take the time to get to know her so you will understand her and I'm sure you will come up with lots of things. She's a very talented lady. You will learn quite a lot about mountain lore and skills in the woods if you want," Maggie smiled as she pulled into the ranger's station. "Well, here we are folks!"

"Thanks for the lift, Maggie." They all jumped out of the jeep and gathered up their gear. "We're not sure if we'll be back tonight, but if we don't we'll see you soon," Josh said as they all hugged her goodbye.

As Maggie watched the young people all climb into their vehicle and drive away, she thought of the days when she had more free time and she and her friends spent all of their free time together hiking and camping in the mountains.

CHAPTER 10

Maggie walked into the main entrance of the Ranger Station. Two of the part-time Ranger's Aids who worked during the tourist season greeted her cheerfully. They were available in the office to give directions and help visitors out when possible.

"Morning!" Maggie called as she walked in the door. "Everybody must be out working today. The parking lot is deserted!"

"Hey, Maggie, come on in and join us. We were just talking about the forest fires. They have some reports that smoke was seen on one of the ridges so everyone left to check it out," Martha greeted Maggie as she walked through the door.

"Do you know where it was seen?"

"It was somewhere off the Skyway close to the Tennessee and North Carolina line. I don't think there is much up there but forest. The Rangers have cleared most of the trails of hikers by now."

"Did Stratton ever make it back in to the office? I know Rena was a little concerned because he didn't show up at the block party last night," Maggie said as she glanced around the office and hoped she would see Stratton walk through the door.

"We haven't seen him around the office this morning, yet. He usually shows up when he's tired of hiking," Martha joked.

"Are you worried about your place, Maggie?" Ranger Dan asked. Dan was also a seasonal Ranger. He and Martha were both local senior citizens who enjoyed the opportunity to work with visitors and have the chance to share their knowledge of the area. Both Rangers volunteered much of their free time when they weren't working.

"Well, I'm always concerned when there are forest fires. There isn't much chance my place could be saved in a major fire, it's too remote," Maggie said thoughtfully as she shook her head.

"They have a lot of equipment around now that helps them detect the fires before they get too out of hand. I wouldn't worry about it too much," Ranger Dan smiled and patted Maggie on the back comfortingly.

"I'm not too worried about my own safety. I think I could get out of danger if there was a fire in my area. You had a very helpful fire safety seminar here last fall."

"So, you remember it is better to try to go downhill if you are on foot because forest fires usually travel uphill?"

"Yes, and once a fire gets to the top of a ridge, it is easier for a forest fire to jump from ridge to ridge so it is better to stay away from the ridge tops even if they don't have a fire on them."

"You are on the right track," Ranger Dan beamed, proud to know Maggie remembered his lessons.

"Also," he continued, "fires generally travel with the direction of the wind. So, keep that in mind if you have a choice in your directions and are trying to get away from one on the trail. Don't forget, if you feel like you are going to be stuck somewhere or trapped, it's better to try to find a stream or natural fire-break than to stay in the woods or in a field somewhere. Fires run through fields rapidly and are more likely to overcome you there. You can't outrun them."

"Thanks, Dan," Maggie smiled, "I'll remember."

"You know, controlled fires are important in forest management. We use them on a regular basis in our line of work to maintain the woods and trails. We often have fire drills where we burn off sections of the forest in order to halt diseases in trees or the migration of certain beetles or insects that are killing native trees in the area."

"I've heard some of the Rangers talk about that before. It just seems a little scary that someone would start a fire intentionally even if it is a Ranger. I'd be afraid it would get out of control and then the whole forest would go up in flames."

Ranger Dan smiled patiently, "We try to keep that from happening. We would never start a controlled burn during this time of year. It's too risky with everything as dry as it is right now."

"That's a relief!" Maggie smiled.

"These young Rangers we have now are pretty good at fighting fires, Maggie. I don't think there has been a major forest fire here for a number of years now," Martha added sympathetically.

"OK, I'm going to finish my errands in town. Tell everyone I stopped by to say Hi," Maggie said as she opened the door. "Oh, by the way, is Sam around today?"

"He's out with the rest of the crew making sure everyone is off the trails. They have everyone out even the top brass like Sam, but by this evening, they'll have most of the trails scouted and cleared. Then, we'll have everyone home again."

"Well, tell him I said Hi. It's been a while since we spoke," Maggie waved and headed for the jeep. The parking lot looked lonely with all of the Forest Service vehicles gone for the day. Maggie shook off her concerns and headed into town.

Maggie drove to the local grocery store to pick up some fresh fruit, a quart of milk and a loaf of bread to take home with her. She then dove across the street to the BP station to pick up a few supplies there. Even though she recently filled the jeep up with gas, she wanted to make sure she had a full tank in case there was an emergency and the station closed down due to fires.

She noticed several of the local men sitting in the booths by the window and stopped by to speak with them and get the latest information on the fires. Neal and Bob motioned for her when they saw her.

"Hey, Maggie! Come on over and join us," Neal said cheerfully. They scooted over to make room for her on the bench as she approached. The group seemed to be somewhat somber as they drank their coffee.

"What's going on fellas? You all seem to be talking about something pretty serious today," Maggie said as she slid in beside them on the bench.

"We're all talkin' about the fires, Maggie. Ain't nothin' much else anybody wants ta talk about any more," Neal said quietly.

"They sure have everybody pretty scared," Bob added.

"Do they have them under control, yet?"

"No, and there are a few more that have started since yesterday. One of them is so big now, it started to jump ridges," Neal said.

"Oh gosh, where are they? Are any of them near homes?" she asked fervently hoping none of the fires were close to her own home.

"Right now, they are all on forest service property but you never can tell which way they will run if the wind picks up," Bob commented as he took a deep drink of coffee. "A small change in the wind can change the course of a whole fire."

"How many crews do they have out now?"

"They've got three teams out now and the Mayor is planning on asking the Governor to have the National Guard on stand-by in case things get worse," Neal said. His eyes were wide and serious. Maggie could see no sign of the playful sparkle he usually had in his eyes.

"That sounds very serious!"

"Yep," Neal started as he shifted in his seat, "The Forest Service already put some evacuation maps out in the local stores jest in case they are needed to help people get off the mountain safely."

"Wow, I didn't know things were already that serious."

"They're 'bout as bad now as they have ever been," Bob said as he nodded his head. "They've had some pretty bad fires in here in the past that destroyed a lot of land. Just about everyone knows it's almost impossible to get fire insurance on a place in the backwoods. That's why most people live in town."

"I don't have insurance on my place," Maggie said thoughtfully as the tension increased in her chest. "Is there any way to protect it if the fire comes my way?"

"The only thing you can do is get off the mountain as quick as you can and hope your house is spared," Neal said as he patted her hand. "They ain't nothin' in your place that's worth riskin' yer life to try and get it!"

The other men at the table nodded in agreement.

"But, surely there is something I could do to help the chance of saving it!"

"Maggie, if you're in your cabin and the fire is even a ridge away, you need to leave as quickly as you can. The only thing that might possibly help save your home would be to wet it down with water, but don't waste time doing even that if you can see and smell fire." Bob said as he watched her intently. "Now, Maggie, you've got to promise us you'll leave that cabin with the first sign of fire in the area."

She hesitated before she answered.

"Maggie, we all know how much that place means to you and how much it keeps you in touch with your Grandmother. But you're much more important than that place, and your Grandmother will be with you no matter where you are," Neal said as his eyes glistened with moisture.

"Ok, I promise I'll leave if it is my only choice."

"And remember, if you're out on the trail and a fire comes your way; make sure you head down hill. A fire is more likely to travel uphill and run to the top of the ridges. If you can't find a way to get out safely, then find a stream or creek and get in the middle of it until the fire passes," Bob said in as serious a voice as she ever heard him use. "Can you remember all that?" He said with a smile.

"Of course," Maggie grinned as she stood up to leave, "I've got a mind like a steel trap. I just have to remember how to open the trap when I need it to remember things."

"That's what we're afraid of, Maggie," Neal said, "Just make sure you don't let yourself get trapped!"

She smiled as she headed out the door and said, "Thanks for the advice!"

'Whew, those were pretty serious words for that crew. They must have gone through fire dangers before,' she said to herself as she contemplated the fire dangers. She shook her head and shoulders in an effort to shake off the feeling of impending danger as she got into the jeep.

CHAPTER 11

Maggie left the BP station and headed through town to Ms. Cates house. As she slowly drove down the shady, rut filled drive that led to her home she thought of her first visit with Ms. Cates earlier in the year. Since that first visit, she continued to make regular visits to the old woman whenever she could. Maggie found Ms. Cates fascinating and very informative about folklore and regional history on days when she was lucid. At times, Ms. Cates seemed delusional when the effects of her Alzheimer's disease seemed more apparent than other times.

When she arrived at the home, she climbed from the jeep and lifted a basket of fresh fruit and vegetables from her garden for the old woman. She made her way across the pathway to the stonewall that wound around the side of the house and disappeared into the woods. She lifted the gate and walked through to the back yard.

No matter how many times she came to visit, Maggie still felt a little uneasy when she first arrived at the old, rundown structure. Just the sight of Ms. Cates' house was a little foreboding. It was impossible to determine just how old the house might be. The boards on the two story structure were weathered and faded through the years and now were a dull gray color. The planks on the front porch seemed to have warped, swayed and even rotted in several places.

The first time Maggie visited Ms. Cates, she glimpsed through the front windows to see stacks and piles of papers and magazines that appeared to be undisturbed for many years. Now, she knew Ms. Cates usually stayed in the back yard or in the kitchen area on the back of the house where she could spend her days looking out over her flowers and herb garden. This was where Maggie headed.

Ms. Cates was an unusual blend of reality and insanity. As a former local schoolteacher n the area, she was bright and alert during her youth. Now, in her eighties and as a victim of Alzheimer's disease, she often appeared confused or disoriented. She was a tiny figure whose body hunched over by years of osteoporosis and hard work. Often, she could be seen wearing bizarre or unusual outfits and even wearing several outfits at once. Although she was very wealthy, Ms. Cates didn't seem to have the desire to spend money on herself or her place.

For the most part the locals thought she was harmless, but a little bit crazy. They all seemed to take care of her needs and watch out for her, even the younger children. Maggie enjoyed spending time with Ms. Cates and listened to her stories even when it was difficult to decide which stories were real and which were a part of Ms. Cates' delusions. At times, she even told stories that seemed to foretell the future. Maggie often wondered if she was some type of seer even though she often looked like a witch. She lived alone now in a home that at some time in the past was probably a mansion for this area. Now, the estate was in ruins and had a ghostly, almost haunted appearance.

Maggie glanced around the yard. There seemed to be some type of flower or brush blooming in every section of the yard. There were pink Coneflowers, golden Black-eyed Susan, Sunflowers and Jerusalem Artichokes. The rich purple shade of Ironweed flowers grew in a broad band and stood out in contrast to the bright orange shade of Butterfly weed that grew around the edge of the woods. Maggie set the basket of fresh fruit and vegetables down on the screened-in back porch and followed the stone wall into the jumble of weeds and shrubs behind the house.

"Ms. Cates, are you here?" Maggie called, "Hello."

She continued to follow the old wall deep into the woods beyond the yard. A small dirt path that followed along the wall was made of many different types of stones. Some were round, flat river stones; others were much larger and of different varieties of stone such as quartz or limestone. The path wound through the woods and came to a clearing near a small stream.

Maggie gasped. She looked in amazement at the pattern she saw before her. The wall and path led around the edge of the clearing and then formed a circle that wound around and around until it stopped in a circular area in the center of the clearing that measured about eight feet in diameter. The whole design looked like a giant spiral. In the center of the circular area, a small stone structure appeared to be some type of altar or place for a ceremony of some sort.

Maggie shivered when she tried to understand the things she saw and wondered how Ms. Cates might use them. She thought of the occasions she often imagined Ms. Cates might be a witch.

"I wonder what she offers up on the altar?" she asked herself when she felt an involuntary shudder run across her shoulders as she imagined some type of ancient ceremony around the stone altar.

As she continued to follow the path around the edge of the clearing, Maggie noticed several sections of the wall had crumbled and fallen down through the years. She stopped in several places to pick up stones from the ground and place them back on the wall. She stopped to pick up a rather flat stone when she noticed there were some initials and a date carved on one side of the stone, RJB 7/23/48.

Puzzled, Maggie examined the carving on the rock closely. As she placed it on the wall and reached for another fallen stone, she noticed it also seemed to be carved. This one had VMD 2/25/52 etched on one side. Quickly, she began to gather more of the fallen stones and pick them up. Each one seemed to have initials and a date on them. Maggie became so engrossed in the stones and reading the dates on the stones, she didn't hear Ms. Cates hurry along the path behind her and brush past her.

Maggie jumped as the hunched little figure brushed past her and scurried along the path to the center of the spiral. The old woman seemed more stooped that usual under the burden of the load she carried. Her arms were full of sticks and branches she piled high on the stone altar in the center of the circle. Maggie watched as Ms. Cates then placed bundles of what seemed to be dried herbs on top of the pile and began to arrange small stones and shells in a pattern around the base of the altar.

"Oh, there you are! Hi, Ms. Cates, it's me, Maggie. I just came by to see you today. Are you doing ok?"

Maggie followed the old woman to the center of the circle.

Today, Ms. Cates looked even more bizarre than usual. She had loosely tucked her hair inside a straw hat covered with brightly colored plastic flowers, which made it seem especially out of control today. She wore an old-fashioned apron over a striped cotton dress that was so long it almost dragged the ground. Her stockings must have come unhooked from their garters and fell to a pool around her ankles just above her dusty boots.

"Is there anything I can do to help you?" Maggie asked as she walked closer to the stone fire pit and peered inside.

Ms. Cates mumbled to herself as she arranged the sticks and herbs on the altar. Maggie listened closely in an effort to understand her more clearly, but was unable to make sense of anything the old woman said.

"Ms. Cates, are you ok?" Maggie touched her arm gently.

She turned to look and stare at Maggie with a blank look as if she was just waking up from a dream or a trance.

"What is that? What did you say?" she asked as if confused and disoriented.

"Hi, it's me, Maggie. I came to visit you today. Are you ok?"

"Maggie! It's you!" Ms. Cates replied with relief and recognition in her voice. "I need to speak with you. It's very important!"

"Sharon told me you were looking for me, so I stopped by to see you and see if there was anything I could do for you."

"Yes, umhmm," Ms. Cates replied.

She seemed distracted as she continued to arrange sticks in the fire pit. She seemed to forget Maggie was even there.

Maggie decided to try to start a conversation in a different way.

"I see you have a beautiful stone wall. This is the first time I've seen the center of the stone circle. Is this a special place?"

"Umhum, special it is … a special place for special things."

"I noticed some of the stones seem to have dates and initials on them. Is there a special reason for that?" Maggie continued to probe and try to get Ms. Cates involved in a conversation.

"Every stone was brought by a visitor sometime in the past. Someone who came to visit, meditate, or search for an answer brought a stone."

"Is that why they have initials and dates carved on them?" Encouraged, Maggie probed further.

"Yes, names and dates of those who came. Each one left a piece of their spirit behind. Give and take," Ms. Cates paused as she gazed at the circular wall. "When you take something away, you must also give thanks and leave something behind. It's the Native way. You must repay the spirits for their gifts."

"This is a beautiful stone wall. It looks like a sanctuary or peaceful meditation place here in the center by the stream."

"Yes, a circle by a stream. It's a place to pray and meditate. It's a Holy place. My mother found it when she was just a little girl and protected it her entire life," Ms. Cates seemed to pause and disappear inside herself again. Then, just as quickly as she became lucid, she changed and began to scurry around the yard once more.

"Need to hurry, no time to waste," she said quickly as she scurried back up the path toward the house again.

Maggie followed closely behind her to the house. When they arrived at the back porch again, she picked up the basket of herbs and vegetables and followed Ms. Cates into the kitchen.

"I brought you some fruit and vegetables from my garden," Maggie said in an attempt to start a conversation again. Now, her curiosity nagged at her and prompted her to get to the heart of Ms. Cates requests for a visit from her.

The plaster walls of the old kitchen were painted green some time in the past and now were dingy and faded from years of neglect. In several places, sections of plaster had flaked and fallen off through the years. Open wooden shelves filled with mason jars lined the kitchen walls. Ms. Cates reached up and pulled a string on a single bare light bulb that hung from the ceiling in the center of the room. It swayed back and forth for a few moments creating eerie shadows along the walls of the kitchen.

She seemed preoccupied with her activities and scurried around the kitchen as she muttered to herself under her breath. It was difficult for Maggie to understand anything the old woman said. Her words at times were incoherent and a jibberish nonsense at best.

"Is there anything you would like for me to do?" Maggie asked.

"Need to talk, no time to waste," she muttered.

"OK," Maggie replied hesitantly, "What would you like to talk about today? Is there anything special?"

"You've got to go get them and bring them here."

"Who? I'm not sure who you are talking about, Ms. Cates. Who do you want me to bring to see you?" Maggie asked patiently, although she could feel her frustration grow as their difficult conversation continued.

"Bring me the woman with the two little boys, the same one who makes baskets and wanders in the woods," she replied as she reached for some of the mason jars and tucked them into her pockets, then reached for more.

"Do you mean, Rena?"

"Yes, go quickly now. We have to save her man."

"Do you mean, Stratton?" Maggie asked as a pang of fear stabbed her chest.

Ms. Cates stopped what she was doing and turned to face Maggie with a chilling stare. She tilted her head and squinted her eye as she looked up into Maggie's face.

"Maggie, the Ranger is in danger. We need his woman's help. If you don't hurry and bring her here, it will be too late," she said in bone chilling clarity. "We have to meditate and ask the spirits for their guidance and help."

"O-ok," Maggie stammered. "I can go get her if you'd like, that is, if they can come today. You want me to bring her back here today?"

"Bring the children, too," she demanded as she began to collect things from the shelves again. "The children have been chosen."

"Ok … well, I can go see if they will come back with me," Maggie hesitated at the door as she thought of how bizarre it would sound to most people for Maggie to come to their doorstep and ask them to come on such a strange mission. "They don't get out much in the evenings. Rena likes to stay home with the baby."

"Got to hurry, don't delay—got to hurry, danger!" Ms. Cates began to mumble to herself. "Ranger danger …, Ranger danger …, don't delay," she mumbled as Maggie slipped out the kitchen door.

Maggie shook her head as she walked back to the jeep. She felt an ominous chill and foreboding sense of danger as she climbed into the jeep and drove up the mountain toward Rena's cabin.

CHAPTER 12

On the way to her cabin, Maggie stopped by the Forest Ranger's headquarters once more. Several agency vehicles were in the parking lot when she arrived. Maggie quickly went inside to check on the status of fire conditions in the area and see if there was any news on Stratton. Several Rangers, who were preparing for an exercise of some type filled the office and talked quietly among themselves. One of the assistant Rangers greeted her at the door and pointed her in the direction of the Head Ranger before she went back about her business of packing a first aide kit.

"Hey, Maggie, it's good to see you," Sam said in a somber voice as he opened the door of his office and allowed her inside. "How are things on your side of the mountain today?"

"Well, I'm not sure. I haven't been home since this morning, but so far things are ok," she said as she searched his face for clues. "Things must be getting pretty serious around here lately."

"Yes, I'm afraid they are," Sam rolled out an area map of one of the ridges that ran along a valley near town. "There are reports of a small forest fire along this ridge. We already have a crew out there to take care of it but with conditions as dry as they are we may be in for more trouble than we care to deal with around here."

"I guess the fire towers are all already manned," Maggie commented thoughtfully.

"Yes, they have been manned for several days now. Our staff is already stretched to the limits and now with this fire, we are looking at several areas where we have very little coverage."

"You could call the local volunteers," Maggie suggested.

"I may have to do that but I don't want to use them until it is absolutely necessary. It wouldn't help any of us if everyone was tired at the same time."

"Is there anything I can do?"

"Well, we may need to use your place as an outpost base if conditions get any worse. It's in an ideal location for the teams to meet on that side of the mountain."

"Sure, you know you are all welcome any time."

"We're still short one man, too. If we don't hear from Stratton by tomorrow, we are going to send a search party out for him."

"That's one of the reasons I stopped by," Maggie said with concern. "Rena is very worried about him. She said he was supposed to be back off the trail last night and she hasn't heard from him."

"We haven't heard from him either but it's nothing for him to be out on the trail for a few days at a time," Sam said thoughtfully. "We may use your place to send a search party out in the morning. If we start from there we can look for him and also follow up on the trails he was supposed to check out."

"We could help. Digger and I are supposed to go on the trail tomorrow anyway; would it be ok if we joined the search team?"

"Sure, we could use your help with tracking if we need to follow his trail. You and Digger are two of the best trackers on the mountain."

"Ok, I'll look for you in the morning then."

Maggie felt as if her stomach was in her throat as she left the Ranger's office and headed up the mountain to Rena's house. After the flurry of activity in the Ranger's office and Sam's anxiety over the fire danger, her fears for Stratton seemed to have intensified. She drove quickly and pulled in front of the path to the house careful so she could watch for the children in case they played in the yard. She quickly ran to the house and called for Rena as she ran.

"Rena, Rena, are you home?"

The front door opened and Rena stepped out on the porch as she wiped her hands on a dishtowel. Anxiety and fear were written across her face as she stepped forward and grasped the rail for support.

"Maggie ..., is everything ok? Have you heard from Stratton?"

"No, Rena. There is no news yet," Maggie answered as she stepped up on the porch and put her arm around Rena's shoulders. "I know it isn't exactly what you wanted to hear, but we haven't heard any bad news either."

"I'm just so worried," Rena whispered.

"I know, I am, too. The Forest Rangers are going to start a search party for him if no one has heard anything by morning and Digger and I are going to be with them."

Rena held her arms around her waist and fought back tears.

"They'll find him, don't worry."

"I just wish there was something I could do. I feel so helpless."

"That's why I stopped by, Rena. There is something we can all do to help. When I went to town the other day, Sharon told me Ms. Cates was asking for me, so I stopped by to see her today."

Rena looked blankly at Maggie as she talked.

"We've talked about her before. Sometimes, Ms. Cates is a little 'off-kilter' in her head but she has moments when she is pretty rational, too."

Rena nodded.

"Anyway, when I stopped to see her today she told me I needed to come get you and the boys. Somehow she knew Stratton was missing and in danger. She said it was very important that she see the boys because they were 'chosen.'"

Rena looked up and stood very still. Silently, she turned and entered her house. She immediately began to pack a small bag for the baby and a few things she thought she might need for the boys. Always a woman brought up with mountain lore and traditions, Rena knew she could not ignore a message from someone who might be able to help her with her crisis. Experience taught her that often people who appear to be a little 'off' mentally were often in touch with a spiritual realm most people ignored or were unaware existed. Maggie watched Rena then walk over to a corner cupboard, take out two small earthen jars and place them in her bags.

"Maggie, would you go wake up the boys? We'd be grateful if you could take us to her house," she said earnestly.

"Of course, I'll take you there; that's why I came!" Maggie replied eagerly. "I wouldn't have it any other way."

She quickly went into the boy's room and gently woke them from their afternoon naps. Zack was asleep with Gertrude curled up beside him on the bed and Jonah was asleep with his arm wrapped around a small teddy bear.

"Hey, boys, how would you like to go on an adventure with me and your mom today?"

Zack smiled, immediately got out of bed and began to put his shoes on and tie the laces. It took a little more encouragement to wake Jonah from his nap because he was such a sound sleeper. He finally turned and rubbed his eyes.

"Is that you, Maggie?" he smiled.

"Sure is! Want to go on an adventure with me today?"

He nodded, and stretched, then turned over and closed his eyes.

Maggie laughed, "Come on, fella. We need to go," she said as she put his shoes on his feet and tied the laces before she carried him to the main room of the house.

"We're ready, Maggie," Rena said. She stood by the door with Abby in her arms and Zack by her side, ready to leave.

"Ok, but before we leave, we each need to find a special stone from the creek to take with us."

Rena looked a little puzzled when she first heard Maggie's request then turned and headed toward the creek. She helped the boys select a small stone for everyone from their creek. Maggie smiled when everyone was back on the path again.

"Ok, let's head out then," she said brightly.

When they were all loaded into the jeep, Maggie slowly drove down the winding dirt road that led to town. She was especially careful because of her precious cargo, and because she was still a little leery of pedestrians on the road after the incident with the jogger, she had earlier in the week in the road.

By time she reached Ms. Cates house, all of the children were awake and watched intently as Maggie drove down the driveway. They had never been to her house before and the new sights were intriguing to their young minds as well as to the adults.

Maggie pulled the jeep to a halt under a large shade tree in Ms. Cates front yard. She opened the door for the boys to climb out of the back of the jeep and waited for Rena and the baby to come around to the front of the vehicle. When everyone was ready, Maggie led the way through the gate and around to the back of the house where she thought Ms. Cates might be waiting for them.

Maggie smiled when she watched the boys walk down the path. They held their stones in front of them securely in their hands and walked gently as if they walked on eggshells. They seemed to drink in everything they saw.

Maggie knocked on the back door.

"Ms. Cates, we're here. Are you in the kitchen?" When she heard no response, she poked her head inside and called again, "Hello, Ms. Cates; are you there?"

"I guess she has already gone to the circle. We could walk down the path and see if she's down by the stream," Maggie suggested.

Everyone nodded in agreement and the little group hesitantly walked down the path toward the stream. As they made their way through the woods in the evening sun they noticed patches of ivy and flowers grew over the stones in some places and gave it an eerie, mysterious look. When the path finally emerged into the small glade where the circle of stones spiraled around the stone altar, everyone in the group came to a stunned halt. Maggie and Rena gasped at the sight.

There in the center of the glade by the stone altar was Ms. Cates. She wore nothing more than what appeared to be a simple doeskin tunic, adorned with shells and stone beads. Her long, wavy hair was undone and hung almost to her waist. She wore nothing on her feet but a small shell bracelet that hung around her ankle. They all watched closely as she scurried around the stone altar fascinated with her movements. Maggie waved when Ms. Cates noticed them and turned to face their direction.

"Hey, Ms. Cates, we're here. I found everyone you asked me to bring tonight," she said as she walked toward the center of the spiral and the old woman.

The boys walked toward her hesitantly, their eyes filled with wonder and trepidation. They had never seen anyone dressed in such an outfit before and were fascinated. As they approached the old woman, they paused briefly in front of her and instinctively held up their hands to offer her their stones.

"Umm, yes," she said in her crackly voice, "You did well, very well indeed."

She took the round smooth stone from Zack's hands and held it up to the sky turning it over so she could see it from every angle then handed it back to him. She then did the same with Jonah's stone. As she turned it over, she smoothed the surface with the palm of her hands before she handed it back to him. She then followed the same procedure with each person in the group until she examined every stone thoroughly.

"Place the stones on the wall now," she croaked and turned her back to the group.

Zack and Jonah quietly walked to the wall and placed their stones on top of the last layer of stones, wiggling them just a little to wedge them into place. Maggie and Rena followed them and did the same, helping Abby with her stone. When they finished, Ms. Cates directed them to sit on ground in front of the stone altar.

She turned her back to the small group, held her hands in front of the fire and began to speak words in a language Maggie recognized as Cherokee. The words were similar to those she heard as a child when her grandmother told her ancient stories in the Native language.

Maggie, Rena and the boys all gasped when she reached inside her robe, pulled out two pieces of flint and struck them against the stone structure. Sparks flew into the sky and lit the bundle of kindling. A small flame immediately burst into a larger flame until the entire bundle of sticks on the stone altar was covered in flames that reached into the darkening evening sky.

As the fire burned brightly, Ms. Cates began to chant a soft melody and pat her feet against the ground. She began to move and sway around the fire as she chanted and tapped her feet until the beads and shells on her garment clinked along in time. Maggie and the boys found themselves moving their feet along in time with the rhythm of the music. Even little Abby seemed to swing her feet and bounce along with the tune.

Finally, Ms. Cates came to an abrupt stop in front of the fire and faced the little group. From what Maggie could tell, she spoke to them in a combination of Cherokee, English and possibly jibberish. As she spoke, she took four bundles of herbs bound into the shape of wands and lit each one. She then blew out each one so that only smoke drifted from the tip of the bundle. She placed one bundle in each direction one facing North, East, South and West. She then began to tell a story.

Many moons ago, the ancient ones traveled upon the face of the earth. They spent their lives devoted to protect the sacred places given by the Great Creator and keep the secrets of the Holy Ones. Many come who try to take away the sacred places and squander the gifts. There are few left who protect those special places and keep the secrets of the ancients.

Many come who believe they can be strong and brave under great danger, but few there are who are able to withstand the challenges and take on the risks. Only few are chosen for the task. Usually one generation passes the task on to the next generation through their bloodlines.

Long ago, a great leader and Shaman among the tribe who was bestowed with the responsibility to protect the innocents and the sacred places was given no children of his own by the Great Creator. So he had to devise a way to choose those who were strong enough to bear the responsibility when his days on earth were done.

He did this by watching the young men of the tribe unobserved. He watched the young men at work and play in the village when they did not know he watched. He wanted to see their character when he knew it was real and not performed. The Shaman wanted to make sure he could find someone of pure motives and honest character who would protect the Sacred Places without personal gain and selflessly give up his life to protect those in need. He wanted to make sure he could pass along this responsibility to someone who could receive it without notice or recognition. ·

In order to do this he passed on the responsibility by giving the new heir a secret gift during the night. For each person he felt was a strong, brave warrior, he left the root of an Ironweed which he blessed. He gave the heir the strength and powers of a bear because the root looks like the claw of a bear. He gave only the strongest, bravest warriors the power of a bear through the bear claw root because they would need the strength of a bear to help them survive their trials.

She then moved toward the boys, reached inside her garment and pulled out two bear claw roots from a dried Ironweed plant. She held a root in each hand held the roots over each of their heads. The boy's eyes grew large and round as they watched her every move in amazement.

"The Great Creator knows your heart and soul. He chose each of you for special gifts so you can help those in need. The great spirit of the bear will help guide you through your trials. You are strong, brave warriors."

With that, she placed a bear claw in each of the boy's hands and touched their head lightly. She then looked into Rena's eyes intently.

"Your love is deep and strong. It will carry you through."

She then turned and disappeared into the forest without another word leaving Maggie and Rena spellbound and staring into the fire. The boys were the first to speak.

"Mom, did you see this?" Zack held his root up for his mother to see more clearly. "Isn't it great! Maybe this will help me find Ranger Stratton!"

Rena nodded absently, lost in thought.

Jonah jumped up and waved his wand around in the air.

"I'm a bwave warrior, now," he said excitedly as he jumped around the fire in an imitation of Ms. Cates dance during the ceremony around the fire earlier and slashed his bear claw root in the air.

Quietly, Rena stepped over to the fire and poured the contents of the earthen jars she brought on top of the coals. The fire sputtered and flamed brightly before going out again. She and Maggie then, gathered the children together and headed up the path toward the jeep.

Both women, caught up in their feelings from the ceremony tried to understand the meaning of everything they had seen and heard. They spoke little on the walk to the jeep. Once all of the children were inside the jeep, they began the trip back up the mountain. The boys chattered with excitement about the ceremony, Ms. Cates' dance and the treasured gift of a bear claw.

When Maggie started to turn onto the road to the Skyway, she had to slow to a halt. She could see several flashing lights from emergency vehicles block the road. It looked as though there was some type of an emergency roadblock up ahead.

Maggie could feel Rena's fear and hear her gasp when she saw the lights. Maggie reached over, touched her hand and patted it trying to reassure herself as well as Rena.

"It's ok Rena," she tried to sound comforting, "Maybe they'll have some good news for us. Don't worry."

Maggie rolled her window down as she neared the roadblock and was relieved to see Sam was one of the Rangers there to stop traffic.

"Hey, Sam, it's good to see you out here tonight."

"Good evening, Maggie, looks like you have a car full tonight," he smiled and poked his head in the window to speak to the children.

"So, what has the entire force of the Rangers out on such a dark night, Sam?"

"Well, we have several new outbreaks of fire here in this section of the county. We have to close the Skyway to visitors until we can get the wildfires under control," he said seriously.

"Are any of the fires close to us right now?"

"No, you all are safe for now. If the wind changes or if any of the fires head this way, we may have to evacuate Indian Boundary and the cabins on the mountain, too."

"Have you heard anything from Stratton, yet?" Maggie asked aware that Rena seemed to be frozen in place while she clutched her arms around her waist.

"No, nothing yet, we still plan to send out a search party to look for him at daybreak. I have you and Digger heading up one team. Something's up or Stratton would be back by now," Sam said seriously, as he gritted his jaw. "Are you sure it's ok for us to use your cabin as a base? It's the closest point to the trail he was hiking."

"Sure, I'll get the coffee going in the morning and have my things ready to go." She nodded as Sam waved her through the checkpoint. She drove through slowly then headed toward Rena's house in silence.

The gravity of the fire situation on the mountain was serious enough but with Stratton still missing, it felt even worse. Maggie realized even the boys were silent and somber after the stop on the mountain. When she arrived at their house they both climbed out of the jeep and trudged into their house without saying a word.

"Hey, boys," she said before they filed into their bedroom, "Thanks for going with me to see Ms. Cates tonight."

"Thanks for taking us, Maggie," Zack said quietly. "I'm going to try to do the things Ms. Cates said we should do."

"What do you mean, Zack?"

"I'm going to be brave and protect Mom and innocent people."

"That's a wonderful thing for you to do, Zack. I'm sure your Mom will be very proud of you."

Zack smiled and headed off to bed. Jonah followed him as he patted his shirt and mumbled something about being a brave warrior.

"They are two special children, Rena," Maggie smiled and hugged her. "Are you ok? You're awful quiet."

Rena nodded.

"I'm just really scared for Stratton, Maggie. Since he came into our lives, he's never been gone so long. I'm just afraid he's hurt or needs us somehow."

"We'll find him tomorrow, Rena. I promise we will."

Maggie hugged her and headed out the door to her jeep. She drove the rest of the way to her cabin in silence thinking about the challenge tomorrow would bring. She knew Stratton well enough to know he would be home if he possibly could. A gnawing fear nagged inside her for his safety.

When she arrived home, Max was there on the porch to greet her and welcome her back. She sat on the porch for a few minutes to pet him and talk to him about the day. Although, Max couldn't actually talk back, you would never know it by the way he and Maggie interacted with each other. He enjoyed her talks with him as much as she appreciated having another living, breathing creature to talk with when she got home.

Finally exhausted from her day's activities, she went inside and prepared for bed. She knew sleep would be difficult but wanted to get as much rest as possible before tomorrow.

CHAPTER 13

After a hot shower, Maggie went into the kitchen and made a cup of Chamomile tea to drink before she tried to sleep. Her mind was still racing from all of the activities and experiences that happened during the day. From the time she awoke until this very moment she had not rested once during the day.

She put on a thin tee shirt and pair of cotton shorts then carried her cup of tea to the porch to sit and think about the day's activities and try to cool off a little. The night air remained heavy and hot even though it was almost midnight. As she began to swing, Max joined her on the porch and sat under the swing. The motion stirred the air enough to cool him a little.

"Hey, buddy, are you hot and tired, too?" she asked as she rubbed his head while he lay under the swing.

Max thumped his tail in response and lay his head down on the porch. His heavy breathing indicated the heat was affecting him also.

As she sat in the swing, she listened to the night sounds around the cabin. She could barely hear the sound of the creek because the water level was so low right now. The crickets were especially active tonight and continued to make a racket until the moon rose. Maggie couldn't remember when she first heard the crickets this summer, but seemed to remember her grandmother tell her once that the first frost of the year would be three months after the sound of the first crickets. This year, she looked forward to cooler weather.

Finally, the soothing effects of the Chamomile tea helped relax her tired muscles and soothe her spirits from the exhausting day she experienced. She patted Max on the head and walked into the cabin to try and get some sleep.

"G'Night, Max. I'll see ya in the morning."

She lay on the bed and listened to the sound of the ceiling fan as she closed her eyes and tried to convince her body to relax. It took awhile for her mind to slow down. The activities from the day and anxiety about tomorrow seemed to keep her brain churning. Finally, the soft hum of the motor and the gentle touch of the breeze against her skin calmed her and lulled her into sleep.

As she drifted off to sleep, her mind again wandered to the scene around the stone altar with Ms. Cates as she danced around the fire in her leather tunic. The rhythm of her soft chant and bare feet as they padded around the fire blended with the jingle of shells and beads on her tunic still rang in Maggie's ears with a familiar tune. The music she heard was a tune she knew from many years before in her grandmother's cabin when their Cherokee friends came to visit. The memory seemed to calm her restless spirit and lull her into sleep …

… a soft breeze blew across her face as she looked down the long deep valley from the high ridge where she stood. The beauty of the valley filled her with a peaceful feeling as she watched the activities below. The scene was familiar and comforting to her.

She could see children play in the village below. The beads and shells that covered their leather tunics jingled and clinked when they moved. The children chased each other in and out among the shelters and seemed to play a game of tag or hide and seek with each other.

She smiled to herself as she watched the fun the children had with each other. Suddenly, two of the children broke away from the rest of the tribe. They moved between two teepees and into the forest. She could see them as they moved deeper and deeper into the woods away from the safety of the tribe.

The smell of smoke drifted to her nose as she watched the children run. She quickly looked across the forest and saw a large fire in the woods ahead. From her view on the ledge that overlooked the village, she could see the path the children took would lead them directly into danger.

She tried to call to the children, but was too far away from them for anyone to hear. She tried to wave her arms from the ledge to get their attention, but they were too far away to see her. She looked ahead to the forest fire and could see it was much larger and more intense. The smoke from the fire billowed and covered the ground below until she could see the children no longer. It began to cover the entire valley floor.

She felt she couldn't breathe. Smoke filled the air and began to choke her. Desperately, she tried to warn the children as she called their names … Zack …, Jonah …,

"Zack! Jonah! Where are you?" she called out desperately as she woke from her sleep with a start.

She gasped for breath and clasped her throat. When she tried to breathe, the smell of smoke made her begin to choke. Maggie sat up in bed and tried to calm down. She began to take deep breaths and slowly walk around the room.

"Whew … that was too real!" she said aloud as she walked around her small cabin and tried to analyze her dream. "Those boys are so special to me. Guess that's why they were in my dreams. The boys, Stratton's absence and the ceremony at Ms. Cates house tonight must have triggered my concerns for them with these fires out of control. It seems like they have all been on my mind."

When she was able, she opened the cabin door and stood outside on the porch. The smell of smoke was much stronger it was when she went to bed. Although, she could see no smoke in the night sky, she could see a faint glow of red in the western sky in the area where Maggie thought the Rangers said a forest fire began the night before. She hoped the fire was under control and prayed for the safety of the ones she knew fought the fire throughout the night.

She clutched the rail of the porch for support. Her thoughts moved from the dream, to the tasks before her. She went inside to make some breakfast and get the day started knowing it would be pointless to try to go back to sleep again.

As she took out the ingredients she needed to prepare breakfast, she again thought of the ceremony with Ms. Cates last night and the mystical story she told of ancient people who lived long ago.

'I wonder if she has dreams, too,' Maggie thought. 'She certainly behaves as if she does. In fact, some of the things she does remind me of Grandmother.'

She thought about the beautiful stonewall and remembered an article about a Native American woman who lives in the West and has a similar wall around her property. The wall in the article was several hundred yards long and filled with stones from many areas of the country that were brought by visitors to the elderly woman.

'I wonder if a similar tribe started both walls, or if Ms. Cates' mother heard about the other wall somehow and preserved this wall because she knew it must be sacred and liked the idea?'

Lost in thought, Maggie continued to prepare a meal.

CHAPTER 14

Brave Warriors

"Come on, Jonah, Get up! You've got to get your shoes on if you're going to come with me," Zack urged.

"I'm not comin' wifout my bear claw," Jonah replied stubbornly. "Bwave warriors haff ta carry their bear claw wiff 'em ALL the time, Mz. Cates sezz, 'n I'm a bwave warrior."

Zack quickly began to toss back the covers on Jonah's bed in search of the dried Ironweed root given him by Ms. Cates that resembled the claw of a bear.

"Where did you put it Jonah?" Zack demanded.

"Can't rweminbur," Jonah replied as his lower lip trembled.

"Ok, look, don't cry—just think. When was the last time you remember having it in your hand? Did you go to sleep with it last night?" Zack urged Jonah to remember.

"uumm—think so. It was wiff me in bed."

Zack crawled under the bed and began to search behind the toys hidden there. He frantically tossed things out from under the bed.

"Here it is Jonah! Put it in your pocket so you don't loose it this time, then, tie your shoes before Mom wakes up!"

"Ya gonna tell Mommy where we're going? She may want to come wiff us, too." Jonah clumsily tied his boots as he talked.

"NO!" Zack whispered emphatically. "She can't come. This is a trip for the men of the family. We've got to be brave and strong."

"I'm a bwave warrior! Mz. Cates sez so," Jonah smiled with pride as he patted the pocket on his shirt that held the dried root.

"Then you've got to be brave warrior who knows how to be QUIET! Come on! We need to go NOW!" Zack whispered as he grabbed his knapsack filled with sandwiches and water bottles.

He poked his head out of the bedroom door to make sure his mother and baby sister still slept, then quietly slipped a note under the sugar bowl on the kitchen table before he gently closed the front door behind them. Bandit popped his head up when the small boys walked off the porch and into the yard. He was ready to follow them immediately. Silently, Zack led the way across the yard to the dark opening at the edge of the woods where his mother often took them to look for herbs. He glanced back at Jonah.

"I'm a bwave warrior," Jonah repeated as he patted his pocket. "I'm gonna find Waingur Stwatton."

Zack nodded, then turned and the two small figures headed deep into the woods and disappeared into the darkness. Bandit was right on their heels.

CHAPTER 15

Maggie made a large cheese and vegetable omelet while a big pan of biscuits baked in the oven and a pot coffee brewed. She didn't often eat a large breakfast, but she knew Digger would be by this morning for their trip and the Rangers would arrive soon to set up their outpost camp in her yard. Maggie was eager to hear from the Rangers and find out about any new developments that happened during the night with the fires.

She set some butter, homemade jam and fresh fruit out on the table while she put a pot of water on the stove to brew some tea. As much as she liked the smell of coffee when it brewed, she was still a fan of tea with her meals.

Just as she was about to get everything completed, she heard Max bark and scramble off the front porch as a donkey brayed in the distance and an old man yelled.

"Digger!" she said to her self and shook her head.

She went out on the porch to greet him. She could see Digger and Nugget as they trudged up the road to her cabin with Max right at their heels. Nugget threw out an occasional hoof when Max came too close and irritated him.

"Maggie, that dang dog of yours is gonna git the best of me, yet!" Digger exclaimed as he tied Nugget to a hitching post under a large oak tree in the yard.

"Good morning to you, too, Digger! Did you have a good trip so far this morning?"

"I've had all the fun I can stand so far, Maggie."

"Well, good then, come on in and get something to eat. I made us a nice breakfast to eat before we head out on the trail. The Rangers are going to set up an outpost camp here while we are gone to monitor the fires and send out search parties for Stratton."

"Is he still missing?"

"Yes, and I'm very concerned about him. It isn't like him to stay gone so long. His office is worried now, too. They're sending out three different search parties. I told them we could take one of the trails since we are going out anyway. Is that ok with you?"

"Sure, 'nuff," Digger said as he filled his plate, "I wouldn't have it any other way. He'd do the same fer you or me."

Maggie turned at the sound as a vehicle drove into the yard. She looked out the window to see Doc climb out of his truck and pull a backpack from the bed of his truck. She motioned to the cabin as he headed toward the porch. She smiled in Digger's direction and headed for the door.

"Looks like Doc's going to join us, too, Digger."

Maggie quickly went to the porch to greet Doc.

"Hey, there! You sure are a welcome sight," she said brightly as she stepped to the edge of the porch to greet him.

Doc looked up and smiled, grabbed her around the waist and kissed her before he stopped to look into her eyes.

"Good morning, Maggie!"

"Wow! Now that's the way to get my day started right!" she laughed as she hugged him. "Come on inside, I made some breakfast if you're hungry."

"Thanks, but I just ate. I'll take some coffee if you have any."

"You may have to pry it away from Digger, but there's a pot full. But, if it runs out, I'll make some more."

Maggie followed him inside, set out some extra coffee cups and checked to see if she needed to start a new pot of coffee, yet.

"We're sort of waiting on the Rangers to get here before we leave. They are going to set up an outpost camp here for the firefighters and for the search parties."

"What search parties?"

"Well, Stratton still hasn't shown up and everyone is starting to worry about him. He'd be back by now if everything was ok. Rena is very worried."

"I'm sure she is. How are you, Digger?" Doc seemed serious.

"Jest fine, good to see you, Doc. It'll be good to have you on the trip with us. I've been having to go slow jest so's Maggie can keep up with me lately," he said with a twinkle in his eyes.

Maggie scowled at him and shook a finger in his direction.

"Mebbe with you around, she'll get a spark in her step agin,'" he continued with a grin. "Her face shore does stay red when you're around."

"You'd best be careful what you say, old man, or you'll end up hiking by yourself!" She said with a grin.

"If I have to spend half my time picking up packs scattered all over the mountain by yer dog again, I'm gonna 'ring his neck and you're neck, too!" Digger spouted off in mock anger as he turned away from them and continued to grumble to himself.

Just about that time, three forest service jeeps drove into the yard and several Rangers walked to the porch and began to carry supplies into the cabin.

"Saved by the bell," Maggie grinned toward Doc as she opened the door for the Rangers and pointed the way to the table where Sam set up his maps.

"Hey, Maggie, thanks for letting us use your place, hope it's not a bother," Sam said as he walked in the door with his arms full of maps and charts.

"Glad to have you, just set up anywhere you like. There's coffee on the stove, help yourself. If you need to make more, I left the supplies on the counter."

Doc cleared the table of breakfast dishes and wiped it off as Sam rolled out the charts and the rest of the crew came into the cabin. They immediately began a strategy meeting on the trails and current fire sites. One of the techs set up a two-way radio system on the kitchen counter. The main room and porch of the cabin soon filled with Rangers and volunteers. When everything was finally set up, Sam quickly started an impromptu meeting.

"Ok, everybody, let's get started. We have a couple of ridge fires that started on the backside of Indian Boundary Lake. Since that's on the North Carolina side, our counterparts on that side of the mountain are going to start working there," he said as he took a gulp of hot coffee and continued to follow a ridgeline with his finger on one of the official topographical maps.

"Since the campground by the lake is on the Tennessee side, we are going to have to take care of any fires that might pop up there. We are going to go ahead and clear the campground of any campers for safety purposes. Smith, you and your crew will be in charge of the evacuation there. Any camper from out of state that can't get home can be moved to the campground at Coker Creek Village in Coker Creek, or the Turkey Pen Resort in Vonore."

"Do you want us to actually move them?" Ranger Smith asked.

"No, we don't have time for that, just make sure they get packed up and headed in the right direction."

Smith nodded and looked at his crew.

"Ok, next, we have a report of smoke on Goldminer's ridge. Hamilton, I want you and your crew to head that way. It's the longest distance, too long to hike and can't be reached by vehicle. You have your horse crew with you today?"

Hamilton nodded and adjusted the cowboy hat on his head.

"Take your crew up the trail and check out the smoke. If you see any sign of fire there, radio us back and we'll send in the chopper with a load of water. We'll need exact coordinates, so take your GPS."

"Ok, we're still missing Stratton. He was last seen here on this trail by first Maggie and Digger and then by the young hikers that came through the trail from North Carolina. Our concern now is that he may be in some type of danger or may be injured. Doc, we're going to send you and Maggie with Digger on that trail. Just start from here and head in that direction. Your main objective is to find Stratton or see if you can find some sign of his trail. Don't worry about trying to find a fire or fighting a fire right now. Your goal is Stratton."

"Are there any questions? Make sure you stay with your party. We don't have time to look for strays. We have enough two-way radios for one per group, please keep it on at all times and keep us informed of your whereabouts. Thank you, travel safely and God bless."

With that said, he headed for the door and began to register the teams of rescuers and firefighters as they left the property. Maggie was shocked when she walked into the yard to see dozens of people in her yard all grouped into teams. There were Rangers, local volunteers and firefighters teaming up in different spaces everywhere she looked. She noticed Josh and Justin were with Amy and CC working at a water booth for the forest service.

A clatter arose when Hamilton's group of horseback volunteers saddled up on their horses and headed down the path at a fast trot. The horses pranced around and reared up in eagerness to leave. Dust flew around the horse's hooves as they clattered down the path.

When the dust cleared, Maggie could see a lone woman with a bundle walk toward her cabin. She looked like she was in a great hurry. Maggie looked closer and realized it was Rena with little Abby in her arms.

"Oh, Gosh!" Maggie grabbed Doc's arm and stared toward the driveway, "Something must be wrong, it looks like Rena is here with Abby."

She ran down the path to greet Rena through the hubbub of people and vehicles in her yard. Rena struggled through the yard as she carried Abby on her hip. She was almost out of breath when she arrived.

"Rena, are you ok? Where are the boys?"

"Maggie, you've got to help. it's the boys. They've gone!"

"What! What do you mean?"

"Look here, they left a note. They must have disappeared sometime last night. I didn't hear them leave," she gasped as she readjusted Abby on her hip.

Maggie grabbed the note from Rena's hand and quickly read it.

Mommy, take care of Abby,
gonna find the ranjur be bak soon
we love you, the warryars

Fear struck deep inside her chest as Maggie read the note. She couldn't believe the words until she read the note twice. She clutched it to her chest and frantically looked up at Rena. She could see the fear and anguish in Rena's eyes.

"They've gone?"

"Yes, Maggie. They were gone when I got up this morning and this was under the sugar bowl."

"Oh, no!" Maggie gasped. "They must have taken everything Ms. Cates said seriously."

"Yes, last night all they could talk about was being brave warriors, especially after they saw the Rangers at the road block on the way home."

"Ok, we're getting ready to head out to search for Stratton right now. We'll look for the boys at the same time, I'm sure they are headed in the direction they think Stratton might be anyway," Maggie said quickly as she began to get her composure back.

"You stay here at the cabin and help keep the hot coffee and sandwiches coming for the work crews. That will give you something to do while we're out looking for the boys and Stratton. I'll tell Sam you're here to help him and let him know the boys are missing, too." Maggie clipped out directions without thinking. Rena quietly followed her to the cabin and nodded her head.

Suddenly, Maggie stopped in her tracks and turned to Rena. She realized Rena was about to burst into tears. She wrapped her arms around her and held her tight.

"It's ok, Rena. We're going to find them. We'll find them all," she said confidently as she brushed a tear away from Rena's eyes. "Now, go get busy, the Rangers need you right now, too."

Rena headed into the cabin with Abby on her hip and began to stir around in the kitchen. Amy noticed Rena with the baby and went inside to see if she could help. She took Abby from Rena's arms and carried her to a corner of the cabin to play with her while Rena made a new pan of biscuits.

Maggie walked over to Digger and Doc and motioned for Sam to come over to their group. She could feel the tension grow in her chest and her stomach tighten as she began to voice the words she didn't want to believe were true.

"We have more troubles. Rena just told me the boys left in the middle of the night to try to see if they could find Stratton. He taught them some tracking skills recently and they got the idea last night that they could find him if they track him."

"Great …," Sam began to grit his teeth. "This puts a whole new slant on the dangers. I didn't expect to have to look for kids, too."

"Well, the good thing is, both of the boys are very familiar with the woods. They go out with their mother all the time when she goes to search for herbs and plants, so they know their way around."

"They're still children," Sam commented, an uneasy look on his face. "And children can get lost or panic in emergencies. I doubt they've ever been into the woods when there was a fire hazard."

"That's beside the point right now. They're out there and we need to make sure everyone is looking for them as well as for Stratton while they're on the trails," Maggie said earnestly.

"You're right. I'll notify the search teams to keep a look out for them. Surely they couldn't have traveled too far from their home."

"Thanks Sam. Rena is going to stay here and help with coffee and sandwiches for everyone when they come in to change shifts or get more supplies. I think she needs to stay busy."

"Ok, good. Be careful on the trail," Sam gave the trio a serious nod as they strapped on their backpacks. "Please keep in touch with your two-way radio. We'll have ours on at all times but turn yours off to conserve the battery if you need to do so."

They all nodded and took one last look around the yard now bustling with activity, before they turned and headed down the trail.

CHAPTER 16

"Come on Jonah, you're gettin' behind," Zack called from the top of the ridge. "Hurry up, will ya? You're slower than mud."

"I'm comin' as fast as I can," Jonah called back as he trudged up the final few steps to join his brother. "Can't we stop yet? I'm gettin' hungry, Zack."

"Ok, we'll stop and rest for a minute and eat one of the sandwiches but then, we've got to keep on going. You heard what Ms. Cates said. She said we are the ones that are supposed to find Ranger Stratton."

"Umhm, she sure did!"

"Yes, she did. Now, eat you sandwich, Jonah and don't give any of it to Bandit until you're finished, either," Zack said as he eyed the little dog suspiciously.

Bandit plopped down beside Jonah and cocked his head to one side. He watched every bite Jonah put into his mouth eager for some small morsel to fall down on the ground or in his lap.

Jonah ate his peanut butter sandwich slowly, savoring each bite. When he thought Zack wasn't looking, he pinched off a few bites for Bandit and tried to sneak them into the dog's mouth without his big brother noticing what he was doing.

Zack stood up and walked to the top of the trail to see if he could see any movement or signs of Stratton ahead of them. The trail was clear as far as he could see. No movement or sign of life was on the trail ahead. When he turned back, he saw Bandit in Jonah's lap licking peanut butter off his face.

"Zack! What are you doing?"

"Him jest wanted ta taste me," Jonah said with a sheepish grin.

"You know Mom wouldn't let him do that. Now get up, we've got to keep going."

"When are we gonna see Stwatton?" Jonah asked as he stood up and put his backpack on his back again.

"I'm looking for him right now, Jonah. Come on, you can help me. Remember how he taught us to track things in the woods?"

"I rwemembur," Jonah said quietly, "I kin twak sum wild aminals, Wrangur Stwatton sez so."

"Well, we don't need a wild animal today but if you can help me find some tracks from Stratton's boots, that would be great."

As the boys made their way across the ridge, they came to a deep valley where the trail divided. Zack paused to look at the trails before him and see if he could determine which one Stratton might use if he was in the woods. So far, most of the area he and Jonah hiked was in familiar territory, but now, the trails headed in directions unfamiliar to him and he began to feel a little uncertain.

He stood at the edge of the trails and worked his way up the side of one of the trails for a few yards, and then back down the other side of the other trail. Soon, his efforts paid off. He saw the imprints of a boot on the trail that led up a ridge he had not hiked before.

A sense of pride and accomplishment sent a thrill inside him when he realized the boot print looked like prints from Stratton's boots. He followed the tracks for a few more feet until he was certain he headed on the right trail. Then, he returned to the mossy area where he left Jonah and Bandit resting.

"Hey, ya'll, come on! I found it! I found Stratton's trail, it's going this way up the mountain!" Zack said excitedly. "Come on, Jonah, it won't be long now. We'll find him, we'll find him soon."

"Oh, boy, come on, Bandit! Wet's go!" Jonah and Bandit jumped up and ran up the trail behind Zack.

After the two mountain men carried their last load of stones and manufactured artifacts from the gravesite through the woods in the final hours of dusk last night, they slept on the ground by their truck. Both were tired and hungry from being in the woods all night with no food and from sleeping on the ground. Both men had enormous hangovers after they spent the evening sampling moonshine from a still they maintained on a nearby ridge.

"Come on Darryl, wake up," Raymond tried to rouse his brother.

When he got nothing but a moan in response, he shoved his brother as he stood up and stretched. He then took his boot and nudged his brother in the ribs.

"Come on Darryl, I said to Wake UP!" Raymond became louder. "We've got ta go check on the 'product' before we head out of here," he said with a chuckle. "Yesterday, it was too dark to tell fer sure, but it looked like sumbody was messin' with our still. Today, I'm gonna ketch 'em in the act."

Darryl rolled over and sat up while he rubbed his eyes. He started to moan "… uuhh …,what time is it?"

"It's time you got up, that's what time it is! Now, git moving!"

"Aww, come on, Ray. My head's splitting right now."

"That's cause you drank too much of the 'product' last night. If you don't get yer rear off the ground, I'm gonna have to split yore head some more. Now, git moving!"

"Dang! You shore do wake up ornery," he said with a scowl as he got up off the ground. "Sumbody ought to just knock you silly a'fore you speak to anyone else."

The two brothers started along the trail that led them across the ridge to one of their moonshine stills. So far, they had a fairly, successful business with their moonshine sales. Each site they selected for a still was in a remote area of the National Forest away from regularly used trails. They made sure they didn't put a still on their own property because they knew if they were caught maintaining the still the Forest Service Agents could charge them a much heftier fine and confiscate their still, 'product' and property, too. They did not intend to lose any personal property to the Forest Service, especially their 'product'. After all, that was their biggest source of income; at least it was until now.

For them, it was a stroke of pure luck to be at the campground delivering a load of firewood when the University Professors were speaking about local artifacts. As frequent travelers in the backwoods areas, both men were familiar with several sites where they often saw strange objects just lying on the ground. Neither brother ever once considered old broken pots or bowls of any value. After all, they were broken.

It wasn't until they heard the strange college men speak about the relics and talk about their value that they thought they might be able to make more money from broken bowls than moonshine. They were so carried away with digging around for the artifacts they even thought they could make some of their own and try to fool the college men. After all, they were looking for things made from just rocks and anybody could make a rock look like a bowl. If it hadn't been for that stupid Ranger coming along and interfering they could get away with it, too. Now, they had to do something with him.

As the two men stumbled their way along the trail, they made more noise than usual in their semi-drunken state. They often stumbled and ran into trees and broke branches and twigs on their way. They made no effort to be quiet as they thought they were alone in the woods and often yelled or cursed at each other as they walked.

Zack heard the commotion of the two men as they came up the trail behind them. He quickly grabbed Jonah and pulled him into the darkness of an overhang of rocks behind some brush then called Bandit to join them. He wasn't sure who was coming up the trail but until he did, he wanted to make sure he and his brother were safe.

"What did ya make us come in here for, Zack?" Jonah asked.

"Shhhh..," Zack whispered, "Be quiet!"

"But, I thought we wuz gonna find the Wrangur."

"We are, Jonah, but you have to be real quiet for now. Here, hold on to Bandit and don't let him get away."

They snuggled deeper into the darkness until the shadows of the overhanging rock sheltered them and hid them from view. Zack's heart pounded with fear as he put his arm around Jonah and held Bandit between them. Just as he could see the men pass in front of their hideout, Bandit tensed and growled. Jonah started to call out to him. Zack quickly wrapped his hand across Jonah's mouth and held Bandit's jaws shut with his other hand. They sat motionless in the shade of the bushes and barely breathed while they waited for the men to move on down the trail.

Lost in thought as he walked, Raymond suddenly tensed when he heard a sound in the brushes along the trail. He stopped immediately on the trail. Darryl wasn't paying attention to him, ran into his back and fell into a bush.

"What the heck are you doing?" he yelled, "You could give me some kind of warning when you're going to stop like that."

"SSHHHH!" Raymond turned dramatically and pointed toward the brushes off the trail where the boys hid.

Darryl immediately stopped; his senses alert and started to look in the brush along the trail. He and his brother were excellent hunters with plenty of experience in illegal production and sales of moonshine, so they knew how to work together as a team. They moved into a position where they had their backs to each other and slowly moved around in a circle until they had time to scan every possible hiding spot on the ridge.

The boys were frozen with fear and remained perfectly still.

Finally, the men moved apart and stood almost directly in front of the boys as they faced each other.

"Well, Darryl, guess we'd best keep on going. Reckon I didn't hear anything after all. We must be imaginin' thangs."

"Yup, we'd best keep on going, Raymond," Darryl said and nodded as both men slowly began to walk up the trail again.

The boys remained in the brushes until they could hear the men's footsteps no longer. Finally, after what seemed like an eternity, Zack breathed a sigh of relief and took his hand off Jonah's mouth and Bandit's jaws.

"Who wuz that, Zack?" Jonah asked excitedly, "Was it sumbody we know? Maybe it was sumbody who was gonna help us find Wangur Stwatton!"

"It wasn't anybody who was going to help us, Jonah," Zack answered seriously, "Now, talk quietly. They might can still hear us. Let's pretend we're Indians and be real quiet, shhh.…"

"I AM a real 'njun, Mz. Cates sez so. She sez I'm a bwave warrjor," Jonah reached in his pocket and pulled out the wooden bear claw root and admired it as he held it in his hand.

Zack and Jonah quietly tiptoed out from the bushes to the path where they took a moment to shake the leaves from their clothes. Bandit stood by and waited patiently. They repositioned their packs and started up the trail again, determined more than ever to find Ranger Stratton.

Just as they started on the trail and rounded an outcrop of stones, Raymond jumped out from behind the stones, grabbed Zack and held him in such a tight grip the child couldn't get away. As he struggled to free himself, Zack gasped for a breath and immediately began to yell.

"RUN, Jonah, RUN … don't let them catch you!" he yelled as he squirmed and tried to escape Raymond's tight grip.

Bandit immediately went into action and bit Ray on the rear end so hard he yelled. Raymond tried to swat at him, but Zack kept squirming. Bandit was too fast and bit him again, but this time Bandit refused to let go. He held on as tight as he could and swung by his teeth from the seat of Ray's pants as Ray twisted and turned in the loose gravel. Raymond tried his best to hold on to the squirming child, and at the same time get rid of the painful critter attached to his backside.

Jonah gasped for breath and tried to run away, when all of a sudden, Darryl whisked him up into the air over his head. Darryl began to shout, spin and shake Jonah in the air. Jonah was so frightened he screamed and instinctively swiped at the man with his bear claw. He lashed out with his bear claw again, striking Darryl across the face.

Darryl dropped Jonah in a tumble and grasped his bleeding face.

"I'm gonna git you, you little devil!"

Jonah scrambled over to help Zack out. He began to hit and kick Raymond on his legs and yell at the top of his lungs.

"You weave my brudder awone! I'm gonna git you!" Jonah yelled as he continued to pound Raymond on the legs.

Raymond screeched, released Zack and spun around. He grasped his rear in an attempt to get the dog off his rump and release the seat of his pants from the dog's jaws.

Both boys took the opportunity to quickly scramble off the trail and down into a ravine. Zack whistled for Bandit who scampered after them. They scooted and slid until they were almost at the bottom of the ridge and hid behind a tree. They hid there gasping for breath, hoping beyond hope they would not hear the sound of anyone follow after them. They stood quietly, almost glued to the bark in the shade of the old oak tree for what seemed like a very, very long time.

On the ridge above, Raymond and Darryl sat in the middle of the trail and rubbed their wounds. Darryl wiped his face with an old rag he kept in his pocket and tried to stop the bleeding. The old rag only smeared the blood and made it look worse.

"I'm gonna catch those kids if it's the last thang I do!" he said angrily. "Nobody draws blood on me and gets away with it!"

"Fergit it, Darryl. We got more important things to do than try to catch them kids," Raymond scowled as he tried to get up off the path.

He tried to look around at the seat of his pants and saw a huge rip in them where the dog bit all the way through to the skin. He stuffed a bandana in his shorts to try to stop the bleeding, then, paused to look at his brother.

"You ok?"

"I'll do," Darryl said glumly, then snorted, "They's purty good fighters, ain't they?" He looked up at his brother and they both smiled and chuckled with admiration for Zack and Jonah. The fighting spirit in the two little boys reminded them of each other when they were small themselves.

"Yep, they shore 'nuff did," Ray agreed, "They 'bout got the best of both of us. Jest let 'em go. We don't have time to chase after any yard apes rite now. We gots the 'product' to tend to and then we need to git off the mountain 'afore anybody sees us around here."

"You're rite, but I still wonder where they come from," Darryl said as they started up the ridge again. "They look like them kids that was with the Ranger the other night."

They trudged on through the morning until they came to the small cove by a stream where their moonshine still was set up. When they visited the site before, they set up a vat to brew sour mash before the distilling could take place. All the ingredients were in the vat and brewing, the only thing they needed to do today was to check on the mash and stir it; then, they could be on their way to town with the ancient treasures they 'discovered' in the woods.

Just as they approached the site, a strange sound erupted from the area where the moonshine still was set up. Both men stopped in their tracks to listen. A loud rumble and grating sound came again from within the thicket where they hid the still. Their greatest fear was that someone discovered the moonshine still and was stealing their 'product'; or worse yet, that the Rangers discovered it and were destroying the still itself. They both looked at each other and made the motion to attack whoever was inside messing around with their 'product'.

On the count of three, both men charged through the brushes and yelled at the top of their lungs. They immediately froze when they reached the inside of the clearing and saw the whole area in a huge mess. They found the still turned over and smashed, bottles and jugs were broken and the sour mash drum on its side. Then they saw a huge black bear with her head and shoulders deep inside the sour mash drum licking the sides of the barrel. She had sour mash all over her fur.

Both men stopped dead in their tracks without a word when they saw the bear. Neither man had a gun or a weapon of any type with them, neither especially had anything to protect themselves from a drunken bear. They stood motionless and waited to see what the bear would do next.

She removed her head and shoulders from the vat of sour mash when she heard the men crash into the clearing and looked up to see what was happening. She growled and wiped a paw across her nose before she tried to stand up. When she stood, she swayed and staggered a little bit. She then reached her paws toward the sky, clawed the air and growled even louder.

Frightened, Raymond and Darryl both screamed as the bear growled. Fear paralyzed them as they watched the bear drunkenly stagger around the glade. Suddenly, she turned and made a dive toward Raymond. He screamed as she wrapped her paws around him in a bear hug and knocked him to the ground.

Darryl moved forward and tried to smash her on the nose with his hat as he yelled.

When she fell on her back and couldn't manage to get up again, Darryl pulled Raymond to his feet and both men scrambled to get out of the glade as quickly as possible. They reached the path and ran as quickly as they could with the wounds they had and quickly headed toward the bottom of the trail. They knew the day was going very wrong and wanted to get as far away from the bear as they could.

In the ravine below, Zack and Jonah waited for long anguishing moments until they heard no further sound from the trail above. When they were certain the men were no longer in pursuit of them they finally began to stir.

"You ok, Jonah?" Zack reached over and hugged Jonah, then held him back a little so he could see if there were any injuries. "Did he hurt you?"

"No, I got 'em wiff my bear claw," Jonah said bravely, his little body still quivered from the attack.

"You were very brave," Zack said as he patted him on the back, "Thank you for helping me out, too."

Jonah smiled. Still trembling, he reached for Bandit and hugged him.

Zack glanced around the woods where they stood and tried to decide which way they should go from where they were. To go back up the ridge would be dangerous. The climb was steep and he wasn't sure the men were gone from the trail and didn't want to be captured again.

As he surveyed the small area where they hid behind the oak tree, he noticed there were some unusual marks in the leaves. Something just didn't seem right. He stood up and walked over to see what they were. He knew from his mother that there was an order and balance to everything in nature. If a person looked carefully enough, they could tell when something was not the way it should be.

"Wait right here for just a minute, Jonah, I'm going to check something out."

He tentatively walked to the bottom of the bank where it looked like something big fell down the side of the mountain from the trail above very recently. He wanted to investigate it further because it was in an area he and Jonah hadn't been before. He could see leaves were disturbed and saw several small bushes filled with broken branches. Then, he saw a stone at the bottom of the bank covered with something bright red that looked like blood.

His eyes followed the line of broken branches and disturbed leaves to see there was a definite trail leading away from the bank. Zack followed the broad broken trail for a few feet when he saw something an unusual shade of green underneath the bushes. He looked closer, reached under the bush with a stick and pulled out what appeared to be a Ranger's hat. His heart skipped a beat.

"Jonah, Jonah … come quick! I found Stratton's hat!" he yelled, hardly able to contain his excitement. "He must be nearby, hurry, Jonah, help me find him."

CHAPTER 17

Maggie and Doc, followed by Digger and Nugget headed across the trail that led to the area where the backpackers last spoke with Stratton. Their description of the site where they set up a camp when Stratton saw them gave the rescue team an accurate point to track Stratton since that was the last location anyone saw him. They walked into the clearing and took off their backpacks while Digger tied Nugget to a tree. Max immediately plopped down in the shade, panting from the heat.

"Digger, are you ready to take a break for lunch yet?" Maggie asked she sat down by Max and poured him a drink of water.

"Sounds good, Maggie," Digger replied. "This heat shore wears a body out quick. It would probably do Nugget some good to take a break for a while, too."

The threesome traveled in unusually quiet moods on their trek through the morning hours. Even Max was abnormally quiet. After the hubbub at the cabin with the arrival of Rangers and departure of the search teams, the quiet, solitude of the trail gave them each time to think. Each was concerned for Stratton because they all knew him so well and knew he would be back at the station if he were ok. They were even more anxious about the two missing boys on the trail. Each of them had a special connection to the boys and wanted to find them.

Maggie handed out apples and sandwiches to Digger and Doc and placed some food on a bandana for Max to eat before she sat down and started to eat her sandwich. She was lost in thought. She felt her anxieties and concerns intensify every moment for Stratton and the boys. The fact that all were missing was almost too much to fathom. She tried to concentrate on the journey ahead and keep the panic from rising in her chest.

"They's been sumpthin' I've been wantin' to tell you both when we got away from the crowd," Digger began seriously.

Maggie and Doc looked up from their meal.

"Is everything ok, Digger?" Doc asked, concerned that the heat and rigorous climbing might have an adverse effect on Digger.

"I'm feeling ok if that's what yer asking," Digger answered with a grimace. He was never one to complain and didn't want anyone to think he couldn't keep up. "They's something I heered in town the other day that has me thinking."

"You said you were going to check something out after the campfire program the other night," Maggie remembered. "Did you find what you were looking for that night?"

"That University fella got me to thinking about a feller over in the Knobs near Vonore," he started as he stretched out his legs. "It's been quite a few years ago now, but they was this feller over in the Knobs who told everybody he discovered some ancient tablets of some sort. He tried to tell everybody they was stone tablets like the ones in the Bible that Moses had up on the mountain."

"You mean the Ten Commandments?" Maggie asked.

"Yep, he said they was written in the very same way as the Ten Commandments, in the same language. He even tried to get some officials to come make a document saying they was real and brought here by the 'Lost Tribe of Israel' many, many years ago," Digger continued as he finished his sandwich. "Some folks even called the people who brought the tablets here the 'Children of the Sun.'"

"I thought you said the Indians who were here before the Cherokee called themselves the 'Children of the Sun', Maggie commented.

"Your right, Maggie," Digger continued, "They called themselves the 'Children of the Sun, from far away'. Some folks say this man who found the tablets was trying to make a connection with the Indian tribe and the 'Lost tribe of Israel.'"

"What happened to the tablets, Digger?" Doc asked.

"Well, there was a big ta-do about it and then it was something everybody argued and fussed about for years. The government took them stone tablets up to Washington and has kept 'em there ever since. It ended up being a big scandal."

"Weren't they called the 'Bat Creek Cave Stones?" Maggie asked, "I think I've read about them before, they're pretty famous."

"Yep, they're called that because the place where they was found was in the Bat Creek Caves," Digger continued. "Anyway, the thing that put a crinkle in the whole discovery was nobody could ever prove if these tablets were real or fake. There was a lot 'o folks at the time that thought the man who found them made the stones himself."

"How would he know how to do that?"

"Well, first of all, he was a stone engraver by profession. Second, he was a preacher who studied the ancient languages. So, whether he faked it or not didn't matter because folks at the time, thought he was guilty jest because he knew how to fake it if he wanted to fake it. They's been folks study it and argue about it for years."

"That's sad," Maggie commented.

"Why would someone fake a discovery like that?" Doc asked.

"Some folks would do it for money and some folks would do it for fame. Who knows what a person's motives are," Digger said as he pushed back his hat. 'This happened a long, long time ago when nobody could prove it one way or 'nother. Anyway, folks in town were talking about that old preacher feller with the old tablets and it got me ta thinkin'. If they was folks that might 'o faked finding ancient things that long ago, they's probably some folks that would fake it now."

"You're probably right, Digger. That's why they have such a rigorous investigation process when artifacts are found. Researchers want to be sure something is authentic before they declare anything is a genuine relic. It takes a lot of testing and research to decide," Doc added.

"When I started thinking about what the University men was saying, I started to remember places I seen before like that. They's been places I've seen that had a lot of things jest laying out in the open, kind 'o exposed like. When I seen 'em, they looked a little different than the ones in the place where I took you, Maggie," Digger continued. "So, I started to wonder if there were some folks here right now that made some things 'n tried to pass them off as the real thing."

"Have you seen any places around here where it looked like someone was trying to fake an ancient site?" Maggie asked thoughtfully. "It would be dangerous for a person to walk up on a place where someone was looting a gravesite, or trying to create artifacts. Maybe that's what happened to Stratton, maybe he ran into someone who was doing something they needed to hide. Maybe it was something so important they would hurt him to keep it hidden."

"You're right, Maggie," Doc added. "I've been racking my brain on the way here, trying to think of things that could have happened to Stratton. Aside from an obvious injury, fall, or natural accident I can't think of any other reason he would be missing unless he ran into something that might involve some type of illegal activity. If something criminal was going on up here and Stratton stepped into it, he would definitely be at risk of harm. Since he was in the wilderness, no one would be around to know about it or help him out."

"Well, what should we do next then?" Maggie asked thoughtfully. "We could try and track Stratton from here, or we could look for Stratton in some of the exposed places you're talking about, Digger if you think that might be a quicker way to find him."

"Since we're here where Stratton was last seen, let's track him first. We have a sure thing if we already know his tracks are here. Finding Stratton is the most important thing right now for two reasons. We know he was here recently and we know the boys are looking for him. It would be risky to go anywhere else first because we don't know for sure if he's been anywhere else. Once we find him, we may find the kids, too. Once we find him, other things will show up," he said with a grin and a wink.

Doc stood up and began to look carefully around the clearing. He saw the area where grass was indented and a ring of stones where small campfire area was set up. He walked over to it and carefully surveyed the site, then motioned for Digger to follow him.

"This must be where the kids set up camp."

"We know they came to my cabin on the trail we just took, so Stratton must have headed in the other direction. The kids said he was going to check something out a little further down the ridge. The trail goes down this way," she said as she pointed to a trail headed along a ridgeline that ran toward the northeast.

She and Digger stood at the head of the trail and looked around for any sign someone had passed that way. Maggie soon saw the print of a boot in the soft dirt at the beginning of the trail. She didn't move but pointed in the direction of the print. Digger nodded and pointed at a few blackberry briars that were bent and broken back to clear a passage on the trail also. They nodded in agreement.

"This must be his trail," Maggie said. Eager anticipation filled her spirit now. She wanted to run down the trail as quickly as possible, but knew she needed to go carefully to keep the trail undisturbed.

"Good, let's load up then," Doc said, "We need to find him."

Maggie put on her backpack and retied the laces on her boots as Digger readjusted the packs on Nuggets back. Max jumped up and wagged his tail, ready to go. They slowly made their way along the trail, careful to avoid stepping on the prints in the trail they followed. Each of them searched for signs as they traveled.

As they trudged on through the afternoon heat, they could smell the smoke from fires somewhere in the forest. It wasn't clear which direction the fires were burning until they came to an overlook and had the opportunity to look out over a large amount of acres in the forest. They could see at least three areas between the Tennessee and North Carolina side of the mountain where smoke billowed out from unpopulated areas of the forest. Doc pointed in the area near the North Carolina side of Indian Boundary Lake where they could see actual flames from where they stood.

"They aren't close to us yet, Maggie," Doc said as he put his arm around her waist to comfort her. "They are still pretty far from your cabin, too. I'm sure they'll get it under control before it gets too close to the populated area."

"Yes, that's all we can hope for now," she said as she eyed the smoke and fires with sadness. "Hope, luck and a little rain would all help right now."

They heard the motor of a helicopter as it flew overhead. A large bag hung underneath the helicopter. They watched as it flew toward the direction of Indian Boundary Lake. Maggie knew it headed that direction for a load of water from the lake to dump on one of the forest fires. She also knew things were bad if the Forest Service was using the water helicopters in their fire fighting efforts.

"We'd better move on," Digger said when the wind began to blow smoke in their direction, "Time's a' waistin'."

Soon, they rounded an outcrop of rocks on the crest of the ridge and came to a bald, stony area cleared of most brush. They all stopped and carefully looked around the area for signs of Stratton. Doc noticed an area where the stones looked as if someone recently disturbed them and went over to investigate. Maggie carefully walked around the perimeter of the area in search of additional signs.

After Digger tied Nugget in the shade, Doc motioned for him to come over and join him in an area where the largest disturbance seemed to be. There they both crouched in the rocks and stones to examine the area closer. Doc picked up a few of the more interesting pieces and handed them to Digger.

"Some of these stones look like they may be artifacts, Digger."

Digger examined them carefully.

"It's hard to tell. I'm not an expert but these don't look anything like the stones I've seen before."

"Maybe, they're from a different tribe," Maggie observed.

"Could be, but I doubt it," Digger said thoughtfully. "See here, these stones have fresh chip marks like somebody just made 'em. They ain't weathered at all around the marks like they would be if they was out in the weather or buried for a long time."

"You're right, Digger. There's a lot of fresh chips around here, too. These don't look like they got here from natural causes, either," Doc commented after observing the stones around them. "There are several places here where the soil is loose, too."

They all looked up when they heard a clatter. Max barked and ran toward the trail. They saw one of the University men jog up the trail towards them. He wore nothing but his jogging shorts, a tee shirt and tennis shoes. Maggie recognized him as the same man who caused her to run her jeep off the road when he darted in front of her. He was the same man who gave the lecture on artifacts at the campground, Professor Morton.

Soon, the second University professor followed the jogger up the trail and joined them. He carried a staff and a backpack and walked at a steady pace. He was dressed as if he were going to a lecture or a field study with his classroom. He seemed very nonchalant and acted as if there was nothing he should be concerned about except a walk through the country.

"Ah, there you are, my fine friends," Professor Watkins greeted them as he topped the ridge. "It's so good to see each of you again."

Digger snorted under his breath and spat a long stream of tobacco juice on the ground, then lowered the brim of his hat when he looked in the professor's direction.

"My colleague and I walked since daybreak in search of you. We stopped by the temporary headquarters at your cabin, Maggie, to offer our services to the Rangers. They said our services weren't needed with any of the search parties, so we thought we would come along on our own."

Maggie, Doc and Digger watched and listened to the man in stunned silence. They could not believe these two men could find their way into the woods, much less out of the woods. No one knew exactly what to say.

"In the course of our conversations with local chaps in town, it was brought to my attention, that you, Digger, were one of the best trackers on the mountain. As you know from the lecture we gave at the campground a few days ago, we are interested in ancient Indian burial grounds. We thought you would be the best person for us to talk to about the trails in this area and thought you might track down some leads we have on a few possible ancient burial sites."

Maggie and Doc stared at the professor in disbelief. They could feel Digger's body become tense and begin to shake with anger.

"Ain't searchin' fer nothin' but that Ranger 'n them little boys!"

Digger's anger was obvious; Maggie could tell he was ready to explode with a string of expletives in his rage. She quickly got up and walked to his side.

"I'm sure Digger appreciates the compliment, Mr. Watkins," she said as she placed her hand on Digger's arm and gently walked with him a few steps away from the professor, but surely you can understand how your timing may be a little off. We are in a critical situation right now and need to concentrate on our search for Ranger Stratton and two little boys who are very precious to us and may be lost in the forest."

"Yes, certainly, of course we understand. We certainly didn't mean to be inconsiderate at all. We wanted to help, too. The Ranger was kind to us this week and allowed us to speak with the campers at the campground."

Maggie shook her head. It was hard to believe anyone could think it would be a good idea to take a stroll through the woods on a day like today. The entire community was on high alert for the dangers of the fires and were either evacuated or on a search party for Stratton and the boys.

"Did you realize the Ranger's are closing the trails? There are some major forest fires in this area right now," Maggie informed them.

"Yes, someone did mention that information. We didn't think anyone would mind if we just came to take a little look at the trail."

"Well, this probably isn't the best time for a voluntary trip to the backwoods. You may want to think about returning to the trailhead. We would help you get back but are just getting ready to head down the trail and see if we could back track Stratton," Maggie said as she pointed them in the direction they entered.

"Thank you, but we think we will just follow along after your group for a while."

Maggie started on the trail, as she and Doc skillfully ushered the professors away from the dig site toward the area where they could see boot prints. Turned in this direction the university men were unable to have the opportunity to see the artifacts Digger and Doc examined when the professors arrived.

"Here, Digger, you lead the way," Maggie said as she headed him on the path. She and Doc exchanged glances as she whispered in Digger's ear, "Let's just go, Digger. We need to concentrate on Stratton and the boys. Besides, these men are idiots. Sooner or later we'd have to show them how to get out of the woods anyway. If they come with us, they won't have time to get into the dig site."

Digger grimaced, grabbed Nugget's lead and grumbled under his breath with every step. The two professors fell in line behind Nugget. Maggie smiled at the thought of the two men following Nugget. She and Doc learned long ago to walk ahead of Nugget because of the deposits and odors he often left on the trail.

The crew followed the trail down the ridge to a place where the trail split off in two different directions. Digger held up his hand for everyone to stop. Maggie, Doc and Digger each observed and surveyed one of the trails ahead. When they gathered as much information as they could from searching a few feet of each trail, they came together.

"Well, what do you think?" Digger asked.

"On this path, there are signs of a lot of recent activity," Doc pointed toward the path he examined, "It has some small boot prints on it that were headed in this direction," he hesitated before he looked at Maggie, "It could be the boy's footprints, they are very small, too small for a woman."

She took a deep breath and nodded, then pointed in the direction of the path she examined, "This trail has two distinctive sets of large footprints headed in this direction. They were very large and probably boots. My guess is they had to be from men. I don't think they were Stratton's prints though because the campers said he was wearing his Ranger uniform and he if he was, he would wear the standard boots. These prints looked like a different type of boot," she looked anxiously at Digger.

Digger nodded and grimaced. "Them little boot prints was headed up this way," he pointed in the direction ahead, "and it looks like some time after the small prints went up the hill, they was followed by the two men because the little prints were stepped on by the larger boot prints."

Maggie stood up quickly, eager to leave, "It's the boys Digger! We've got to hurry, they may be in danger."

Digger nodded. The three quickly followed the trail across the ridge every sense alert, every eye searched for signs of the boys or Stratton. So caught up in their concentration, they completely forgot about the Professors who followed them and silently, watched their every move.

CHAPTER 18

The boys and Bandit eagerly scoured the bushes and shrubs around the bottom of the ridge in search of Stratton. They began to see definite signs of drag marks through the leaves as they walked through the dense undergrowth in the woods. At times, they could see spots of what looked like blood on rocks.

They came to a small ravine where the leaves scraped away from the edge and the disturbed soil made it obvious something recently fell over the edge. The boys lay on their stomachs and looked over the edge of the ravine.

There at the bottom of the ditch, partially hidden under the side of the bank lay Stratton in a crumpled heap. He lay on his side with his knees drawn up to his waist. It looked like he was trying to get close to the stream. Bandit began to bark furiously and dash down the bank toward Stratton.

"We found him!" Jonah said excitedly.

"Let's go get him," Zack said as both boys scrambled down the edge of the gully.

They both reached his side and began to shake his arm.

"Stratton, Stratton," Zack called as he touched his face. "Ranger Stratton, are you ok?" he said as he leaned over Stratton and placed his hand on his chest.

Stratton moaned slightly when he heard the boy's voices.

"Wake up, Waingur. We're here to take you home," Jonah added as he grabbed his hand and tried to pull him up.

"Wait a minute, Jonah, we have to be careful," Zack cautioned as he began to check out Stratton's injuries.

Jonah sat down and watched as Zack looked closely at the blood on Stratton's head. A large gash bled for some time and left a pool of blood under his head. There was a large blue welt on the other side of his head. As Zack examined further, he could see nicks and scratches on Stratton's hands where he tried to drag himself along the path. He looked down and noticed Stratton's leg turned at an odd angle.

"OK, Jonah, here's what we're gonna do," Zack said slowly as he sat back and tried to think of all the remedies his mother would use in a situation like this.

He and Jonah were with her numerous times on outings through the woods to gather herbs and medicines to use during the winter. She helped him fix the leg of a dog they used to have when the dog broke his leg and nursed all of their various injuries when they were growing up, so he had an idea of things he could use for healing.

"First of all, he needs water," Zack started, "Mom always says when a person is sick they need to drink lots of water."

"Him kin haf my water, Zack," Jonah offered his canteen to his brother.

"Ok, thank you Jonah." Zack tried to pour some of Jonah's water into Stratton's mouth. "Wake up Ranger Stratton. You need to drink some water." He tried again to pour some water into the Ranger's mouth. More of the water seemed to run off his face and onto the ground than down his throat.

"Ok, we'll try more after while," Zack paused to think. "Next, we need to fix up his head. We need some of that plant Mom uses to put on our cuts when we fall down and get scrapes. Do you remember what it looks like?"

"Is it the one that grows in the fields with the big leaf and the tall, skinny flowers?"

"Yes, Mom says the Indians call that one 'White Man's Foot' because the white people brought it here from other countries and it started to grow everywhere they went. You go get some of that and wash it off in the creek; then bring it back here."

Jonah jumped up and ran into the field with Bandit on his heels to gather some of the Plantain that grew there. He quickly grabbed several hand full of the leaves and flowers and stuffed them into his pockets before he headed to the creek to wash them off. When he returned, Zack took off his shirt and headed to the creek.

"You wait right here, Jonah, I'll be right back."

Zack ran to the stream, and quickly took his shirt and tore it into several pieces by tearing it at the seams. He put two pieces in his pants pocket and placed the other two pieces in the stream to get them thoroughly wet. He then ran back to Jonah and Stratton.

"Ok, we've got to fix his head first," Zack said as he started to wash the wound on Stratton's head. He washed as much of the blood off the Ranger's head as he could. He then ran again to the stream to rinse out the rag so he continue to clean out the wound.

"Jonah, you take the plants you brought and put them inside this piece of shirt and then hit the shirt with a rock over there," he directed Jonah toward two large flat rocks by the stream.

Jonah immediately put a hand full of plantain leaves in the shirt and ran to the rock. He pounded the shirt over, and over again until green sap saturated the shirt. Then he ran back and handed it to Zack.

"Here ya go."

"Thanks, Jonah," Zack said as he opened up the rag, took the crushed leaves and plastered them against the wound on Stratton's head. He then wrapped the rag around the head wound and tied it on the side of his head. A small amount of blood continued to seep through the poultice and material.

"Here, Jonah, come put your hands on his head like this." Zack demonstrated how to put pressure on Stratton's wound.

As Jonah held his hands against Stratton's wound, Zack ran back to the stream and walked along the bank for several yards until he found a small willow tree. He reached up, and broke off several branches from the willow tree and ran back to Jonah.

"Ok, this will help him feel better, but we've got to help him drink some more water, first," Zack said thoughtfully. "Let's see if we can help him lay on his back."

"But whut about his head?" Jonah asked.

"Let's see," Zack said as he contemplated the situation. "Ok, give me your shirt."

"But what if the skeeters decide ta bite me?" Jonah asked.

"You can go over to the creek and put some mud on your arms and chest. Mom says that keeps the mosquitoes from biting so bad. We need your shirt to put under the Ranger's head so it won't hurt him so bad."

"I want ta help the Waingur," Jonah nodded.

"Sure, you do," Zack added, "That's why we're giving him our shirts. Besides, if we put mud on us we might look like real Indians!"

"Oh, boy! I can be a real 'njun, now!" Jonah immediately took off his shirt, gave it to Zack and ran to the stream to rub mud on his chest and arms.

Zack rolled the shirt into a long roll and slid it under Stratton's neck, then tried to push his shoulder and roll him onto his back. Stratton moaned, and fluttered his eyes as Zack pushed him over. Zack patted him on the shoulder.

"It's ok Ranger Stratton; we'll take good care of you."

Zack tried to pour a little more water down his throat and seemed to get more into his mouth this time. He could hear Stratton swallow once or twice. He smiled, pleased with the progress.

He then picked up the small willow branches he gathered from the tree by the stream and tried to pull the bark off the branches. It was difficult to do without a knife, but he managed to get most of the bark off the twigs. He took several of the striped twigs and slid the stripped ends of them inside Stratton's mouth beside his tongue.

"There, that should do for now," he said, pleased.

He looked up as Jonah ran back toward him. Except for his eyes, his body was entirely covered in mud from head to foot. His red hair stuck out all over his head. Zack couldn't help but laugh when he saw him.

"Jonah, you look like a mud monster," Zack laughed.

"I'm a 'bondabul mud monstur," Jonah grinned, his white teeth sparkled through the mud on his face.

"Ok, you watch the Ranger, I'm going to go put some mud on me too," Zack said as he ran quickly to the stream.

When Zack came back from the stream, the boys continued to clean Stratton's wounds and plaster them with crushed plantain leaves until they treated every wound they could see, except for his distorted leg.

Stratton's leg was at an odd angle and each time Zack tried to touch it or move it, the Ranger moaned or called out in pain. Zack decided to leave it alone for the time being until he could decide what to do.

"What cha gonna do next, Zack?' Jonah asked.

"I'm not sure," Zack replied as he glanced around the area where they sat.

"My tummy hurts," Jonah fussed. "When do ya think we kin make sum dinner?"

"We can't cook on the trail, Jonah," Zack replied.

"But, I smell some smoke. Somebody might be cookin' sum dinner. We could ask 'em if they could make us sumptin' ta eat," Jonah said innocently.

"I don't think that's a campfire, Jonah," Zack replied as he unconsciously rubbed his stomach, too. It was a long time since they ate lunch and they were walking since the wee hours of the morning on the trail. "What do you have left in your back pack?"

"Me gots a peanut butter sandwich, 'n a 'nanna," he said as he searched through his bag.

"Ok, you eat the sandwich and let me have the banana."

Jonah gave his banana to Zack and started to devour his sandwich. Zack peeled opened the banana, broke off a small piece of the banana and placed it in a clean piece of material he tore from his shirt earlier. He took the small willow twig out of Stratton's mouth and used it to mash the banana. He then placed a small bit of it into Stratton's mouth and then tried to wash it down his throat with water. He smiled when he heard the Ranger swallow.

While Jonah ate, Zack continued to feed Stratton some of the mashed banana and dribble water down his throat. While they ate, he took the opportunity to survey the surrounding area for other things he might need.

As he looked around the area where they sat, he saw a spot near the edge of the field where some wild raspberry bushes grew. He also saw the dark green leaves of beechnut trees near the stream. When he finished giving Stratton as much of the banana as he could, he stood up.

"Jonah, I'm going over to the edge of the field to see if the raspberry bushes have any ripe raspberries on them. You stay here by Stratton and protect him while I'm gone, ok? It won't be long."

"I'll take care of him," he said as he jumped up, pulled out his bear claw and bravely stood over the unconscious Ranger.

Zack smiled and ran quickly to the edge of the field. He quickly picked several hands full of ripe berries and placed them in a corner of the cloth he carried in his pocket. He then walked over to the stream to examine the Beech tree. He selected several of the seedpods that looked long enough to have full seeds in them and hurried back to Jonah and Stratton.

"Jonah, go wash your hands in the creek," Zack directed him, "I need you to help me feed Stratton."

Eager to help, Jonah washed his hands as well as he could and quickly came back to help. Zack gave him the small bundle of berries.

"Here, take one or two of these at a time, squish them between your fingers and put the berry juice in Stratton's mouth."

Jonah began to crush the berries over Stratton's mouth and dripped the juice inside. He then placed the crushed berry on his tongue. The Ranger seemed to roll his tongue around in his mouth and swallow the berries.

While Jonah worked with the berries, Zack examined the Beechnut pods he gathered from the edge of the stream. He took one of the long, husk-like seedpods and opened it to find the dark brown, triangle-shaped nuts inside the shell. He carefully broke away the shell with his fingernail and gently removed the sweet white kernel inside. When he had several of the kernels peeled and gathered, he carefully put them inside the lid of his canteen.

"Here, Jonah, give me a few of the raspberries for a minute."

Jonah gave him the few remaining berries and watched as Zack took a small stone and crushed first the nuts, then added the berries and crushed them together with the nuts. When he had a fine paste made, he handed the mixture to Jonah.

"Here Jonah, take one of the little willow sticks we have and try to put some of this on his tongue."

The afternoon wore on as the boys continued to place the mixture of ground berries and nuts on Stratton's tongue until they were almost out of water. When Zack noticed the evening was ready to turn to dusk, he started to feel more concerned. He and Jonah had never slept on the trail alone without their mother before and this trail had some scary strangers on it. He hoped Stratton would somehow wake up and be himself again. He tried to rouse Stratton once more.

"Ranger Stratton, are you ok?" he asked as he gently shook his shoulder, "Ranger Stratton, can you wake up?"

Stratton moaned and fluttered his eyes. He moved one of his hands to his head and groaned again, then opened his eyes and batted them several times to try and clear the confusion from his head.

"Zack? Is that you?" he hoarsely whispered.

"Are you ok Waingur Stwatton?" Jonah asked excitedly as he stuck his head right in the Ranger's face.

"Jonah? Where are we?" He blinked his eyes a few more times and tried to understand Jonah's unusual appearance. When he tried to sit up, he immediately fell back down, closed his eyes and slipped into a semi-conscious state again.

"Him must be sweepy," Jonah decided as he continued to stare in Stratton's face.

Zack nodded. He looked intently at the Ranger. His fears increased as the evening sun set. The smell of a woods fire became more intense and he wasn't sure what he would be able to do if the Ranger didn't wake up.

"I'm gettin' sweepy, too, Zack." Jonah said quietly.

"Me too, Jonah," Zack said as he put his arm around his brother. "Here, you lay down real close to Stratton and try to keep him warm. I'll lie down on the other side. Mom says when people get hurt they have to stay warm or they'll get sick."

As he tucked Jonah in by Stratton's side, Bandit curled up beside him and lay beside Jonah and Stratton. Zack then quietly lay down on his other side, wrapped his arm around Stratton's chest and laid his head on the Ranger's shoulder.

"Everything's going to be ok," he said as he patted the Ranger on the chest in an effort to reassure himself as much as everyone else. "We'll get somebody to help us tomorrow. Everything will be ok when the sun comes up in the morning."

As his eyes became heavy and he drifted off to sleep, he could hear moans and a light rattling sound come from Ranger Stratton's chest when he breathed. He knew he would have to do something to get more help tomorrow. He wished more than anything his mom was there to help him. She would know what to do.

CHAPTER 19

As the afternoon wore into the evening hours, Maggie, Doc and Digger continued to trudge across the mountain trail. The two professors tried to follow along behind Nugget and keep up with the crew. By early evening, no one was in a mood to talk. Digger was out of sorts and grumbled under his breath. Maggie was so concerned for the boys she didn't want to concentrate on a frivolous conversation with the professors and Doc didn't like to talk to strangers, especially strangers as obnoxious as these two.

They continued to follow along the trail they thought belonged to the boys and Stratton. The boy's tracks were easy to follow as they were often in middle of the path. The two adult tracks tended to veer off to the side of the path or travel across areas where they were more difficult to follow. One thing was evident to each of them, all tracks were headed in the same direction.

"Surely, they couldn't have gone too much further," Doc said as he walked alongside Maggie, "They haven't been gone too long, and we've already walked quite a distance."

"You'd be surprised how far kids can go," Maggie said, "Especially when they are on a mission."

Doc nodded.

Suddenly, Digger stopped and held up his hand.

"Shh …"

Everyone quickly stopped and held their breath while they listened and waited for Digger to tell them what he heard. Soon, they could all hear the sound of running footsteps on the trail and men's voices yell as they approached the crew. They all quickly stepped to the side of the trail to avoid a collision.

Suddenly, the two mountain men ran down the trail gasping for breath. Maggie recognized them as the men she saw at the campsite the night of the lecture on ancient artifacts, only today, the men were bloody and covered with scratches and cuts. The look of terror on their face was frightening. As both came to a halt, they gasped for breath when they saw Digger and his search party.

"What in the world happened to you?" Digger asked as he stared at the two men and surveyed the scratch marks and wounds that covered their arms and face.

"Bar …, bar …," Darrel gasped as he started to speak. His whole body trembled and shook. He tried to speak again but was so out of breath, no sound would come out.

"We were attacked by a black bear," Raymond gasped and finished the sentence for him, as he wiped away a stream of blood that ran down his face.

Maggie quickly went to their side, grasped Raymond's arm and led him to a large flat rock where he could sit down. He gingerly sat on one side of his rump. Doc was already digging into a large pack tied onto Nugget's back that contained medical supplies. They both automatically went into action when they saw the seriousness of the men's wounds and worked together easily with few words. They seemed to know the other's needs without speaking.

Darrell hobbled over to the rock as the university men watched the commotion in stunned silence. The professors were accustomed to participating in digs that were a little more civilized than ones where people were rude and ignored them, bears attacked or forest fires raged while they studied their trade. They were used to getting what they wanted when they wanted it. Maggie quickly handed a bucket to the University men and directed them to the stream at the bottom of the trail.

"Here, make yourselves useful," she briskly ordered. "We need clear water, so don't step in the stream before you try to fill the bucket."

Digger took the opportunity to loosen the packs on Nugget's back and walk the mule to a place further down the stream than the spot the men chose to gather water. Max followed Digger and walked out into the water to cool off. They both stayed by the water long enough for Max and Nugget to cool off from the late afternoon heat.

When the men left their place in the stream and carried the buckets of water back to Maggie and Doc, Digger took the opportunity to use the two-way radio and call the Rangers at the base station in Maggie's cabin. He wanted to wait until he was alone and away from the mountain men and professors to call.

"Breaker …, breaker …, this is Search and Rescue Team Two," he spoke into the small speaker. "Breaker …, Breaker …, Sam come in."

The speaker crackled and sputtered before he heard Sam's voice on the other end of the radio.

"Breaker …, breaker …, this is home base, Sam speaking." The words crackled and came in among broken static, "What's your location …, over."

"Digger here …," he began, "We're about three miles along the east ridge. We've got a situation here and need a medical team to head this way …, over."

"What's the situation? … over."

"We've got two fellers we found on the trail that's been attacked by a bear. They bin walkin' but I don't think they kin walk much further. It sure looks like they lost a lot of blood …, over."

"Roger, we'll send a team that way. It may be morning before they can reach you. The team has to come on foot because the choppers are tied up with the fire …, over."

"Got, ya …, we'll see if we kin head 'em up that way to meet the team by themselves. We've got something more important to do. We seen some sign of the kids and Stratton 'n are trailin' them …, over."

A few moments of silence followed before Sam responded.

"Digger, you need to find them as soon as you can …," he paused, "the wind has changed direction …, over."

Digger knew the implication in the words Sam didn't say and didn't have to ask for an explanation. He didn't respond for a few moments as he thought about the gravity of the situation.

"Breaker …, breaker …, are you still there?"

"Roger …, understood. Search and Rescue Team Two …, over and out."

He grimly placed the radio back in his pack as he watched Maggie and Doc hard at work on the two mountain men. He clinched his jaw and gritted his teeth as he tried to decide what to tell the crew.

Maggie took out some clean cloths, poured water on them and cleaned some of the wounds on Raymond's back and arms. She brought a few of the more serious wounds to Doc's attention. When he finished his work on Raymond, he brought the bottle of antiseptic to Darryl and cleaned his wounds.

"I don't have any suture material here with me, but I can put some butterfly Band-Aids on the serious cuts until we can get you to a hospital for proper treatment," Doc said as he tried to hold Darryl's wounds together with narrow strips of tape.

"Here, Maggie, you're going to have to try to hold the skin together while I put the suture tape on his face."

Maggie immediately tried to hold the skin in place while Doc taped Darryl's skin together as well as he could. After they closed as many of the wounds as they could with tape, they covered the rest with gauze and padding. When they finished, Raymond and Darryl both looked like they belonged on a movie set as an extra for zombies. The tape and gauze that covered them almost completely covered their faces.

"What happened to make a bear attack you?" Doc asked Raymond as he worked on his brother. "Did you notice anything unusual?"

Doc already smelled an odor of stale whiskey on the men's breath and the peculiar odor of sour mash on their clothing. He already suspected the men were drunk when the bear attacked them. Darrell and Raymond looked at each other. Darryl winced as Maggie continued to pull his skin together.

"Ouch! Dang-it, that hurts!" He complained in pain.

"Sorry," Maggie said sincerely, "It's hard to do without hurting you, there are so many cuts."

Doc continued to ask them about the attack.

"You were going to tell me about the attack," he said as he looked Darryl in the eyes before he continued to work on his wounds. "What was it that made the bear want to attack you?"

"Ahh, ya may as well tell him Ray, they's gonna find out anyway," he said as he squirmed in his seat while Doc taped his wounds closed.

"Well, the thang is," he began, "We run across this moonshine still in the woods."

Darryl rolled his eyes and Doc looked Ray's direction.

"We came up on this moonshine still and they wuz a big bear rite in the middle of it. She had her head 'n shoulders inside the mash drum and had done eat almost all our mash!" Raymond continued. "When she seen us, she took out after us and almost killed us both! It's a pure miracle we both got away."

He stopped when he realized he identified the mash as something that belonged to them. He cleared his throat and shifted in his seat as he tried to avoid Doc's intense stare.

"Looks like the worst one is the one on your face here," Doc said as he examined the wound on his face. "What happened here?"

Raymond laughed.

"Aww, he didn't git that one frum no bear. Tell 'em how ya got that one Darryl," he said as he laughed and sneered at his brother.

Doc looked at him and waited for an answer.

"No, it ain't frum no bear," he grumbled.

"Naw," Raymond sneered, "He got that one frum sum little kid that wasn't big enough ta swat a fly," he laughed at Darryl's discomfort.

Maggie froze. She felt her temperature flare and immediately turned around and grabbed Darryl by the shoulders.

"Ouch!" he screamed.

"What kids?" she demanded, "Tell me, what did they look like?"

"They wuz jest little kids," he whined. "One had dark hair and one had red hair, they wuz jest scruffy, little kids. They had some mean little dog with 'em, too."

"Yeah, tell 'em how the dog bit you in the butt," Darryl snorted.

Raymond glared at Darryl.

"Where did you see them?" Maggie demanded.

"We saw them 'afore we run into the bear on the trail up ahead," Darryl said. "We saw them 'n then they took off when we headed up the trail."

"You left those little children on the trail when there was a bear up there?" Maggie felt she couldn't contain her anger and got right in Raymond's face so close he could feel her fury.

"We didn't see the bear until after those kids scooted off," Darryl said defensively, "They wuz done gone when we run into the bear."

Maggie trembled with fear for the children and rage that these men left two children on the trail alone, especially when there was a violent bear in the area. She let go of Darryl's shoulders when Doc touched her arm. She cleared her throat.

"Why don't you tell us exactly where you saw the boys?" she asked calmly.

"It's like we told you earlier," Raymond said defiantly, "When we seen them kids, they wuz walkin' on the trail about half a mile ahead o' where we are now. They scooted off the trail 'n we went on ahead. That's whur we run into the bear."

Maggie looked at him and searched his face to see if she could tell whether he told the truth or not. Something about his story didn't add up right. She took a step closer to Darryl and looked at him.

"How did one of the boys scratch you on the face if they scooted off the trail so quickly?" She asked as she stared into his eyes.

"They were jest crazy," Darryl added, "Plain 'ole crazy," he said as he firmly closed his mouth and refused to speak any more.

"Were the boys in good condition when you saw them?" Doc asked patiently. "We've been looking for them all day."

"They sure was in good enough condition to attack us!" He said defiantly as he glared at Maggie, "And they wuz mean little critters, too!"

The professors moved to the side when they saw Digger return from the stream with Nugget and rejoin the group. The serious look on Digger's face frightened Maggie when she saw him. She knew by the look on his face, that there was some serious news.

"Is everything ok, Digger?"

He motioned for Maggie and Doc to join him at the edge of the clearing away from the group before he answered her.

"I jest spoke with Sam," he started as he gritted his jaw. "He said we've gots to git folks off the trail as soon as we can."

"What's going on, Digger?" Doc asked.

"They gots all the choppers out workin' on the fires," he continued. "Sam says they can't send a chopper our way, so they've got to walk in a team to us."

Maggie and Doc exchanged a glance.

"Then, he says the wind's changed."

"You mean the fire is headed this way?" Maggie asked as her heart began to pound in her chest. She felt her stomach clinch into a knot.

"Yep, that's about the size of it," Digger said seriously.

Maggie looked at Doc as her mind began to churn with the new information from Digger and decisions they needed to make.

"Do you think these two can make it out under their own power? They seem pretty weak."

"They've lost a lot of blood, but I think if we can fill them with fluids tonight, they can make it up the trail tomorrow. They at least can make it as far as the rescue team and the medics can deal with them."

"You can send those University men with 'em as fer as I'm concerned. I ain't got no use fer those two," Digger said. "If they was gone, we could travel faster."

"We could give them something to do and ask them to walk back up the trail with the two brothers," Maggie said as she thought through the situation. "They've been on the trail they need to take on the way down here. Hopefully, they can follow it back up the mountain, especially if we head them in the right direction."

Doc nodded.

"I agree. The brothers will be sore by morning and may not get too far, but as long as they stay hydrated, they'll be ok."

"We need to go ahead and start after the boys, then. If there's a bear out there that attacks people, we need to find them and Stratton, too," Maggie said urgently.

"Maggie," Digger said patiently, "It's dark now, 'n ye know as well as I do we can't go searchin' fer nobody on this trail when we can't see where we are going."

"But, Digger," she continued, alarmed, "The boys never spent the night on the trail by themselves before …, and the bear …"

"I know yer worried, girl, I am, too, but we ain't gonna do those boys any good if we take a wrong step 'n walk off the edge of the mountain."

"Digger's right, Maggie," Doc said quietly, "The boys are pretty resourceful or they wouldn't even be on the trail. Their mom and Stratton have both taught them well. We'll just get up at the crack of dawn and send these folks on their way so we can continue to follow the boy's trail."

Reluctantly, Maggie nodded. She clutched her arms around her waist and felt an overwhelming sense of danger as the evening shadows deepened and the smell of the forest fire increased. She fought back tears as she returned to the clearing and unhooked some of the packs on Nugget so he could rest for the night. Then, they placed their supplies under a tree as Doc informed the rest of the travelers of the plans for tomorrow.

He looked toward the professors before he began.

"We're going to need your help."

They both nodded in agreement.

"Tonight, there isn't much we can do because it is already almost dark, so, we are going to set up camp here for the night. We have a few extra bedrolls and groundcovers we can share so everyone has something to sleep on tonight."

The professors nodded.

Maggie divided the ground covers and bedrolls among everyone and returned to the packs to gather some of the trail food they packed for the trip. She tried to decide how to portion it out among everyone fairly and reserve enough for the boys.

Both of the mountain men sat quietly. The pain from their wounds began to set in as the effects of the alcohol wore off. They started to feel uncomfortable.

"It's very important for each of us to stay together. The dangers from the forest fires have increased and anyone on the trail right now is at risk. The Rangers informed us they are unable to conduct a helicopter rescue because all of the helicopters are busy fighting the fires." Doc continued as he looked into each face.

"This means, each one of us is going to have to do their part in order to get out of this situation alive," he continued. "Tonight, I want you two to drink as much fluid as you can and rest," he said as he looked in the direction of the two mountain men. "Tomorrow is going to be very difficult for you because you are going to have to walk up the ridge to meet the rescue team."

Both men hung their heads and glowered at him. The pain they felt was already intense, but the pain of their wounds was secondary to the terrible headaches they both felt from the effects of the moonshine.

Doc then looked at the professors.

"We need for you two to go with these men, help them to the top of the ridge and then leave the forest with the wilderness rescue team. It's very important that Maggie, Digger and I have nothing to worry about except the children and Stratton," he continued as the professors nodded in agreement. "Right now, we have a good lead and an excellent trail to follow but we don't need to have extra people around we have to keep up with and protect."

"Who's this Stratton feller ya'll keep talkin' about?" Darryl asked.

"He's a Ranger that's been missin' fer a few days," Digger said as he watched the two mountain men. "We've been following his trail."

Raymond and Darryl glanced at each other then looked away.

"So, tonight, we'll share some of the trail food we have in our packs and then hole up for the evening. Everyone needs to drink plenty of water and get some rest. We're going to need all of our strength tomorrow."

Everyone nodded and headed towards their sleeping area as Maggie handed out a trail bar, an apple and a bottle of water to each person. When she came to the mountain men, she gave each of them two bottles of water so they would have extra to drink. Then she came to Digger. She paused and gave him a big hug and a pat on the back as she tried to hold back her tears.

"I know ye want to go out there tonight, girl, but we're doing the right thang, you know we are. Them boys is gonna be ok. If ya remember, they were able to fight off those two critters over there today and get clean away!" He said with a proud grin.

Maggie smiled and nodded her head.

"You're right, Digger. I'm just worried. I want them to be safe."

"I know it, girl. They'll be jest fine," he said as he smiled and placed his hand behind her head and rubbed her hair. "Them's tough boys. They shore took care of our moonshine pals over there. Yup, them kid's something to be proud of fer any man."

Maggie nodded and made her way over to where Doc sat on his bedroll and leaned against a rock. She sat down beside him and leaned against his shoulder as she munched her apple in silence. Weary from the tension and physical exertion of the day's activities, sleep soon overcame her and she fell asleep against his shoulder. Doc quietly wrapped his arms around her and slept, too.

CHAPTER 20

In the wee, dark hours just before dawn, the sounds of the forest die down and come to a rest before the sun awakens the day. This is the darkest hour, the time when legends and fables speak of spirits that haunt and ghosts that travel. Just as the night reached its darkest hour, a quiet stirring arose from one area of the campsite.

One of the mountain men slowly moved as he tried to get up quietly without disturbing anyone else in the campsite. He stiffly stretched out his legs and tried to rotate his arms without screaming out in agony. Excruciating pain filled very move he made. When he was finally able to stand up, he quietly moved over to his brother and nudged him in the side.

"Come on Darryl, git up," he hoarsely whispered. "We got ta go."

Darryl moaned and moved slightly but did not wake up.

"I said git up!" he shoved his brother more harshly. "We gots ta go 'afore anybody else wakes up."

"Whut on earth for?" Darrel ask angrily as he tried to sit up. He groaned in pain. Every inch of his body filled with unbelievable pain.

"If we don't leave now, they's gonna find out sooner or later that we's the ones that got rid 'o that Ranger. Then all hell's gonna break loose," Raymond said urgently.

"They can't prove nothin'!" Darrel snorted.

"And if they don't find those kids, they won't be a place in the South we'll be able ta hide. Come on now, git yer sorry butt up! We gots ta go!" Raymond urged.

Darrel slowly got up and stiffly followed Raymond to the edge of the campground. Just as they reached the edge of the clearing and started to head onto the trail, a ghost like figure stepped out on the trail in front of them.

Both men immediately stopped, frozen with fear. Generations of folk tales and stories about haints that traveled the woods at night during this hour flooded back into their memory. Although, they were afraid to move a muscle, their bodies shook and trembled involuntarily.

The figure stepped forward, stopped in the center of the trail and blocked their passage. They looked closely and could tell it was the old mountain man, who traveled with the mule and camped with them during the night.

Raymond snorted, relieved to see a human and not a spirit.

"Git out 'o our way, old man," he sneered.

Digger silently took a step closer to them, lifted up his double barrel shotgun and held it across his chest. The barrel of the shotgun glistened in the moonlight.

"You'd best be settin' rite back down 'n waitin' till morning for the rest o' us 'afore you try to leave," he said without a smile.

Both men knew Digger was deadly serious and both knew from the look in his eyes he would like nothing better than to have an excuse to fill their backsides with buckshot. They grimaced, then turned and carefully sat back down on their bedrolls.

Maggie turned and snuggled a little closer to Doc. Her sleep was restless and filled with dreams during the night that allowed her little true rest. She was eager for the morning to arrive so she could be on her way to the boys and Stratton. She thought she heard a commotion around the trail but couldn't see anything, so she closed her eyes once more and snuggled a little closer to Doc.

When she finally couldn't remain still any longer, she decided to get up and wash her face in the stream. She quietly made her way down the path to the small stream that flowed along the edge of the clearing. She took off her shoes and stepped into the stream. She soon saw Max head toward her from the woods.

"Good morning, Max," she greeted him as he stepped into the water beside her. "Was your night as restless as mine?"

Max wagged his tail and licked her leg before he headed on into the stream to swim. He was perfectly content to swim alone or together, as long as there was water, he was happy.

As Maggie washed her face, she noticed the air felt very heavy and humid for such an early time in the morning. No breeze blew. The smell of smoke was worse than yesterday and seemed to hang in the air where they camped. Although the air was uncomfortable and heavy to breathe, she was grateful the wind hadn't picked up again and spread the wildfires any more.

When she went back to the campsite, several people were stirring around and preparing for the day. Both of the professors were awake and moved about, the mountain men both sat up and glared at everyone from their bedrolls. She looked at them, puzzled by their glum expressions.

'Guess they're just sore,' she thought as she glanced around and looked for Doc and Digger. She finally saw them stand together by Nugget and quickly walked over to speak with them.

"Good morning!" she said eagerly, "Is everything Ok?"

"Yes," Doc replied, "We're just getting ready to radio the Ranger station and let them know the professors are headed their way with Ray and Darrell."

"Good, let's head them out. I'm ready to get on the trail an find the boys."

Maggie stopped when two men didn't say anything.

"What?" she asked alarmed, "You aren't telling me something."

"Digger suspected our two bear wrestlers might do something to try to escape during the night, so he waited up to see what they might do," Doc started. "When they tried to leave early this morning, he overheard them talk to each other about how they got rid of a Ranger."

Maggie gasped.

"Did they say exactly what they did, or explain what happened?"

"No," Doc continued, "They don't know what happened to him. Evidently, they attacked him and he escaped or at least didn't follow them anymore. They were trying to get out of camp before we found out about it or found ..., umm ..., Stratton."

"Then we need to let Sam know so they can pick them up when they get with the rescue party," Maggie said emphatically.

"That's just what we're getting ready to do," Doc smiled to reassure her.

"Let's hurry then, we need to go," Maggie said urgently and turned to leave.

"Maggie," Digger hesitated, "Maggie, you need ta be prepared."

"Prepared for what?" she asked, a little bewildered.

"Prepared for the worst," he looked at the ground as he continued. "Thangs could be purty bad," he said as he looked at her with genuine concern in his eyes.

Maggie gasped. She stopped and looked at him and then at Doc.

"I won't accept that," she said as she fought back tears, "I won't accept that at all. We're going to find them and they're all going to be OK!" She turned and quickly walked away from the two men before they could see her fear and tears.

Doc and Digger exchanged grim glances then Doc phoned Sam.

"Breaker, breaker …, Search and Rescue Team Two calling home base …, come in, Sam …," Doc spoke into the small radio. When there was no immediate response, he spoke again, "Breaker, breaker …, Team Two calling home base …, come in …"

"Home Base to Team Two …, this is Sam, go ahead …,"

"Sam, this is Doc. We're sending the two injured men on the trail toward you this morning accompanied by the two professors. They are stable and in fair condition, go ahead."

"Roger, Medics are prepared to leave home base within the next 15 minutes and should be able to meet them on the trail by mid-morning …, go ahead."

"You probably need to send law enforcement along with the medics," Doc continued. "There are indications the two injured men have something to do with Stratton's disappearance, go ahead."

There was a moment of silence on the radio before Doc heard a response.

"Roger," Sam's voice crackled over the two-way radio.

"We'll continue on the boy's trail …, over."

"Roger, use caution, wildfires still only 30 percent contained and out of control on the north ridge, over."

"Roger, over and out." Doc closed the two-way radio then looked grimly at Digger before they turned toward the group.

"Ok, folks, it's time we got up and moving," Doc started as he looked toward the professors. "The current report from headquarters is that the medics are leaving home base at this time and plan to meet you on the trail. They expect to rendezvous with you and the injured men by mid-morning, noon at the latest."

The professors nodded in silence.

"We put together a couple of small packs that have water, snacks and additional bandages in them in case you need them. Please be careful, the latest report is the fires are still mostly uncontained at this time. Walk at a steady pace and take lots of breaks, these men are going to be pretty uncomfortable."

The professors nodded as they strapped on the packs Maggie prepared for them then walked over to the two mountain men. As their group headed out to meet the medic team, Maggie, Doc and Digger gathered up the rest of the bedrolls and reloaded Nugget before they headed in the opposite direction toward the boy's trail.

Stratton began to stir a little just before daybreak. He moaned, tried to open his eyes and looked around. He blinked his eyes and tried to remember where he was. He saw Jonah curled up under his arm by his side with Bandit. Confused, he tried to lift his head. Excruciating pain, a flood of nausea and dizziness made him lay back down again. He saw a movement and glanced over to see Zack wash something in the stream. He blinked his eyes and tried to remember what happened.

Bandit lifted his head when Stratton moved, wagged his tail and barked. When Stratton placed his hand on Bandit's head the dog jumped up, wagged his tail in excitement and barked again. Jonah stirred and looked at Bandit. When he realized Stratton was awake, he leaned over, nose to nose and looked into Stratton's eyes.

"You ok, Waingur?"

Stratton chuckled, "Well, I'm not sure. What are we doing here?"

"Me 'n Zack com ta save you," he said seriously.

Stratton, still confused, looked at Jonah with his face covered in mud and his bright red hair sticking out all over his head and chuckled. He closed his eyes when a wave of dizziness flooded over him. He wasn't quite sure if this was real or a dream.

Jonah jumped up and yelled, "Zack, Zack, hurwee, quick! Waingur Stwatton opened his eyes!"

Zack quickly finished washing the plantain in the stream and ran across to the overhang where Stratton lay. He quickly checked him to make sure he was still breathing and then sat down beside him.

"He must be resting again Jonah," Zack said as he started to undo the bandages from Stratton's head. "We've got to clean his wounds again, Jonah. Can you help?"

"Sure," Jonah jumped up, excited to be able to help.

"Ok, take these bandages down to the stream and see if you can wash them out a little bit. They got a little bloody during the night."

"Ok, I kin do that!"

"If you have any trouble getting them clean, rub some of the sand from the edge of the stream into them to help wash them out like Mom does when we're out on the trail. Just make sure to wash it out real good if you use the sand."

Jonah grabbed the bandages and quickly ran to the stream.

While he left, Zack carefully removed the old poultice of crushed plantain leaves from Stratton's head. He carefully wiped away blood that dried around the wound during the night then poured water from his canteen over the wound to wash it.

Jonah ran back from the stream carrying the dripping bandages with him as Bandit ran along beside him.

"Here ya go, Zack, how's that?"

"That's great, Jonah. Now, take this piece of cloth and crunch it up with a rock just like you did yesterday, ok?"

Jonah took the bundle of plantain wrapped in the rag and began to pound it between two stones. When he finished, he handed the bundle to Zack.

"Here ya go, Zack."

"Thank you, Jonah. Now could you do me one other favor?"

"Sure," Jonah said as he jumped up eager to go.

"Ok, go over to that willow tree and pick me a few more branches from it so we can put them in his mouth."

"What cha gonna do that for, Zack?"

"It's what Mom uses when we have a headache or hurt somewhere."

"But, Mommie makes us tea out of it."

"Yes, but remember, we can't make tea without a fire, so we'll just peal some and put the sticks in his mouth, that way his head won't hurt so bad."

"Don't want him ta hurt," Jonah said as he looked at Stratton.

"I don't either, that's why I need you to get the willow branches, hurry up, ok?"

"Ok." Jonah ran off to the willow tree by the stream.

While he was gone, Zack took the plantain poultice, and gently placed it on the wound on Stratton's head and wrapped the long piece of shirt on it again to hold the poultice in place. He then cleaned and redressed each of Stratton's wounds.

When he finished, he hulled and peeled some of the remaining seeds from the beech tree he gathered last night. He placed them in the lid of his canteen and ground them together with a few of the raspberries and some banana then sat by Stratton and gently touched his shoulder as Jonah ran back from the stream with a handful of willow branches.

"Ranger Stratton," he said as he gently shook his shoulder. "Ranger Stratton, can you wake up?"

Stratton's eyes fluttered open and he looked up to see Zack, covered in mud, lean over him. He moaned and tried to shake his head and clear the confusion.

"Hey, Zack," he mumbled weakly. "Where are we?"

"We're on the trail. You had an accident but Jonah and I are going to fix you up," Zack said confidently.

Stratton's eyes rolled back in his head when he tried to lift his head and became dizzy. He groaned in pain.

"Here, we made you something to eat," Zack said as he took one of the willow sticks, quickly stripped it then placed some of the fruit and nut mixture on his tongue."

Stratton slowly worked the mixture around in his mouth, then swallowed. He tried to open his eyes again as Zack poured water in his mouth and swallowed again.

Zack continued to place the fruit mixture on Stratton's mouth until it was gone, then gave him some more water. When he finished, he placed another stripped willow twig on Stratton's tongue.

"What is this," Stratton asked.

"It's a willow branch," Zack quietly replied. "Mom uses it when we have a headache, just let it sit in your mouth and it will make you feel better."

"Umm, nature's aspirin," he smiled, "How'd you learn so much about remedies?"

"Momma taught me. She knows a lot about healing people."

"Yes, she does," Stratton smiled as he closed his eyes and drifted off to sleep. "She certainly does."

"Is he sweepin' agin, Zack?" Jonah asked.

"It looks like he is, Jonah. I think he's resting just fine," he said as he patted Stratton on the chest.

"What we gonna do now?"

"We need to get some more berries and nuts for Stratton to eat before we do anything else," Zack answered unable to think or plan much further beyond the immediate crisis.

"Want me ta go git the berries, Zack?"

"No, you wait right here and watch him while he's sleeping. I'll go over to the beech tree and get the nuts, then get some raspberries while I'm there."

"Will ya git sum fer me? My tummy's hurtin' agin."

"Sure, I'll get plenty for all of us."

Zack quickly ran down to the stream and found the beech tree. He filled his pockets with as many of the long, slender pods as he could stuff inside then ran to the raspberry bushes. As soon as he got there, he noticed a large path of crushed raspberry canes that went right down the middle of the patch. He glanced at it, even though he didn't pay much attention yesterday, he didn't think there was such a wide path when he picked berries last night.

He quickly tied the corners of his bandana together and picked raspberries until the bandana could hold no more, then ran back to Jonah and Stratton. Zack knew there were other things his mother taught him he could eat if he was in the woods but he was afraid to leave Jonah alone with Stratton for too long.

As he started back, he noticed a flurry of motion on the left side of the field. He stood very still. He suddenly saw a bear that was acting funny at the edge of the field. The bear looked like she couldn't walk straight. When she got up, she fell down again.

Zack screamed, dropped the bundle of berries and ran as fast as he could toward Jonah and Stratton. He scrambled inside the overhand beside Stratton and gasped for breath as the bear awkwardly stumbled through the field after him.

"What's wrong, Zack?" Jonah asked.

"It's a bear," Zack pointed in the direction of the raspberry bushes where he last saw the bear. "She's coming this way!"

The bear tried to run then slowly made her way across the field. As she staggered and lumbered through the field, the bear swayed her head. Occasionally, she stopped, reared up on her hindquarters, swiped at the air and growled. When the bear reached the small bandana Zack dropped filled with ripe raspberries, she stopped, sat down and began to eat the berries. After an angry growl, she stood up again, shook her fur, and headed in the direction of the boys and Stratton.

CHAPTER 21

At daybreak, after they headed the professors, Raymond and Darryl in the right direction, Digger, Maggie and Doc then headed up the other trail in the opposite direction. They soon saw tracks when they scouted the trail. They walked slowly until they saw little boot prints in the soft dirt on the trail again. Maggie pointed to the tracks, as soon as she saw the first print in the dirt. Doc immediately crouched down to examine them closely.

"Looks like they came this way, alright," Doc said as he examined the prints. "Their dog was still with them here."

"This must be before they ran into Ray and Darrell," Digger commented, "Their tracks are after the boy's tracks right here."

Maggie nodded in agreement and quickly stood up to continue. She walked in silence most of the time now, lost in thought as she concentrated on the trail and searched for signs of the boys or Stratton at each turn.

She paused when they came to a turn in the trail where a large outcrop of boulders hung over and shadowed the trail. She pointed at the disturbance in the path. Numerous prints from the boy's small boots and larger adult boots scrambled over each other across the path. In some places, the dirt looked as if someone dug their heels into the ground. On top of everything were prints from a small dog. Maggie crouched down and held Max while she waited for Digger and Doc to examine the signs for themselves.

"What do you think, Digger?"

"This must be where them boys got the best of our mountain bear wrestlers," Digger said with a wide grin across his face. "Them boys is something' else. Looks like those men was hiding behind them rocks 'n tried to catch the boys."

"They sure put up a scuffle, didn't they," Doc commented.

"Shore did," Digger beamed with pride.

"It's hard to tell what happened from here," Doc continued.

Maggie stood up and released Max.

"Here Max, find the boys," she said as she pointed at the scuffle marks around the rocks. "Go find Zack and Jonah."

She stood up, slowly turned around and looked in each clump of rock or brush for some sign of where the boys disappeared. There was one place where she could see a definite disturbance in the bushes around the trail. She carefully walked around the edge of the trail to examine it more closely. Max followed her and sniffed the edge of the trail.

"What is it Max, Do you smell the boys?"

Max wagged his tail furiously and barked. He charged into the bushes and dove down the bank at full speed. Maggie was right behind him. She didn't wait for Digger or Doc to follow. Somehow, instinctively she knew this was the route the boys used to escape Raymond and Darrell. She scooted and slid down the bank until she came to a crashing halt at the bottom of the hill and ran full force into a holly bush.

"Ouch!" She yelled as she finally came to a stop. She carefully examined her legs and arms to make sure nothing was broken, then stood up and brushed off her clothes.

"Maggie, are you ok?" Doc called from the trail above.

"I'm fine," she called after him, "We just took the quick way down the hill. Are y'all going to come too?"

"We're on our way," Doc answered, "It may take a few minutes longer with Nugget, but we're coming down the path, it's a little longer."

"Ok, I'll check out the trail."

She stood up and looked for Max. When she saw him a few feet away, she followed him and looked for signs of the boys and Bandit. Carefully, she looked around the thicket until she saw an area about twenty feet away, where leaves and branches were scraped off the bank from the top all the way to the bottom.

She slowly made her way to the path and scoured the ground with every step. When she finally made her way to the scrape marks, she saw her first sign of the boys. Several little boot marks were around the trail and led to a large oak tree where it looked like the boys stood by the tree for a length of time.

"Digger, Doc, come quick! I've found their trail, they were here!" She called out to the men excitedly as she continued to scout their trail.

Digger and Doc worked their way down the bank into the woods where Maggie stood and looked as she pointed to the bank where the boys slid down the hill and then stood behind the large oak tree.

"It looks like they hid from Ray and Darrel behind that tree," Doc commented, "They must have been pretty scared."

Maggie nodded. She fought back her fears and tears as she continued to follow the trail through the dense undergrowth of the forest. It became more difficult as the leaves became thicker. Soon, they saw a small break in the dense undergrowth. Just as they started to go through the opening, they heard the sickening sound of a bear roar and all froze. The hair stood up on the back of their necks with the chilling sound. They looked at each other when they heard the sound again followed by screams of children.

"It's the boys!" Maggie cried as she dashed through the opening.

They all climbed through the brush and immediately stopped to see a small glade with a field and a stream. There, they could see a large black bear as she stood in front of an overhand of the bank. She was angry, stood on her back haunches and roared loudly in the direction of the bank.

Maggie looked toward the overhang where she saw a barely conscious Stratton lay on the ground and wave a stick at the bear. Standing over him were Zack and Jonah. They were half-naked and covered with mud. Both boys held their bear claws in their hand as they jumped up and down, then yelled and growled back at the bear as loud as they could. Bandit pranced around in front of them, with his teeth bared he barked as loud as the bear growled.

"Oh, no!" Maggie gasped when she saw the terrifying scene. "What can we do?" she said as she tried to run toward them.

Doc quickly grabbed her arm and held her back, "Wait a minute, Maggie," he said gently. "Watch out."

"I've got 'er," Digger said as he quickly slid the shotgun out of the sleeve on Nugget's pack. He quickly took aim and shot the bear's backside full of buckshot. "Don't worry, it won't kill 'er, it'll jest skeer 'er away."

The bear howled in pain, turned away from the bank and started to run across the field. Bandit immediately jumped out from the overhang and joined Max as they chased after the bear, barked and nipped at her legs as she ran. She quickly disappeared into the woods on the other side of the field. Bandit and Max remained on the edge of the woods and continued to bark as loudly as they could.

Maggie and Doc quickly ran to the overhang.

"Zack, Jonah," Maggie called as she ran. "Are you ok?"

She quickly ran to their side, grabbed them and held them as tightly as she could. Their little bodies trembled as she hugged them. The mud from their little bodies rubbed off on her and covered her with mud, too. She held them back and looked at them through her tears, then hugged them again.

"You look wonderful!" she cried through her sobs and tears.

"Aww, Maggie," Jonah said bashfully, "Yer gonna mess up our 'injun decorwations.'"

"Oh, boys," she said as she tried to hold back her tears, "We were so worried about you. Are you both ok?"

"We were ok, Maggie," Zack said calmly, "We had to save the Ranger."

"We found him, Maggie," Jonah added as he grasped her face with both hands and looked into her eyes, "We found Waingur Stwatton, 'n me 'n Zack fixed him up!"

She smiled and looked over in Stratton's direction. Doc crouched beside him as he leaned over and checked out his wounds. When he finished the exam, he looked up.

"Did you boys put these things on Stratton?" Doc asked.

"I did," Zack answered solemnly, "Jonah helped me out."

"How did you know how to treat him?"

"Momma showed me how," Zack said in a solemn voice, "She likes to teach us all about the medicine she learned from her Momma."

Doc smiled his approval.

"You did very well, Zack," he said sincerely. "Would you mind coming over here so you can teach me about the things you used, so I can understand and use them, too?"

"Sure," Zack smiled and walked over to Doc to explain about the crushed plantain and feeding Stratton the willow branches, berries and nuts.

Doc patted Zack on the back.

"You've done very well, Zack. You probably saved his life."

"Him had his eyes open this mornin'," Jonah chimed into the conversation as he leaned over and put his face directly in Stratton's face. "But him couldn't git up cuz his head hurt."

"Yes, it looks like he got a pretty good bang on the head," Doc observed, "But, you and your brother fixed it up pretty good."

"We did everything we could, but we couldn't fix his leg," Zack said as he pointed toward Stratton's leg that was turned at an odd angle.

"You did the best you could, Zack," Doc said and patted him on the back. "You did very well with the things you did for him. It would be difficult to fix a broken leg out here even for a doctor."

As he crouched down to examine Stratton's leg, the two-way radio began to crackle and sputter.

"Breaker, breaker ..., this is home base, come in Rescue Team Two ...," Sam's voice came across the waves. "Breaker, breaker ..., this is Sam, come in Team Two ... over." Maggie quickly grabbed the two-way radio and responded.

"Breaker, breaker, this is Team Two, Maggie here, over."

"Just to inform you, we have the two injured men in custody. They confessed to everything. They're on their way to the ER for treatment and then to the county jail," Sam informed them through the crackling sound of static. "The rescue team intercepted them around noon today and successfully brought them and the professors out safely."

Maggie smiled and breathed a sigh of relief.

"Sam," she started then stopped as she took a moment to hold back her tears, "Tell Rena," she paused, "We found the boys."

"What's the situation ... over," Sam interrupted.

"The boys are fine," she continued, "Tell Rena the boys are uninjured and will walk out with us ... over."

"And Stratton," he hesitated, "... over."

"He's alive, Sam, he's alive!" She burst into tears and cried when she heard a roar of cheers from Sam's side of the radio.

"He has a head injury and needs to have immediate treatment as soon as we can get him out of here," she continued, "We're going to have to rig a travois on Nugget to get him out because it looks like he has a broken leg, too ..., over."

"Roger ..., we have a wilderness medic crew headed your direction, they should be able to meet you at your last campsite around evening ..., over."

"Roger ..., that's a 'can do'. We'll meet the medic team at the last campsite, over."

"Maggie ...," Sam's voice hesitated as he continued, "the fires are still going strong, be careful, and ...," he paused, "Be quick."

"Roger ...," she answered, "Rescue Team Two, over and out."

Maggie quickly ran to Doc and Digger to tell them about the new information from headquarters. As she approached, she could see Stratton was awake and able to talk to Doc and Digger.

"Hey, Stratton," Maggie greeted him, "It sure is good to see you! You sure gave everybody a scare."

"Hi, Maggie, I can't tell you how good it is to see you three," he grinned. "I think the boys had their hands full taking care of me."

"How's your head?"

"Well, it's doing a little better but I don't think I can sit up yet. I keep passing out when I try."

"You probably have a concussion," Doc told him, "It would be better if you didn't get up. Just rest, we'll take care of everything else."

"We may need to think about that," Maggie started.

"Saw you talkin' on the radio, is everything ok?" Digger asked.

"Yes and No," Maggie continued. "The Medic Team found the professors with Raymond and Darryl. They have all four of them off the mountain. The mountain men are now in custody and on the way to the ER right now."

"That's the good news, what's the rest of the story?" Doc asked.

"The rest of the story is the Forest Service is having trouble containing the fires and we aren't safe here. We need to get off the mountain as soon as we can."

"Can Stratton be moved?" Digger asked.

"I'll do whatever I need to do," Stratton said, "I don't want anyone risking their life for me on the trail."

Doc looked at him thoughtfully as he contemplated what they needed to do.

"We could build a travois and hook it to Nugget's pack to pull you out of here, but we would have to put a splint on your leg first and that will hurt like hell."

"You do whatever you need to do, Doc," Stratton said as he grabbed his hand. "I don't want anything to harm those two little boys. They mean everything to me."

"Digger, I'm going to need your help when we set his leg. We also need to build a travois. Do you have an axe?"

Digger nodded.

"If you could cut us down some long poles for a rig, Maggie and the boys can work on that while we set Stratton's leg. We are going to need some young Elm saplings, too, for the bark to use as a temporary cast," he said as he began to look around the clearing for Elm trees.

Digger pulled out his axe from his pack then motioned for the boys to join him.

"Come on fellers, we gots to find something to fix the Ranger's leg with, then, we gots to help Maggie build a rig. We need something to help carry him out of the woods," Digger said as he and the boys went to the edge of the woods to look for trees they could use for the travois.

"Maggie, this is going to cause Stratton some pain," Doc said earnestly, as he looked at Stratton. "It might be better if you and the boys were occupied on the cart while we set his leg. I don't want to traumatize the kids anymore."

She nodded.

"We'll have to straighten the leg and then bind it with splints and Elm bark," Doc continued. "Just setting it will probably make him pass out again from the pain but if he does, it will make the rest of the procedure a little easier."

Stratton looked a little green and nauseous, but bravely smiled, "I don't want anything to alarm those boys, they're brave, but they're still little kids."

"Ok, we'll get the carrier ready then I'll try to find something for the boys to eat while you set the leg."

Doc nodded and left to find the Elm trees as Stratton lay back, closed his eyes and tried to prepare himself mentally for the procedure.

CHAPTER 22

While Zack and Jonah helped Digger find some poles for the rig that would eventually be hooked up to Nugget's pack, Maggie went down to the stream to see if she could find any wild food for the boys to eat on their trip back to.the cabin. She thought she packed enough for the trip but sharing the things she had with the professors and the mountain men drained her supplies.

She found some Jerusalem Artichokes near the stream and pulled up the plants to find some good size tubers in the soil. She quickly broke off the flower tops and took the tubers to the stream to wash them off. While she was there, she found some Passion Flower vines and selected a number of fruit that looked ripe. She then moved on to the Beech Tree where Zack picked the Beechnuts he ground up for Stratton.

She looked across the field while she picked the nuts and laughed when she saw the boys with Digger. While he chopped down one tree, the boys carried another tree back to the shelter where Stratton lay. They looked so funny as they carried the pole on their shoulders and tried to run through the grass. The grass in the field almost covered up their little legs as they carried the pole across their shoulders and ran as fast as they could.

When they arrived with the first pole, they hurried back to Digger to get the second pole and quickly placed it on their shoulders, then repeated their journey. They soon had both poles in the shelter and waited for Digger to come help build the travois.

Doc was in the other area of the field stripping bark from several young Elm trees. The bark of the Elm was slippery and excellent to use to set bones. It became as firm as a cast when wrapped around an injury. He brought his supplies back to the shelter also and prepared to set Stratton's bone.

He glanced around the field as Maggie approached.

"Hey Doc, do you have everything you need?"

"I'm looking for something to put on his skin to keep the Elm bark from chafing his skin. I need something soft," he said as he looked around the field. Normally, I could use the down from Cattails, but I don't see any Cattails around."

"I think there are a few down stream a little bit, do you want me to get them?"

"That would be great, thank you, Maggie," he smiled as he leaned over and kissed her. "Everything's going to be fine. We'll all be out of here in no time."

She nodded, and then paused before she left.

"You know, Zack is going to want to help you. He's spent a lot of time trying to mend Stratton lately. He may feel left out if you set the leg without him."

"When the worst of it is over, I'll signal you and you can send Zack over to help me put the splint on Stratton's leg."

She nodded and smiled, then quickly ran down to the stream to gather some of the mature Cattail reeds. She placed them in a pile next to Stratton while Doc gave Stratton a drink of water.

"We're ready now, Maggie. Tell Digger we're ready for him."

She nodded and walked over to the boys who were helping Digger devise an old-fashioned type of travois to strap to Nugget's pack. She watched for a moment as the boys helped Digger fold several ground cloths over each other on one end and lash the top of the material to the poles.

"Hey, guys, can I help for a minute?"

"Sure, Maggie, come on," Zack answered.

Maggie motioned for Digger to join Doc and Stratton.

"I'm sure glad you guys know how to lash poles together. I was getting a little rusty. This is going to be the perfect rig for the Ranger. Before long, we'll have him out of here and on the road home."

They continued to lash the poles together when suddenly they heard a loud, brief shout from the shelter. The boys quickly stopped what they were doing and looked up. Zack stood up and started to walk towards the shelter. Maggie stood and wrapped her arm around him.

"It's ok, Zack, Doc had to set his leg so we could move him. He said it might hurt a little bit, but I think the worst part is over now."

Zack continued to watch Doc and Digger, a little apprehensive about what he should do. He wanted to run to his side, but felt afraid to leave the security of being with Maggie since his mother wasn't there.

"Momma had to set my arm one time when I fell out of a tree."

"She did?"

"Yes, and it hurt pretty bad," Zack said as he remembered.

When Doc waved toward her, Maggie leaned over and whispered in Zack's ear.

"I think Doc may need your help, now," she said and smiled as she watched Zack run across the field as fast as he could.

She watched Doc show Zack how to break open the Cattails, pull out the soft down from inside and pack it around Stratton's leg before they placed the splints on his leg. When they finished placing the Cattail down on his leg, Zack helped Doc wrap Elm bark around it.

Maggie turned back to Jonah and helped him finish the carrier. She then gave him Nugget's lead rope and they walked back to the shelter to join the rest of the crew. Zack finished stuffing Cattail down under the Elm bark now in place on Stratton's leg. Maggie noticed Stratton was either sleeping, or out cold from the procedure. Either way, he looked much more peaceful than he did when he was awake.

Digger joined the crew and paced nervously around the shelter while Doc finished the splint and looked his direction.

"Is everything ok, Digger?"

"Doc, we need ta git outta here likkity-split," he said anxiously.

Doc stopped what he was doing and looked at Digger.

"What do you mean? Is the fire closer?"

"I jest walked on the ridge to take a look-see, 'n some 'o the new fires are purty close. If we don't leave soon, we won't have a way out," Digger said seriously.

"Ok, we'll be ready soon. We're done here," Doc said as he patted Zack on the back. "You've been a big help, Zack. I think everything is ready, all we have to do is get Stratton on the rig."

They all paused and looked up when the dogs barked and rushed toward the edge of the woods. The dogs barked and pranced around until Josh and Justin emerged from the woods where Maggie and her crew discovered the field and the shelter where they found Stratton and the boys. Maggie felt an enormous rush of relief when she saw the two young hikers walk down the bank to the shelter. She and the boys rushed over to greet them.

"It's so wonderful to see you both," she cried, "How did you ever find us?" She said as she hugged each of them. She watched Zack and Jonah grasp their hands as they all walked back to the shelter.

"You left a big enough trail, Maggie," Justin teased. "We would have to have our head in the clouds to miss it," he said as he grinned and took his backpack off.

"Hey, ya'll," Josh smiled, "We're a little ahead of the rescue crew that's supposed to meet you. They took a short break, but we couldn't sit down when we knew ya'll were still out here on the trail."

"Thanks," Doc said as he shook their hands. "So, you have a Medic Team waiting at the last campsite?"

"Yes, they're waiting there with medical supplies and food," Justin said, "We decided to come ahead and see if we could help get you from here, to there," he grinned.

"We are more than grateful for the help," Maggie added.

"How's Stratton?" Josh asked.

"He's stable," Doc answered, "We've put a splint on his leg and tried to stabilize his neck, but he needs medical attention."

"The biggest safety risk right now, is the fire," Justin said as he told them of the most recent outbreaks in the area. "We need to get moving as soon as possible."

"We built a carrier for Stratton," Digger commented, "If ye boys kin help us git him on there, we'll jest tie it to 'old Nugget 'n head outta here. Nugget can pull him the whole way."

"We can do that," Josh said as he took his pack off.

They helped Doc work a ground cover underneath Stratton then the four men together lifted the ground cover with Stratton on top to the travois. After they secured him on the padding, Josh and Justin lifted the front end of the poles and Digger quickly lashed the poles to Nugget's chest harness.

Doc took a few moments to secure several tee shirts behind and around Stratton's neck to prevent it from moving on the journey. He then took several bedrolls and secured them around his broken leg to help reduce the jarring movement as they traveled.

Just before they left the area, Digger lifted Jonah and Zack to the top of Nugget's packs where they could sit on the trip back up to the cabin. He knew the boys were tired and their travel would be much easier if the boys rode.

Maggie and the rest of the crew strapped on their backpacks and headed out of the little glade to the steep bank. After a slow, struggle to get to the top of the bank, Nugget finally made it to the trail above. Everyone else followed at a much slower pace.

When the crew finally reached the trail, the smoke was much more intense. There was a dramatic difference in the air on the top of the trail than the air in the little valley below. The distinct odor of the fires now consumed the air and the burn and sting of smoke filled their eyes as they traveled.

By the time they reached the campsite where the rescue team waited for them, it was late afternoon. The crew was ready to relieve them of Stratton's care and quickly unhooked him from the travois. They secured him in a trail basket and prepared to carry him the rest of the way up the trail. After a discussion about the trail and a moment to plan a strategy to leave the area, they all decided to stay together due to the increasing smoke and hazardous conditions on the trail. Stratton drifted in and out of consciousness as they traveled. The Medic trail crew traveled as gently as they could, but the path was narrow and the steep trail made the journey difficult.

Josh and Justin walked alongside of Nugget so they could talk to Zack and Jonah and keep them occupied. They shared their trail food with the boys when they realized the boys hadn't eaten much all day. The boys loved the attention they received from Josh and Justin and soaked up every moment of it.

When they reached the overlook at the head of the trail, the crew stopped so look out over the vast acres of wilderness forest between Tennessee and North Carolina. Everywhere they looked, smoke drifted from hot spots where the wild fires raged. At times, huge fireballs broke away from burning tree, and blew through the sky until they landed some distance away and started new fires.

In some areas, smoke billowed, and the sky glowed intense yellow and crimson hues from the flames. Intense smoke blew in their face and felt like fires were right on them. The smoke made it difficult to breathe and they often choked and gasped for air.

"We'd better keep moving folks," Doc broke the silence, "This looks pretty serious; we don't need to waste any time."

They all nodded and continued to move on along the trail.

"We gonna haff a fire by our house, Maggie?" Jonah asked.

"Well, I certainly hope not, Jonah. I think the Rangers are doing everything they can to put it out," Maggie said confidently.

"I wonder if Mom is ok," Zack thought aloud.

"Hey there buddy," Justin answered, "Your Mom is going to be just fine. We talked to her before we came on the trail to meet you and do you know what she told us?"

"No, what?" Zack asked a little timidly. He was afraid to admit how very concerned for his mother he was and how much he missed her.

"She said for us to tell you she loves you both very much!"

Zack smiled and nodded.

"I wuv my Mommy, too," Jonah chimed in as he lay his head down on top of one of Nugget's packs and fought back tears.

Josh rubbed his back, then he and Justin took off their bandanas and wet them with water from their canteen. They tied them around the boy's nose and mouth to protect them from the smoke. The boys both lay their heads down on Nugget's packs as the crew wearily trudged on again while the dense smoke increased.

They picked up their step when they began to hear the sound of other hikers come up the trail in their direction.

Maggie paused on the path when she thought she also heard the sound of distant thunder. She stopped Doc as he passed to see if he heard the sound, too.

"Hey, did you hear that?" she asked excitedly.

"It sure sounded like thunder," he smiled wearily.

"We're going to make it, aren't we?"

"It sure looks that way, Maggie," he said as he gazed into her eyes. "Everything is going to be just fine. You were wonderful on the trail."

"I'm not the one who was so wonderful. You did all the hard work setting Stratton's leg. I know that was really hard to do without your usual tools," she said as she hugged him close.

They smiled wearily at each other and gently kissed as the reinforcement crew appeared on the trail in front of them. They all quickly picked up their step and followed the crew to the Ranger's headquarters in Maggie's cabin.

They stepped from the path through the trees into Maggie's yard as Rangers and Medics who wanted to help them, immediately surrounded them and tried to check them out. Josh and Justin protected the children from the commotion and lifted the sleeping boys off Nugget's packs. They carried them into the cabin where they could be with their mother in some privacy.

Doc stepped over to the Medics and gave them a report on Stratton's condition. The Ranger's eyes fluttered open as Doc spoke.

"Hey, Doc," Stratton said hoarsely, "I just want to …," he started to speak and drifted into unconsciousness again. He opened his eyes again and tried to speak. "Doc …, thanks …, for everything," he smiled weakly and tried to grasp Doc's hand.

Doc smiled in return and patted Stratton on the back of his hand.

"Tell the boys," Stratton continued weakly, "Tell the boys how much I love them. They were so brave," his voice trailed off as he continued to drift in and out of consciousness, "... so very brave."

Just as the Medics placed Stratton on the stretcher and prepared to load him into the ambulance, Rena ran out of the cabin. She quickly grabbed first Digger, then Maggie and Doc and embraced each one tightly as she wiped away her tears.

"Thank you so much," she cried, "Thank you, from the bottom of my heart. I don't know what I would have done if something happened to my children." She quickly looked around the crowd. "Is Stratton with you? Is he ok?"

"He's going to be fine, Rena," Maggie smiled.

"I think he would love to speak with you, Rena," Doc said gently as he held Rena's elbow and led her to Stratton's side.

When Rena saw Stratton on the stretcher, she burst into tears and wrapped her arms around him. She could hardly speak because she was crying so hard. He reached up and gently touched her hair as she hugged him.

"I love you, Rena," he said quietly as he tried to wipe away her tears, "With all my heart."

"I love you, too," she gulped.

The Medics shifted their feet and moved toward the stretcher.

"We really need to go," they said, "Are you coming with us?"

She paused and clutched her chest, then looked at Maggie.

"Go, Rena. The boys will be fine with me until you get back," she smiled, "Don't worry about a thing."

"But," she hesitated, "I haven't been with the boys either and I hate to leave them right now," she said as she clutched Stratton's hand tightly afraid to let him go.

"They'll be fine, Rena," Maggie reassured her, "They're probably already asleep on the bed. The hikers are here and the boys really love to spend time with them. We'll just make it a big slumber party for everyone. Don't worry for a minute about the boys, Stratton needs you more than anyone right now."

"Thank you, Maggie, thank you so much," Rena said as she hugged her tightly then climbed inside the ambulance with Stratton. The ambulance pulled away into the night as the lights and siren blared, and Rena waved through the window of the van.

Maggie and Doc slowly walked over to Digger as the commotion in the yard died down and work crews changed teams and left the yard.

"Is there anything we can do for you tonight, Digger?" Maggie asked wearily. "You can camp out here in the yard if you'd like, I think the kids already pitched a tent and Rena's boys are asleep in the cabin."

"Thanks, Maggie," Digger answered, "But it's still early. I think I'll jest git on home. I'm purty tired, 'n my own bed would be nice to sleep in t'night."

Doc stepped over to Digger and shook his hand.

"It's always a pleasure to be on the trail with you, Digger," Doc smiled, "You're a fine traveling companion and someone I'd want in my corner in any situation."

"Same to ya, Doc," he said as he grinned, tipped his hat and headed down the road with Nugget. "It's always good to have a doctor on the trail."

As they stood and watched Digger and Nugget slowly walk down the trail, Sam came over and stood beside them.

"He's something else isn't he?"

"Yes, he sure is," Maggie smiled, "I wouldn't have him any other way than exactly as he is."

"How are Raymond and Darrel?" Doc asked, "That bear really tore them up. Did they get the medical treatment they needed?"

"Oh, yes," Sam filled in the couple on the treatment of the mountain men. "We took them directly to the ER and between the two of them, they had over 200 stitches."

"Wow!" Maggie exclaimed, "They're lucky it wasn't worse."

"The one injury they complained about the most was the one the boys gave them during their scuffle," Sam laughed. "Raymond kept saying something about a rabid dog bite on his rear end."

Maggie and Doc laughed.

"They're in jail now; waiting a hearing on charges they assaulted a Forest Ranger. They will also face charges they devastated an ancient burial ground and made fake artifacts for profits."

Sam then turned to look at them, "Are you two going to be ok? That was a pretty grueling experience. You must be tired."

Maggie and Doc looked at each other as a soft rain began to fall and thoughts of the trip raced through their head. They both smiled and laughed as the rain increased.

"Yes," they both said in unison and then laughed.

"We'll be fine," Doc smiled as he leaned over and kissed her gently in the rain, "We'll be just fine."

CHAPTER 23

Maggie finished the article she was writing and glanced out her cabin window. The woods around her cabin now burst with beautiful colors of gold, red and bronze. True to her Grandmother's ancient predictions, the first frost came this year around the first of the month, almost three months exactly to the day Maggie first heard the crickets chirp. The frost brought with it the wonderful and greatly anticipated change of seasons.

The mountain now exploded with colors. Areas burned or damaged by the late summer fire began to show signs of re-growth. Although, the Rangers and firefighters were able to save the woods and campground at Indian Boundary Lake from the devastating forest fires, the ridges beyond the campground suffered the loss of many acres. Much of the wildlife and trees damaged were now on the mend.

She looked across the field and saw Max lay in the sun between the main entrance to Basil's den and his escape route. She watched closely to see if Max was asleep. He must have sensed she watched him, because he began to thump his tail and twitch his nose. Suddenly, he stiffened and began to sniff the air as soon as Basil stuck his head and shoulders out of his den.

When Max saw Basil, he jumped up and ran toward Basil's den in an attempt to catch him, or chase him at the very least. Basil immediately scooted inside and disappeared in his den. Maggie watched a few minutes longer then smiled when she saw Basil waddle out of his escape route and into the woods while Max continued to bark at the opening of his den.

"At least you're learning how to keep Max occupied while you hunt for food, Basil," Maggie thought aloud.

She smiled, then turned back and looked at the clock.

"Oops! I'd better hurry, it's almost time to go," she said to herself as she quickly went into the bedroom and dressed. She chose a long cotton skirt with a small peach flower print and a soft white blouse to go with it. She then brushed her long hair, and gathered it up into a clip allowing a few curls to drape down her shoulders.

She quickly gathered her purse and a light, cream colored, hand-crocheted, shawl together and headed for the door of cabin. When she stepped out onto the porch, Max bounded across the field to greet her.

"Hey, buddy," she said as she held her hand out, "Don't get me dirty. I've got to stay clean today."

He sat down in front of her and wagged his tail in response. She patted him on the head before she got into the jeep.

"I'll be home soon," she called as she drove down the mountain and headed toward Rena's cabin.

She smiled, as she rolled down the window of the jeep and thought about the wonderful things in store for the afternoon. As the wind blew her hair, she could smell the rich fragrances of fall. She felt such a peace and contentment with her life on the mountain. It was everything she hoped it would be when she moved.

She reached Rena's house about the same time Doc drove up in his truck and parked along the road in front of the path to Rena's house. She smiled and waved when she saw him, then quickly walked over to meet him.

"You look beautiful, Maggie," he said as he leaned over, smiled and kissed her gently. He held her in a tight embrace.

"You look great, yourself," she said as she stood back to look and admire his suit. "It's not everyday I see a handsome man in a real suit."

"I don't usually wear them unless it's a very, very special occasion; and this ranks as a pretty special occasion," he smiled.

"I agree," Maggie smiled, and grasped his hand as they walked toward Rena's house. She felt as light as a feather as they walked together.

Zack and Jonah greeted them at the door when they stepped on the porch. Both boys came bouncing out the door to meet them. They each had on dress pants and royal blue shirts with neckties to match.

"Maggie, you're here!" Zack shouted excitedly. "It's almost time to go!" He said as he reached up and grabbed her hand.

"I know! Are you ready?"

"Yes, we're all ready, even Abby. She has a new dress, too."

"I'm ready, too Maggie. Did ya see my new shurt?" Jonah asked as he ran over so she could feel his shirt.

"That's a wonderful shirt, Jonah and it is just like your brother's shirt, too. I like that!" She smiled as she helped tuck the tail of his shirt into his pants. "Where's your Momma?"

"She's inside putting on her dress," Zack replied as he went over to sit with Doc on the swing. "She wants to look pretty."

Maggie smiled and went inside the little cabin to find Rena.

"We're here, Rena, are you ready to go?"

Maggie didn't see her in the main room of the cabin, so she walked towards Rena's bedroom as she talked.

"Are you in the bedroom?"

When she didn't hear a response, Maggie walked into the bedroom and found Rena sitting on the edge of the bed holding a tissue in her hand. She was dressed in a beautiful cream color dress she made herself. Her hair was swept up into a beautiful braid, adorned with several small flowers.

"Hey, there, is everything ok?" She asked as she quickly sat beside Rena and wrapped her arm around her.

"Oh, Maggie," she began and started to cry.

Maggie quickly handed her a tissue and held her tight as she tried to reassure her, "It's ok, Rena, I know you're scared."

"It's not that, Maggie," she said between sobs, "I just never thought I could be so happy again."

Maggie tried to comfort her by rubbing her shoulders.

"When my husband died, my whole world changed. With a new baby and three mouths to feed," she paused and wiped her eyes, "I just kept busy working hard to make ends meet so I wouldn't have to feel just how lonely I was. It never entered my mind that someone as special as Stratton would enter my life and love not only me, but the children, too. I know he loves them with all his heart."

"He's a special man, Rena, and he loves each one of you so much. It's easy to see how much he loves you, because it's written all over his face. He practically glows."

"Yes, I know," she said as she burst into tears.

"Then, why all the tears?" Maggie asked a little confused.

"I'm just sooo happy," she sobbed as she wiped her tears away.

"I know," Maggie cried with her as she reached across her for a tissue to wipe her own eyes. "Isn't it wonderful!"

Doc came into the room and stopped when he saw both women sitting on the bed crying. He wasn't sure what he should say, if anything. He hesitated before he came into the room any further.

"Umm, is there anything I can do?" He hesitated.

"No," Maggie said through her tears, "We're fine, we're happy."

"Ok," he started, a little confused and unsure as to what he should do next, "Umm, well, it's almost time to go. We don't want to be late. You'd better get moving!"

Maggie and Rena both looked at each other and started to giggle as they wiped their tears away and stood up to leave. After a long, endearing embrace, they gathered up the children and loaded them into Maggie's jeep. Rena joined Doc in his truck and they all headed down the mountain to Bald River Falls.

When they arrived near the falls, several Rangers on the road directed traffic to park along the side of the small road or in the parking lot of Baby Falls a few yards away. Dozens of cars already parked along the side of the road, and numerous people congregated on the bridge. They walked around and spoke with each other, as they looked at the waterfalls and decorations. They each enjoyed the music until everyone arrived and the ceremony began.

Huge bouquets of fall wildflowers, marigolds, sunflowers and zinnias decorated the bridge. An impromptu arch, hand-made of willow branches were covered with streamers of fall leaves and crimson ribbons that blew in the breeze.

When they arrived, Sam directed them to walk over to the right side of the falls and wait there while he found the rest of the party. Sam then directed the minister to the center of the bridge and called out to get the attention of the crowd. With the dramatic waterfall at Bald River Falls as a backdrop and the beautiful brilliant colors of autumn around the river, a small band began to play bluegrass music and the ceremony began.

As the music started, Stratton slowly walked across the bridge with his cane. The smile on his face was so broad and bright, it was impossible for anyone to look at him and not break into a large smile. He grinned when he saw Rena, Abby and the boys stand on the edge of the bridge with Doc.

When the music played louder, Doc wrapped Rena's arm around his and walked with her and the children together to meet Stratton in the center of the bridge, under the arch. He smiled, kissed Rena on the cheek and stepped aside to stand by Maggie. Everyone smiled as the preacher began the ceremony.

"What a wonderful occasion to bring us all together," he began. "This is truly a day to bring the whole community out for a common purpose. We are here to celebrate the fact that there are people among us who might not be here with us if the whole community hadn't come together when disaster struck."

Everyone smiled in response and nodded their heads.

"We are also here to rejoice with Rena and Stratton and honor the love they have for each other as they begin their lives together as a family," he said as he looked at the couple and continued the ceremony.

Doc wrapped his arms around Maggie's waist as the ceremony continued. The ceremony was so tender; it touched everyone in the crowd, community members and visitors included. When the minister came to a pause, he placed his hand on Stratton's back and gently nudged him forward.

"I'm not going to take up all of the time we have for this ceremony," the minister continued, "Stratton would like to say a few words before we continue."

Stratton stepped a little closer to Rena and the children, cleared his throat, and looked down at his feet before he started.

"Guess I don't have much to say most of the time. Ya'll know me to be kind of a quiet guy," he grinned as a snicker rolled through the crowd. "There aren't many words I could say right now that could genuinely express the feelings I have." He cleared his throat and looked at Rena with tears in his eyes.

"It's not every day, you are lucky enough to meet the person you're meant to spend your life with," he said as he reached for her hand. "And I'm here to tell you, Rena, and to tell you all. I not only have met the person I want to cherish for the rest of my life, but, I've also met three other little people I couldn't possible love any more than I already do."

"I love you, Rena, with all my heart and nothing would make me happier than for you to be my wife and spend the rest of my life with you," he smiled. "My life is richer and fuller with you by my side." Tears ran down his face as he touched her cheek tenderly then looked at the boys.

"Boys, and Abby," he said as he smiled at each of them, "Since the day I met you, my life has never been the same. You saved me," he began, then paused to clear his throat, "not only on the trail, but, saved me from a life of not knowing what true love and self sacrifice really means. You fill my life with so much happiness and joy. I can't imagine spending a single day of my life without you in it. I would be honored if you would allow me the chance to be a part of your family."

Zack beamed from ear to ear as he stepped over to Stratton and wrapped his arms around his waist. Jonah tucked his lower lip inside his mouth and looked up at Stratton. His eyes sparkled as he wrapped his arms tightly around Stratton's leg. Stratton chuckled, reached for Rena and Abby then held the family close.

First, a hush, then a soft ripple of ooh's and ahh's ran through the crowd. Soon, the crowd cheered and became so moved with the touching scene, they could no longer hold back their emotions. Everyone began to smile, chuckle and finally burst into cheers and applause for the happy family. Couples hugged each other and became so filled with excitement they rushed in to greet the couple. The preacher held up his hand and spoke loudly to get everyone's attention.

"Wait a minute; they haven't said 'I do', yet!"

Rena and Stratton smiled and immediately said, "I DO!"

As the crowd in unison shouted, "THEY DO, THEY DO!"

The band played a tune as everyone burst into laughter and hugs and danced in the middle of the bridge. Each person, filled with the warmth and love they felt for the happy family greeted them and celebrated their union. Soon, Sam came onto the center of the bridge to make an announcement to everyone at the celebration.

"Folks, I know you are all having a wonderful time and we want everyone to continue the celebration. If you would be so kind, please head up the short path to the top of the falls. The Rangers and some of the women of the community have a wonderful reception on the picnic tables at the top of the falls," he said as he and several Rangers pointed and guided the crowd toward the falls picnic area.

Stratton walked slowly with his cane and held Rena's hand as she carried Abby and they followed the boys up the trail. The crowd quickly followed them to the top.

The rich colors on the fall trees and the brilliant blue autumn sky made the winding path up the hill even more beautiful. Well-wishers adorned every turn of the trail with a bouquets of fresh sunflowers or marigolds. Someone even decorated the sides of the rushing stream that ran along the picnic area with flowers and ribbons that hung from the trees and gently blew in the breeze.

When they arrived in the picnic area at the top of the falls, they were stunned to see the picnic tables covered with checked tablecloths, mason jars of fresh flowers, and tray after tray of food.

A beautiful three tiered cake decorated with fresh golden marigolds was in the center of one table. Sandwiches, vegetables and every kind of finger food imaginable were on the other tables. Each of the women brought their best dish for the celebration. The newlyweds cut the wedding cake and everyone went through the tables and filled their plates with food as the band set up and played.

When Maggie saw a break in the crowd that surrounded Stratton and Rena, she walked over to them and gave each of them a heartfelt hug. She wiped away a tear when she saw them together and could feel the happiness and love between both of them. Doc came over and gave them both a hug when he joined them.

"Do you have any big plans for a honeymoon?" He asked.

Rena blushed as Stratton looked at her and smiled.

"We decided to do something with everyone as a family since we are starting out together. So, we plan on taking the kids on a little camping trip to Joyce Kilmer Forest in a few weeks when my leg heals completely," Stratton said as he gazed into Rena's eyes. "For right now, we're just going to go home and be a family."

"That sounds like a wonderful plan," Maggie smiled at both of them, "If you two decide you want some time alone, just let me know. I'll be glad to have the kids come over to my house for a weekend if you'd like."

"Thank you, Maggie," Stratton said, "But, for right now, I think we just want to go home and be together."

"I don't blame you for that," Doc shook Stratton's hand, "Best wishes to all of you; I know the boys are so happy to have you in the family now."

Maggie hugged each of them again as Doc grabbed her hand and led her away from the couple toward the stream where they could get a few moments to speak to one another. They stood by the river and held each other as they watched everyone eat, dance and celebrate together.

"I'm so happy for them," Maggie said, "It's the most wonderful thing that could happen for Rena and Stratton. The greatest part is that it's especially wonderful for the kids, they love him so much."

Doc held her close then gently kissed her. He smiled as he gazed into her eyes and swayed slightly with the music.

"Maggie, it's a wonderful feeling to find the person you want to spend the rest of your life with, especially when you know without a doubt that you can't go on another day without them."

She looked up at him, and knew in her heart, he spoke the truth.

"I feel as though we have known each other our entire lives," he continued, "Even though we have known each other for only a short time, it certainly feels as if we've been together for a long time, perhaps even in another lifetime."

"That's true," she smiled. "Isn't it funny how sometimes you can meet someone, and in an instant feel as though you know everything about them. Maybe that's what my Grandmother used to mean when she talked about how 'soul-mates' seek each other out and know each other long before their conscious minds are aware that they are supposed to be together."

Doc nodded quietly, then continued.

"These last few years, I've hidden myself away here in the mountains. All my time was spent trying to recoup some of the things I've lost through the years. I gave so much of my life up to my career that I ended up loosing everything I loved."

"I can understand that," she nodded. "A career can easily take over a person's life. Mine did in a lot of ways when I worked in the city."

"Maggie, There was never a person who touched my life as you do and every day I spend with you is an adventure and a love for life. Not only have I learned how to feel again, but I've learned how to enjoy life and live again."

She became very still as the impact of his words hit her.

"I guess what I'm saying is that I'm ready to move ahead and stop hiding away in the woods while I nurse my emotional wounds," he said as he gazed into her eyes. "I'm ready to live again and to love again. For the first time in a long time I've found someone I'd like to spend time getting to know and love."

She trembled, yet knew in her heart, she felt the same way.

With the soft music from the band in the background and the rushing sound of the water as it made its way over the falls, Maggie held him tight and closed her eyes. She felt more warmth and love than ever in her life.

"Yes," she smiled as she wrapped her arms around his neck and kissed him, "That sounds wonderful, I'd like that very much, too."

REFERENCES

Hutchens, Almar R., "Indian Herbalogy of North America", Boston, Massachusetts: Shambhala Publications, Inc., Boston and London, 1991.

Jackson, Jason Baird, "Yuchi Ceremonial Life", Bloomington, Indiana; Nebraska Press, Lincoln and London, 2003

Speck, Frank G., "Ethnology of the Yuchi Incians", Nebraska, University of Nebraska Press: Lincoln and London, 2004.

Krochmal, Arnold and Connie, "A Field Guide to Medicinal Plants", New York, New York: Times Books 1973.

Cyrus, Thomas, "Report on the Mound Explorations of the Bureau of Ethnology," Smithsonian Press, 1985.

Science Frontiers Online, "A New Look at the Bat Creek Inscription", No. 63: May-Jun 1989.

Mainfort, Jr., Robert, and Mary L. Kwas; "The Bat Creek Fraud: A Final Statement", Tennessee Anthropologist, Vol. XVIII, No. 2, Fall 1993.

Kirk, Lowell, "The Bat Creek Stone", 'The Tellico Plains Mountain Press'.

White, M.D. Linda B, and Steven Foster, "The Herbal Drugstore": Saint Martin's Press, Rodale Books 2000.

Mainfort, Jr, Robert C. and Kwas, Mary, "The Bat Creek Stone: Judeans in Tennessee?" Tennessee Anthropologist, Vol. XVI, No.1, Spring 1991..

"Wilderness Survival", SA Wildlife Program, www.wildlifestudents.com

American Botanical Council, "Herbal Medicine, Expanded Commission E Monographs", Blumenthal/Goldberg/Brinckmann, 2000.

978-0-595-41336-
0-595-41336-6

Printed in the United States
66272LVS00006B/151-249